MARSUPIALS AND MURDER

An Isle of Man Ghostly Cozy

DIANA XARISSA

❀ Created with Vellum

For marsupial lovers everywhere.

AUTHOR'S NOTE

Before I sat down to begin this book (book thirteen in the series), I went through a bunch of title ideas with my daughter. Men and Murder, Mansions and Murder, Myths and Murder and many others. Just for fun, I threw in Marsupials and Murder and she loved the idea. The neat thing is, the Isle of Man has a wild wallaby population of around a hundred animals, all descended from a breeding pair that escaped from the island's Wildlife Park many years ago. The title sent my imagination into overdrive and this book is the result.

I always recommend reading my books in order (alphabetically), but every title should be enjoyable on its own if you prefer not to do so. The characters and their relationships do change and develop throughout the series, however. This series is primarily written in American English as my main character was raised in the US and made her home there until the events just before the first book in the series. When she's talking to her friends and neighbors on the island, they speak in British (or Manx) English, though. I try to keep this consistent, but I'm sure I make mistakes. Please let me know if you find any, and I'll correct them.

This is a work of fiction and all of the characters come from the author's imagination. Any resemblance to actual persons, living or dead, is entirely coincidental. The shops, restaurants, and businesses in this story are also fictional. The historical sites and other landmarks on the island are all real, however, the events that take place within them in this story are fictional.

Please feel free to get in touch. You can find all of my contact information on the About the Author page at the back of the book. I'd love to hear from you. I have a monthly newsletter that gives all of the details for upcoming releases. You can sign up on my website. Thank you for coming with me on another adventure with Fenella and her friends.

"Why are we doing this again?" Daniel Robinson asked as he stared at her from under his umbrella.

"It sounded like a good idea at the time," Fenella Woods muttered in reply. She pulled her raincoat more tightly around herself and shivered.

Daniel chuckled. "Surely we don't really have to stay out here for a full hour?"

"I signed up for an hour. I'm going to stay. You don't have to, though."

Daniel looked at her for a moment and then slowly shook his head. "You aren't getting rid of me that easily. I took a day's holiday to spend some time with you and I'm going to do just that, even if that means spending the day standing around in the rain watching nothing happen."

"It's only an hour. And we've already been here," she glanced at her watch, "six minutes."

Daniel laughed. "I gather you thought we'd been here longer."

"A good deal longer, like maybe half an hour," Fenella admitted. She sighed and then, again, pulled her coat tighter around her body. It was a cold, rainy day, which was fairly typical for March on the Isle of Man.

She should have realized that they'd be miserable standing in a field in the rain.

"Tell me again why we're here, then. Talking will make the time go faster."

"Except talking may well scare away the wallabies."

Daniel made a face. "I'm not sure that I care," he whispered.

Now Fenella laughed. "Okay, I'm going to have to agree with you on that one," she admitted. "I'd love to see a wallaby in the wild, but I'm not going to be too upset if I don't manage it, at least not today."

Daniel took a step closer to her and slipped his arms around her. "Maybe we could warm ourselves up a little bit," he suggested in a whisper.

"I don't know about that," she said, tipping her head back. When their eyes met, she felt a rush in the pit of her stomach. The chemistry between them was strong and when he lowered his lips to hers, she forgot all about the wind, the rain, and the wallabies.

"I do beg your pardon," a loud voice said.

Daniel lifted his head and gave Fenella a rueful grin. "Hello," he said to the new arrival.

"I don't believe we've met," the man said, his tone disapproving. He was probably fifty, with dark black hair that almost certainly had to be dyed and beady little eyes that seemed to be staring hard at Fenella. He was wearing Wellington boots, waterproof trousers, and a heavy rain-coat with a hood. His umbrella was still folded in his hand, in spite of the falling rain.

"I'm Daniel Robinson and this is Fenella Woods."

"Ah, Ms. Woods, yes, Darrell told me that you'd volunteered to help out today. I must say, I believe when he wrote to you that he was expecting a monetary donation, rather than you giving up your very valuable time."

Fenella swallowed a smile. Now that she'd been on the island for a year, it seemed as if every charitable organization had decided at the same moment that she'd had enough time to settle in and could now be approached for donations. For the first twelve months, her mailbox had been mostly empty, but for the last several weeks it had been stuffed nearly every day with appeals for donations from more organizations than Fenella thought the island could reasonably support. "He invited me to join you today, and I thought it sounded interesting," she replied. "Assuming you work with the Manx Wallaby Society, that is."

"I didn't introduce myself, did I? That was very remiss of me. I'm Rodney Simmons. I'm Darrell's assistant with the charity, as well as with the rest of his life. I usually organize the rotas for these events, but Darrell insisted on doing this one himself for some reason. Now I'm wandering around the Curraghs, trying to find people, some of whom I've not even met yet."

"Like us," Fenella said.

"Exactly. But I must stop talking and let you get back to watching. Remember that you're meant to be sitting or standing silently, watching for wallabies. I'd rather you saved your, um, other activities, for later, if you don't mind. We're desperately keen to record some wallaby activity in this area. It's the best way to protect the Curraghs from development."

"We'll keep watch," Fenella promised.

"Excellent. I'm sure someone will be along to take your place in an hour or so. Please wait here until they arrive. It's important to have continuous coverage, you understand, for the entire twelve-hour period. Are you doing additional shifts later?"

"No, just this one, as it's my first," she told him.

He nodded. "I suppose that's wise," he said, sounding disapproving again. "I'll let you get back to watching. I need to find the rest of our volunteers and make certain that everyone is where they're meant to be."

Fenella watched him walk away and then turned back to Daniel. "He didn't like me."

"He didn't care for either of us. I don't think we're meant to be enjoying ourselves out here."

"We're supposed to be enjoying looking for wallabies."

"And why, exactly, are we here?"

"It truly did sound like a good idea at the time," Fenella sighed. "In the past two weeks, I've received over fifty different appeals for money from various charities on the island. For some reason, the first anniversary of my arrival on the island seems to have opened the flood gates in terms of people asking me for donations."

"I'm surprised anyone waited that long, really."

"I am, too, actually. I mean, everyone on the island knows that I inherited a fortune from Mona. Most people probably knew more about that than I did, when I got here."

Fenella's aunt, Mona Kelly, had left her entire fortune to Fenella, her sister's only daughter. Fenella had four brothers, but Mona had chosen not to leave them anything. The inheritance had given Fenella a chance to start over at forty-eight. She'd sold her little house in Buffalo, New York, quit her job as a university professor at the same school where she'd studied, and ended her ten-year relationship with another professor. When she'd arrived on the island, she'd known only that she'd inherited an apartment and some cash, but over time she'd learned that Mona had owned a great deal of property all over the island. There was antique furniture, stocks and shares, jewelry, and other valuables. Fenella would never need to work again and she could live quite lavishly if she chose to do so. And she could afford to give generously to charity, something it seemed as if everyone on the island knew.

"Your being flooded with requests for money doesn't explain why we're standing in the pouring rain in the middle of a soggy field."

"I get two types of letters. The first type is straight appeals for donations. Those get sent to Breesha, Doncan's assistant. She sorts through them and then sends me a list of which requests they recommend I support. Thus far, I've simply agreed with their advice. It seems easier."

"I didn't realize that your advocate dealt with such things," Daniel said.

There was something in his tone that suggested that the idea made him uncomfortable. That was fair enough, it made her uncomfortable, too. The idea of having a lawyer and his assistant handle her finances was still strange to her. She'd always worked hard for her money and done her best to be frugal. Having a fortune at her fingertips was proving to be a large adjustment. It was also causing difficulties in her relationship with Daniel.

The pair had first met over a dead body. Daniel was an inspector with the island's constabulary and he'd been put in charge of investigating that murder. At that point, Fenella had had no idea of the extent of her fortune, so it hadn't been an issue between them. Their friendship had developed into something more before Daniel had been sent to the UK for several months for some additional training. While in Milton Keynes, he'd met another woman who'd sparked his interest. Circumstances meant that he and other woman, Nancy Weston, couldn't pursue a relationship, and Daniel had returned to the island. It had taken some time, but he and Fenella were now starting to spend more time together, even though Fenella's money sometimes caused friction between them.

"It's all rather overwhelming," Fenella tried to explain. "I don't know anything about any of the charities, either. Apparently, in the first twenty-five letters that I gave to Breesha, there were two from charities that were completely made up."

"I hope she rang someone at the constabulary about that."

Fenella frowned at his policeman's voice. "She did, actually, but if I hadn't given her the letters, I might have simply sent checks to everyone. I didn't realize, in the first few days, just how many letters I was going to be getting, of course."

"So you've had a lot of appeals for money. What else do you receive?"

"Save the date cards and invitation to events. I believe there's going to be some charity event on every single Friday and Saturday evening from now until the end of time and I've been invited to every last one of them."

"And you're complaining?"

Fenella laughed. "Do you want to go to some charity auction or fancy dinner with barely edible food, just so you can be asked for a huge donation as the evening progresses?"

"Is that how it works?"

"I assume so. I used to go to a lot of these things with Donald. I never understood why he always took me to charity events, but now I do. He's a businessman on the island, so he needs to make an appearance at most of them and they're happening all the time. And I do mean *all the time*." She took a deep breath, aware that she'd nearly shouted the last three words.

Donald Donaldson was wealthy and sophisticated with a reputation for going through women at a rapid pace. He'd taken Fenella out several times when he'd been on the island, but his nearly constant business travels had kept their relationship from developing into anything serious. When his daughter, Phoebe, had been badly injured in a car accident, he'd spent months in New York with her. Now he and Phoebe were in London, where she was getting round the clock care from a team of experts. The last Fenella had heard, Donald was falling for one of Phoebe's nurses and Fenella was more than happy that he had given up on pursuing her.

"How is Donald?" Daniel asked.

"He rang me last week, actually, to let me know that Phoebe is doing better. She's still got a very long way to go, though. He'd love to come back to the island, but the care she needs isn't really available here, at least not as readily as it is in London. He may come across for a few days soon to get away, and to deal with some business concerns. Obviously, he's been neglecting his business for the past several months."

"But you were explaining why we're here," Daniel said, dragging the topic back around.

"Oh, right, well, the thing is, I get invited to all sorts of charity balls and fancy luncheons, some of which Mona probably wouldn't have been invited to, because of her racy past," Fenella said.

When Fenella first arrived on the island, she'd been shocked to discover that her aunt, whom she'd only remembered vaguely from visits that Mona had made to the US when Fenella had been a child, had lived a wild life. She'd met Maxwell Martin, the wealthy businessman who'd showered her with riches, at eighteen. He'd moved her into one of his hotels and she had lived there, supported by his generosity, until he'd decided to turn the hotel into luxury apartments. He'd had the largest and most luxurious apartment built for Mona, and that was the apartment that Fenella had inherited. While Mona and Max had been devoted to one another, they'd never married, and there was a small portion of the island's population that had never approved of Mona. It seemed as if those people were prepared to ignore the source of Fenella's fortune, however, if she were willing to donate to their favorite charitable cause.

"Do you get Doncan to deal with the invitations, too?" Daniel asked.

Fenella made a face. "That sounded like an accusation of something, but I'm not sure what."

"I'm sorry. The money thing is weird for me," Daniel said, looking at the ground.

Fenella had recently met Daniel's sister and she'd told Fenella a few things that helped to explain Daniel's attitude. "The money thing is weird for me, too," she said softly. "I'm really hoping that having some money in the bank isn't going to change me. I hope I'm going to stay the same person and keep the wonderful friends that I've made on the island. I don't want the money to come between us."

"I don't want that either, but, well, it's difficult."

"I know it is. We should talk about it, rather than ignoring it, though."

"We should talk about a lot of things," Daniel said.

Fenella nodded. "Where would you like to start?"

He grinned at her. "You still haven't explained why we're standing in this soggy field."

Fenella laughed. "It's a wetland," she told him. "And I was getting there, but I keep getting sidetracked. Anyway, among all the invitations for fancy lunches and overpriced dinners, was an invitation to help the Manx Wallaby Society with their monthly wallaby hunt."

"Surely we aren't hunting for the little guys?"

"Not hunting as in killing, but hunting as in trying to find. The society tries to keep track of where the wallabies are living so that they can help protect their habitats as more and more developers try to build around the island."

"The island does need more affordable housing."

"Yes, I know, but there are lots of places that are more suitable for that than the Ballaugh Curraghs. This is wetland, for a start. And it's a long way from Douglas or any of the other towns or villages that might offer employment for the men and women who need this affordable housing."

"It is miles from everywhere," Daniel agreed, looking around. "It would be a wonderful place to have a house, well away from everyone and everything."

"But the commute to work, to the shops, to everything, would be a pain."

"You're right, of course. So you were asked to help with today's hunt?"

"As Rodney said earlier, I suspect the man in charge of the society was hoping that I'd read his letter and simply send him a check, but the idea of spending an hour enjoying nature and watching for wallabies seemed quite appealing as I read the letter."

"Was it sunny and warm outside that day?"

Fenella shook her head. "It was rainy and cold, but that was nearly two weeks ago. I was just dumb enough to think that it might be spring by the time today rolled around."

Daniel looked up at the sky and then back at Fenella. "From my experience, this is spring on the Isle of Man."

Fenella sighed. "Anyway, after I read the letter all about how the society spends an entire day in the Curraghs, every month, working in shifts to watch for wallabies, I called Darrell and agreed to come and donate an hour of my time."

"Darrell?"

"Darrell Higgins is the man's name. I'm afraid I don't know much more about him than that."

"I should have asked you for all of this before I agreed to come along. I could have done some discreet investigating."

"Why? The man is simply enthusiastic about wallabies. That isn't a crime, is it?"

"Of course not, but I still feel as if I should have done some background checks. It comes with the job, I suppose."

"I can't imagine being suspicious of everyone and everything," Fenella told him.

"I don't think I'm that bad. I just want to learn more about a man whose idea of fun is standing in the rain watching the shrubs for signs of life."

"I shouldn't have invited you along."

Daniel shook his head and then moved closer to her again. "I'm glad you invited me along. There isn't anyone I'd rather stand in the pouring rain with than you."

This time the kiss wasn't interrupted and when Daniel finally lifted his head, Fenella was very aware that a hundred wallabies, riding bicycles and singing show tunes, could have thundered past her during the kiss and she wouldn't have noticed.

"We need to watch for wallabies," she told him, blushing fiercely.

"Of course we do," he chuckled, a sexy sound that made Fenella's toes curl.

"What was that?" she asked a moment later, pointing toward several large shrubs in the distance.

Daniel looked over and then shrugged. "Wallabies are small kangaroos, right?"

"They look like kangaroos, anyway. They aren't actually kangaroos, though. I can't remember everything I read in the brochure that Darrell sent me, but I remember that much."

"Well, whatever you saw over there, it wasn't a small kangaroo."

Fenella sighed. Daniel was right. She hadn't seen a wallaby. In truth, she hadn't seen anything moving. She was simply trying to distract him before he could kiss her again. Things were moving in the right direction with their relationship, but she didn't want to find herself in over her head. It felt too soon to sleep with the man, even if his kisses did make her weak with desire.

"Are we allowed to walk around?" Daniel asked a minute later.

"We're supposed to be as still as possible, so as not to disturb the animals."

"I'm freezing over here, though."

"I know. I'm freezing, too. I should have worn more layers. I'm pretty much soaked through, too, in spite of the raincoat and the umbrella."

"Umbrellas can only do so much when the rain is coming down sideways."

"Yeah, that's true."

"The next time you decide to go to one of the charity events to which you've been invited, maybe you should take Shelly as your guest," Daniel said as he began to stamp his feet on the ground.

Shelly Quirk was Fenella's next-door neighbor and closest friend on the island. If Daniel hadn't agreed to join Fenella today, she might well have asked Shelly instead.

"I'm really sorry. I promise I won't invite you to anything other than fancy balls and dinners from now on."

He looked at her and then laughed. "Actually, all things considered, I think I'd rather be out here in the rain. I'm never quite certain how to behave at posh events."

"That makes two of us," Fenella sighed. "Mona was a natural at such things. I'm told she thrived on them, even, but I feel odd and out of place every time I go to anything."

Which frustrated Mona to no end. Fenella did her best not to think about the ghost who haunted her apartment, but there was no doubt that Mona's ghost played a huge role in her life. The dead woman offered advice, mostly unwanted, about Fenella's love life, how she spent her money, how she dressed, and just about everything else. Whenever Fenella complained about not knowing how to behave at social events, Mona questioned whether they were truly related. Of course, Mona had warned her not to attend the wallaby hunt.

"It will be cold and wet and horrible," she'd said. "Darrell Higgins will expect you to stand out there for hours on end, no matter what he told you on the phone, and then, when you're finally done, he'll still expect a huge financial contribution."

"Well, he won't be getting one," Fenella had said firmly.

"Darrell's an expert at manipulating people. Wait and see if he doesn't persuade you to write a check. He even talked me into donating to his latest projects once or twice and I was a lot more difficult to convince than you'll be."

"His latest projects?"

"Oh, Darrell goes through charities in the same way most men go through wives. Having said that, he's gone through a few wives, as well. He's wealthy, mostly due to inheritance, and he's bored, so he gets involved with one charity after another, throwing money at them and giving his time generously. Eventually, he gets bored with the cause or fights with someone on the staff, and then he moves on to his next project. The Manx Wallaby Society is unique, in that he started it himself, but he'll still get bored with it eventually."

As Fenella remembered the conversation, she frowned. Was it possible that she and Daniel were going to be stuck out here for more than an hour? When she'd met Darrell that morning, he'd insisted that another watcher would be there to replace her and Daniel at ten o'clock. She glanced at her watch. It was quarter to ten.

"Fifteen more minutes," Daniel said. "I can't wait to get into my car and put the heater on as high as it will go."

"That sounds like a little bit of heaven," Fenella sighed.

"I'm almost afraid to ask what you have planned for the rest of our day together."

"We're supposed to go back to the charity's office in Ballaugh as soon as we're done. That's where all of the reports of sightings are being coordinated. They're supposed to have tea and coffee and food all day."

"And after we're warm and fed, Darrell will try to talk us into taking another shift," Daniel guessed.

Fenella gave him a rueful grin. "You're starting to understand how these things work."

"I may need to invent something urgent that requires me back in Douglas immediately," Daniel said thoughtfully.

"Only if it needs me back in Douglas, too."

"We came in the same car. If I left you here, you'd be stuck."

"I'm sure someone from the charity would be happy to drive me home later," Fenella said. "Charity people are always incredibly helpful in that way."

Daniel laughed. "Especially when it means they can keep their volunteers working for longer."

"Exactly."

The next fifteen minutes dragged past slowly. Fenella found herself pacing in a small circle, trying to stay warm. No doubt the wallabies were all snuggled up together somewhere sheltered, laughing at the people who were dumb enough to stand out in the rain.

"It's ten o'clock," Daniel announced eventually. "We can go."

"We're supposed to wait for our replacement to get here, remember?"

"I remember, but I was hoping you'd forgotten."

Fenella laughed. "He or she should be here soon."

"Do you know who is replacing us?"

"I've no idea. When I ran into the office this morning to get our instructions, Darrell was the only person there. I've not met anyone else involved with the charity."

"But there is someone coming to replace us, right?"

"Darrell assured me that there would be someone here at ten. He had a chart with all of the different locations around the area and the names of who was meant to be covering each area on an hour by hour basis."

"So why isn't someone here yet?"

"Remember that it took us about ten minutes to walk here from where you parked your car. Our replacement is probably just walking in now," Fenella said, trying to stay optimistic.

"We didn't see anyone else as we walked here. Aren't there meant to be people all over the area?"

"There are, but everyone has been given their own specific GPS coordinates, the same way we were. I'm sure Darrell has us spread out to cover as much area as possible."

"Or maybe we're the only two people dumb enough to be out here in the rain."

"We saw Rodney," she reminded him. "He said he was checking on everyone."

"Which could mean twenty people or three."

"From what Darrell said when we spoke on the telephone originally, it's a fairly large operation. I remember him saying something about having dozens of volunteers to coordinate for the day."

"At this point, I'm only interested in one volunteer, the one who is replacing us."

"I can try to call Darrell if no one turns up soon, but I don't have great reception on my phone out here."

Daniel pulled out his mobile and frowned at it. "I don't have any service at all. It's a good thing I'm not on call today."

Fenella was just about to try to ring Darrell when she heard a sound. "What was that?" she asked.

"It sounds as if a herd of elephants is heading this way," Daniel told her.

A moment later, they spotted someone approaching them. The woman was stomping through the grass, her raincoat rustling as her umbrella rattled in the wind.

"Wallaby lovers unite," she shouted when she got a bit closer.

"Hello," Fenella called back. The new arrival was probably somewhere in her sixties, with grey hair that was caught up in a messy pony-tail under the hood of her coat. She had generous curves and a bright smile on her face as she stopped in front of Fenella.

"Hello, hello. What a lovely day for wallaby watching. I'm so excited to be here. Please tell me that you saw dozens of the wonderful creatures during your hour," she said without pausing for a breath.

"Sadly, we didn't see a single wallaby," Fenella replied. She introduced herself and Daniel.

"Oh, it's very nice to meet you both. I'm Gail Greer. I'm a retired civil servant who's more than a little obsessed with wallabies. I lived in Rugby for years and years, but when I retired, I decided that I wanted to live somewhere that had wild wallabies. Australia was tempting, but it's a long way away from Rugby, you know? I was all set to fly down and take a look at it, when I heard that the Isle of Man had its own wallaby population. That was three years ago. I've been here ever since."

"Have you seen many wallabies in the wild then?" Fenella asked.

Gail frowned. "Not really, actually. When I first moved across, I used to just drive around and look for them, but I never found any. About a year ago, Darrell started his charity and began having these hunts. I've been on every single hunt for the past twelve months. Once I found some wallaby tracks in the mud and another time I saw some movement in some shrubs, but I couldn't actually see what was there. I'm sure I'll see a wallaby soon."

Fenella and Daniel exchanged glances. The woman's enthusiasm was admirable. Fenella couldn't imagine spending that much time watching for wallabies and never seeing any. She was frustrated about the single hour she'd spent today.

"Anyway, I'm here for a two hour shift now. I'm sure I'll see a wallaby this time. If not, I'm doing another two hours this afternoon and then another two hours in the evening. That's probably the best time to see them, of course, as it starts to get dark. They're a lot more difficult to spot, but they're more likely to be out and about."

"Are they nocturnal, then?" Fenella asked.

"They're classified as nocturnal, but they're really more crepuscular. That's more active around dawn and dusk, though their active period can continue after dark."

"Well, good luck to you," Daniel said.

"Are you taking any more shifts today?" Gail asked.

Fenella shook her head. "This was our first experience with the Manx Wallaby Society. We thought we should limit ourselves to a single hour for the first time."

"Except you didn't see anything. I'm sure, if you ask, Darrell will be able to find you another shift later in the day. You can't give up on seeing a wallaby in the wild, not after only a single hour."

"Yes, well, sadly we have plans for the rest of today. Maybe another month," Fenella told her.

"Oh, that would be good, too. We usually have our best results in spring and autumn for some reason. That's why I'm so sure that today will be a good day."

"Yes, well, good luck," Daniel said. He took Fenella's arm and began to lead her away from Gail. "I hope you see several wallabies as the day goes on."

"Now, I mustn't be greedy," Gail laughed. "I'll settle for just one, really."

Daniel nodded and then began to walk faster. Fenella shouted "good-bye" over her shoulder as they went.

"I think you can slow down now," she said after a few minutes of rapid walking. "She isn't following us."

Daniel grinned at her. "I wasn't worried about that. She's too eager to see a wallaby. She'll stay in her spot all day, I'm sure. I'm just trying to get to the car as quickly as possible so that I can put the heating on and warm up a bit."

"I don't mean to be difficult, but are you sure you're going in the right direction?" Fenella asked a minute later. "I don't remember that cluster of pine trees on the way in."

"We were following the GPS coordinates on the way in," Daniel replied. "I wasn't paying enough attention to our route."

"Me, either. I don't suppose you have the coordinates for where you left your car."

"I wish I did," he sighed.

They continued along the barely visible path, both looking for any other path leading off of it. Eventually, Daniel stopped and pulled out his mobile. "Luckily, I have a signal," he told Fenella.

Using the maps function, he was able to work out where they were in relation to the nearest road. "We must have taken a wrong turn somewhere," he sighed as he showed Fenella the map. "Let's stop worrying about the path and cut straight across this bit."

"Are you sure?"

"No, but it's the best idea I can come up with when I'm freezing."

Fenella nodded and then followed him as he began to walk across the large field in front of them. They were nearly across it when Fenella saw something out of the corner of her eye. Something bright orange stood out under some nearby bushes.

"What's that?" she asked, stopping in her tracks.

Daniel looked in the direction she was pointing. "It looks like someone is trying to take shelter under those shrubs. Presumably, it's another of our intrepid wallaby hunters."

"Maybe we should have tried sheltering under a bush."

Daniel chuckled, but he was still staring at the splash of orange in the distance.

"Let's go," Fenella suggested.

"I think I want to get a closer look at whatever is over there," Daniel replied.

Fenella didn't question him. She'd felt as if there were something wrong with what she'd seen from the moment she'd spotted it. There wasn't any path between them and the orange object, but they slogged through the wet field together. It wasn't until they were practically on top of what Fenella had seen that they could make out what they'd found.

"He's dead, isn't he?" Fenella asked in a quavering voice.

Daniel crouched down next to the man on the ground to check for a pulse. When he pulled his hand away, it was covered in blood.

❧ 2 ❧

Daniel muttered a few choice words. "Ring 999 on here," he said, handing her his phone. "I can't do it with one hand."

She nodded and punched in the numbers.

"I'll talk to the dispatcher," Daniel added.

When the call was answered, she handed the phone back to Daniel. He spoke in short, sharp sentences, detailing the situation and their location.

"Someone will be here soon," he told Fenella as he pushed the end call button on the phone. He dropped the phone into his pocket and looked back down at the body. "Any idea who we've found?"

"It's Darrell Higgins," Fenella told him. "Or rather, it's the man who introduced himself to me as Darrell Higgins this morning in the office where I picked up our instructions."

Daniel frowned. "I was really hoping this was going to be nothing to do with us."

"It is nothing to do with us. We didn't know the man, after all."

"But we were here as part of the day that he'd arranged. We're part of it, whether we want to be or not."

"We're part of it because we found the body, anyway."

"Yes, of course," Daniel sighed. "Tell me everything you know about Darrell Higgins, then, while we wait for the police."

Fenella frowned. She knew very little about Darrell, aside from the few things that Mona had told her. This was not the time or the place to try to explain Mona to Daniel. "I'm afraid I don't really know anything about him. I should have asked someone about him, shouldn't I?"

"All things considered, yes," Daniel said. "You didn't discuss him with Doncan or Breesha?"

"I told Breesha that I was going to be helping with today's hunt and she told me that she wanted to hear all about it when I got back. She said it was something she'd considered volunteering with before, but she hadn't found the time, yet."

"She didn't say anything about Darrell?"

"Not that I remember. I've heard some things about him from various sources over the year or so since I've been here, but it's all hearsay and I don't know that I can recall who said what, if you know what I mean."

"At this point, I'm more than happy to hear gossip and innuendo. We're just talking. This conversation doesn't need to go into your formal statement."

"Someone told me that he was a bored, rich man who spent most of his time working with his favorite charity. That favorite charity changed fairly regularly, though."

"And the wallaby thing?"

"Was the first charity he'd ever set up on his own. He'd been running it for about a year, which was, as far as I was told, quite a long time for him."

"Interesting. Any signs that he was getting tired of the little marsupials?"

"Not that I'm aware of, but I'd never even met the man until today."

Daniel sighed. "I should have come in with you this morning and met him myself."

"Because you should have known that he'd end up murdered by the end of the day?"

"Considering your track record, maybe."

Fenella felt as if she'd been slapped. She took a step backwards and took a deep breath to stop herself from blurting out a hasty reply. Before she could speak, Daniel held up a hand.

"That was out of line and I didn't mean for it to sound the way that it did. Even you have to admit that you've found more than your fair share of dead bodies in the past year."

"One was more than my fair share," Fenella said steadily.

"Yes, of course, but with everything that's happened, I should have been more diligent when you told me about today. I should have done some discreet checking into Darrell and his wallaby organization, and I should have made a point of meeting the man myself this morning."

Fenella opened her mouth to reply, but before she could speak, a voice called from behind her.

"Inspector Robinson? Hello." The uniformed constable wasn't very tall and he seemed to be struggling to get through some long grass.

"Hello," Daniel called back.

"I'm Constable Harrison," he said when he finally reached them. "I was closest, so I was sent to secure the scene."

"You can start with crime scene tape," Daniel told him. "You'll have to try to find trees to string it around, rather than just shrubs."

"Yes, sir," the younger man said smartly.

Fenella stood and watched as the constable began to stretch crime scene tape from one tree to another. Even though it was only a thin strip of plastic, Fenella began to feel slightly trapped as the constable completed the large circle around the body with Fenella and Daniel on the inside.

"What next?" he asked eagerly when he was done.

"Now we wait for the crime scene team," Daniel told him.

The constable nodded. "Yes, sir. How did you happen to find the body, though? I mean, what were you doing out here today? It's not a very nice day for a walk through the Curraghs, is it?"

Daniel glanced up at the sky and shook his head. "It's not a nice day, at all."

"What are you doing now?" a loud voice demanded.

Fenella spun around and frowned as Rodney Simmons walked toward her.

"This isn't your assigned section," he said crossly. His eyes narrowed as he looked at the constable. "And what do you think you're doing?" he demanded.

The constable looked at Daniel and then cleared this throat. "I'm sorry, but this is a crime scene. I'm going to have to ask you to take a step back, please."

Rodney shook his head. "Crime scene? I don't know what's going on here, but these two people are meant to be somewhere else altogether. Where is the person who's meant to be watching this section?"

"Who is assigned to this section?" Daniel asked.

"I wish I knew. As I told you earlier, Darrell insisted on doing the rota himself for today, and I can't make heads nor tails of what he's done. The sections are all different to how we normally divide them. Some areas don't seem to have anyone covering them at all and other areas have more volunteers than they need. Everything is going wrong and I can't seem to reach Darrell to get it straightened out."

"You've been trying to ring him?" was Daniel's next question.

"All morning. He isn't answering his mobile, but if he's out here somewhere, that isn't surprising. Reception out here is patchy, at best. It's also possible that he's ignoring me, of course. We exchanged a few angry words about his sudden insistence on taking over everything. Knowing Darrell, he doesn't want to talk to me because he knows things are going badly."

"How badly are they going?" Fenella asked, certain that they were going to get a lot worse once Rodney spotted the body behind Daniel.

"As I said, the sections are all different to how we normally arrange things. That's confusing our volunteers. Some of the new sections are too large to be monitored by a single person, and some are quite small with people nearly tripping over their neighbors in the next section. I don't know what Darrell was thinking when he changed everything, but we'll be going back to the old system next time, mark my words."

Fenella and Daniel exchanged glances before Daniel spoke again. "How many sections are there?"

"Ten now. There used to be eight. That's another problem, of course, because now we need two additional volunteers every hour. It should mean that everyone's section is smaller, but that isn't the case, either. Some are smaller and others are larger," Rodney complained.

Movement some distance away caught everyone's attention. Fenella watched as several men and women in white suits approached the area.

"What is going on here?" Rodney demanded. "Who are they and why are they here?"

"It's a crime scene team," Daniel told him.

"What crime scene?" Rodney asked. He looked at Daniel and then slowly looked around. To Fenella it seemed as if he hadn't noticed the police tape before, even though he'd stopped just short of it. "What's going on?"

"We're just waiting for an inspector from the Ramsey Constabulary," one of the men in white told the constable.

"He's an inspector from Douglas," the constable replied, nodding toward Daniel.

The other man shrugged. "We were told to wait."

"What is going on?" Rodney repeated his question.

Fenella began to wonder if the man was dumb or guilty of something. In his place, she would have taken a few steps closer to the police tape and tried to see what was happening, not just stood in one place, demanding answers.

As Fenella thought about it, the idea seemed to occur to Rodney. He took a step forward and began to try to see around Daniel.

"I'm going to ask you to stop there," the constable said. As he took a handful of steps toward Rodney, it became more obvious what he and Daniel had been blocking from view.

Rodney stopped in his tracks. "Is that a body?" he asked hoarsely. "It is, isn't it? But whoever it is, he's wearing Darrell's favorite raincoat. We always tease him about wearing bright orange out here. The walla-bies can see him coming for miles, can't they? I always feel as if it's his fault if we don't see any wallabies, since he's so obvious. I tell the volunteers to wear dark colors so that they blend in with the trees and shrubs, but Darrell never listens to me. He never listens to me about anything else, either, not just about what not to wear on our wallaby hunts."

He stopped and drew a shaky breath. One of the women in white crossed to him. "Sir, I think you should take a few steps back. Tell me why you're here today."

Rodney looked at her and then slowly shook his head. "One of the volunteers must have turned up without a coat. Darrell must have lent the volunteer his coat, that's the only thing that makes sense. I'll just ring Darrell and ask him who he lent his coat to, shall I? The poor man or woman must have had a heart attack, I imagine? How terribly unfortunate."

He pulled his mobile phone out of his pocket and tapped on it anxiously. The constable looked at Daniel, who shrugged. After a moment, a loud ringing noise could be heard from behind Daniel.

Rodney frowned. "Darrell's phone must have still been in the coat's pocket when he let someone borrow it. That will be why I haven't been able to reach him all morning." He looked at Daniel. "I know all of our volunteers. If you'll just step aside, I can get a look at the man's face and let you know who has sadly passed away."

"We'll wait and see what the inspector from Ramsey wants to do," Daniel told him.

For a moment, Fenella thought that Rodney was going to object, but instead, he dropped his head and then shuffled backward a few feet. More movement across the field signaled the arrival of another group of investigators, including the promised inspector.

"Daniel, this is a surprise," the man said as he approached them. He appeared to be close to sixty, although his bald head may have made him look older than he actually was. Everything about him seemed average, from his height to his weight to the cost of the suit he was wearing.

"Alfred, I wasn't expecting to see you today," Daniel replied. "Not that any of what's happened today has gone to plan."

The other man raised an eyebrow. "We'll have a lot to talk about later, I'm sure. For now, introduce me to everyone."

"This is Fenella Woods, my, er, we were here together for the wallaby hunt put on by the Manx Wallaby Society," Daniel began.

Fenella smiled as Daniel stumbled over the introduction, grateful that she hadn't been the one to try to define their relationship for the other inspector.

"I'm Inspector Alfred Patrick from Ramsey CID," he told her. "You're Mona's niece, aren't you?"

"Yes, that's right." It was something Fenella was asked on a regular basis. The question was usually followed by an outrageous story about her aunt.

"Mona was something else," Alfred told her. "I stopped her once for speeding when I was still in uniform. She laughed and told to me ring the chief constable before I wrote out the ticket. I wasn't sure what to do, actually, so I ended up letting her off with a stern warning, just in case she truly was friends with the chief constable."

"Did you ever find out if she actually did know the chief constable?" Fenella had to ask.

"Oh, she knew him alright. In fact, she was driving his car that day," Alfred laughed. "This was many years ago now. The chief constable at the time had a collection of fast cars that he used to like to drive across the mountain. He'd lent one to Mona and that was what she was driving when I stopped her."

Fenella shook her head. "She led an interesting life."

"She did indeed. There was something magic about that woman," he replied, shaking his head and sighing. "But back to the business at hand. You are?" he asked Rodney.

"Rodney Simmons. I'm Darrell's assistant," he replied.

"Darrell?" Alfred asked.

"Darrell Higgins," Rodney told him, his tone indicating that he felt as if the inspector should have known without asking. "Darrell is the driving force behind the Manx Wallaby Society, among other things."

"Right, and why are you here, exactly?" was Alfred's next question.

"It's our monthly wallaby hunt today. We've volunteers scattered throughout the Curraghs, watching for wallaby."

"Why?"

"Why? Because it's important to keep track of how many wallaby are living in the wild. If nothing else, it's data that can be used to help protect the Curraghs from development."

Alfred shrugged. "How many people are scattered throughout the area, then?"

"I'm not absolutely certain. There should be ten, based on the way Darrell divided up the sections, but he took charge of everything this time. There have been times when we've failed to recruit enough volunteers to cover every section for the entire twelve-hour day, you see."

"I think we need to start rounding up the volunteers," Alfred said to the uniformed constable.

"Rounding them up? You can't do that. They're here to perform a valuable service," Rodney protested.

"I'm afraid our investigation is going to have to take precedence over your wallaby watch today. You'll have to reschedule the watch for later in the month, maybe," Alfred told him.

"But Darrell is going away tomorrow. He won't be back for several weeks. This was the last possible day to have the watch this month," Rodney countered. "He's going to be absolutely furious with you for canceling. I don't know that he knows the chief constable well enough to borrow his cars, but he certainly does know him."

"I'm sorry, but under the circumstances, I'm going to have to insist that you call off your hunt for today," Alfred replied. "I can send my men into the Curraghs to try to find everyone, or you can simply ring them and ask them all to report to a central location immediately. Which do you prefer?"

Rodney opened his mouth and then snapped it shut again. After a moment, he took a deep breath. "I'll ring them. What should I tell them?"

"Tell them that, due to unforeseen circumstances, the hunt is being postponed and that everyone should report, well, somewhere. I can arrange for a location if you don't have one to suggest," Alfred replied.

"They can all go back to our headquarters building in Ballaugh. That's where they were all meant to report after their shifts, anyway," Rodney said. He gave the inspector the address.

Alfred made a note in his notebook. "Right, if you could ring every volunteer and ask him or her to go straight from here to there, I would appreciate it. We'll have someone there to start taking statements shortly."

"I did offer to identify the body," Rodney said hesitantly. "I know all of our volunteers, well, our regular volunteers anyway. There were a few new ones today."

Something in his tone suggested that he wasn't happy about that turn of events. Fenella frowned at him, but bit her tongue.

Alfred glanced at Daniel who slowly shook his head. "Thank you, but I think we'll leave that for right now. If you'd like to go with Constable Howard, he'll take notes as you ring through your volunteer list."

"Notes?" Rodney repeated.

"We'll want the names and addresses of all of the volunteers," Alfred explained.

"I have all of that," Rodney assured him. He held up a small leather satchel. "It's all in here."

"Excellent. Constable Howard will take you back to where he's left his car. You can ring everyone from relative comfort there."

"If I can get service," Rodney muttered.

"Let me know how you get on," Alfred told the constable as he walked over to Rodney.

Fenella watched as the pair walked away.

"I can't believe he just walked away without trying to get a better look at the body," one of the crime scene team said.

"Maybe he was afraid of who he would see," Daniel suggested.

"Or he already knew who we've found," Alfred said.

Daniel nodded. "Now what?" he asked.

"Can either of you identify the body?" Alfred asked as he stepped inside the police tape.

"It's the man who introduced himself to me as Darrell Higgins this morning," Fenella said. "I'd never met him before today, though."

Alfred made a face and then looked at the body. "I've met him several times. It's Darrell Higgins, all right, although we'll need to have that officially verified by someone else." He sighed. "This is the last thing I need right now."

"I'd offer to help, but I doubt the chief constable would agree,"

Daniel said.

"Seeing as how you're a witness and all that, you won't be able to officially help. You're perfectly positioned to help from the inside, though," Alfred told him. "It goes without saying that you won't be a suspect, not as far as I'm concerned anyway. Ms. Woods won't be on my list either, but I never said that."

Fenella smiled at him. "I never heard it."

He nodded at her and then looked around. "We need a tent over the body," he announced. "We'll have to clear away some of the shrubbery around it, but we'll need pictures first. Let's go."

Daniel crossed to Fenella and took her arm. "That's our cue to get out of the way," he told her in a low voice.

"I'll need statements from both of you," Alfred said as he followed them outside the tape. "How long have you been involved with the charity?"

"Three hours," Fenella said.

Alfred laughed. "Really? This was your first time volunteering with them?"

"First and last," Daniel muttered.

"That would explain why you'd never met Darrell before, anyway," Alfred said. "Daniel, you never met him?"

"No. I drove to the office this morning, but only Fenella went inside. She got our instructions and we came out here."

"And found this."

"Only after standing in the pouring rain for over an hour watching for wallabies," Daniel told him.

"Did you see any?"

Daniel shook his head. "We didn't see anything, aside from Rodney and a woman called Gail Greer."

Alfred pulled out his notebook. "Gail Greer. Tell me everything."

"She came to replace us, actually. She's been volunteering for the charity for over a year but she hasn't actually seen any wallabies yet."

Alfred made a note. "Describe her."

Daniel complied, condensing the woman's appearance into a succinct description. Fenella made a mental note to try to emulate his technique if the police ever asked her to describe someone again.

"Ms. Woods, what can you tell me about Ms. Greer?" Alfred asked.

"Please, call me Fenella. I'm afraid I can't tell you anything more than Daniel. I'd never met her before and he's described her perfectly."

"What did you think of her?"

"She seemed pleasant enough. Maybe a bit obsessed about wallabies."

"Obsessed enough to kill for them?"

Fenella blinked several times. She hadn't exactly forgotten about the dead body, but she had put it out of her head. "I don't know," she said slowly. "It's difficult for me to imagine anyone killing another person over anything at all, but regardless, Darrell ran the island's foremost charity in support of wallabies. Surely, he'd be the last person she'd target."

Alfred shrugged. "You never know. If this was your first time volunteering, does that mean you've not met any of the other volunteers yet?"

Fenella shook her head. "Darrell was alone when we stopped at the office this morning. We were supposed to go back there after our shift. Darrell told me there would be hot drinks and snacks available all day for people before and after their shifts."

"And that's where you were heading next?" Alfred asked.

"Yes, although we probably weren't going to stay long," Fenella told him. "I was pretty sure someone was going to try to talk us into taking another shift or two."

Alfred nodded and then looked at Daniel. "Can I have a word?" he asked.

The pair walked a few paces away. Fenella looked over at the team of constables who were struggling to erect a tent around the body. The wind was picking up and that seemed to be hampering their efforts. Daniel was back a moment later.

"Okay, we're going," he told Fenella.

"Going?"

"We're heading to the office with the rest of the volunteers," he told her in a low voice.

"Oh, okay," she replied, trying not to sound as surprised as she felt.

"We need to follow the path," he added as he took her arm and began to lead her away.

Fenella was still feeling more than a little lost. She could only hope that the path would take them out of the wetlands somewhere near to where Daniel had left his car.

Just as Fenella was starting to think that they were hopelessly lost, she saw a car drive past surprisingly close to them. "It's the road," she said.

"You thought we were lost."

"Totally and hopelessly."

Daniel chuckled. "You should have more faith in me."

"You weren't worried?"

"I was a little worried," he admitted. "Alfred assured me that the path would come out at the road eventually, though. I trust him, more or less."

"Why did he..." Fenella stopped when Daniel held up a hand.

They were at the road now and Fenella could see a long row of police cars parked along both sides of it. Daniel's car was visible some distance away. There was another car parked behind Daniel's that was clearly not a police vehicle. It was an older four-door car that had seen better days. Fenella could see a few dents in the doors and the rear bumper as they approached the out of place car. There was someone sitting behind the steering wheel and when they reached the car, Daniel knocked on the window.

The window was slowly rolled down. "Oh, hello," Gail said, blinking several times at him. "I was just trying to think."

"To think?"

"I don't understand why there are so many police cars here. Do you know?"

"I believe we're all supposed to go to the charity offices in Ballaugh," Daniel told her.

"Yes, that's what Rodney said, but why? I've done this many times before and we've never canceled a hunt. What could possibly have happened to make them cancel this one?"

"Maybe we'll learn more once we get to the office," Daniel said.

Gail nodded slowly. "I was thinking maybe I should just go home, though. I mean, if the hunt is canceled, why have us all go to the office? They can simply email us with the new date and our assigned times, can't they? This is all very odd."

"Which is even more of a reason to do exactly as you were asked," Daniel told her firmly. "Perhaps the police want to speak to all of the volunteers."

"The police? Why would they want to speak to me? I don't know anything about anything. I don't want to talk to the police," Gail said, her voice rising in pitch as she spoke.

Daniel frowned. "I think you would be wise to go straight to the charity office."

Gail shook her head. "I don't want to and you can't make me," she said, nearly shouting. She rolled the window back up and then started the car. As she pulled away, Daniel pulled out his mobile. Fenella listened as he talked to Alfred, giving him the woman's plate information.

"He's going to have her picked up and taken in for questioning," he told Fenella after he'd ended the call.

Fenella nodded. "Will she be in much trouble?" she asked as they climbed into Daniel's car.

"Probably not. Whatever Rodney is telling people, he can't make them go to the office from here. I'm sure Gail won't be the only one who decides not to bother."

"Except you told her to go to the office."

"But I never identified myself as police," he pointed out. "For the moment, I'd prefer it if no one at the Manx Wallaby Society was aware that I'm an inspector. We're simply doing what we were asked and reporting to the office after our shift, nothing more."

"So you're undercover?"

"Nothing that sophisticated. I'm just not going to volunteer any information about my job, that's all. The first person we meet may well know me, which will make this a wasted exercise, anyway."

"But Alfred thought it was worth trying."

"He thought I might overhear something at the office that would be useful."

Fenella nodded. "At least we'll be out of the rain."

❧ 3 ❧

Five minutes later, they pulled up to the small cottage that housed the offices of the Manx Wallaby Society. When they'd been there earlier that morning, the parking lot had been empty. Now it was full of cars and there were others parked along the road near the cottage. Daniel found a space a short distance away and the pair walked back. He opened the door and held it so that Fenella could walk in first.

"Who are you?" someone demanded as they entered the building.

"I'm Fenella and this is Daniel," Fenella replied. "Our shift finished at ten and we were told to come back here once we were done."

"It's gone eleven. You took your time," a voice suggested.

Fenella flushed. "We got a bit lost on our way out of the Curraghs," she said sheepishly.

She looked around the small room. It had presumably once been the cottage's living room and it was still similarly furnished with couches and chairs. There were about half a dozen people lounging around the room. A large coffee maker stood on a table in the corner. "Is there coffee?" she asked.

"There is," another voice replied. "A pound a cup."

Someone laughed. "Don't mind Jody. She's always trying to get money out of people. The coffee is free for volunteers."

Fenella quickly crossed to the machine and poured two cups of coffee. After handing Daniel a cup, she took a slow sip and then sighed as the warmth began to spread through her wet and cold body. After another sip, she glanced around again.

"I wasn't expecting there to be so many people here," she said tentatively.

"There shouldn't be anyone here. We should all be out in the Curraghs, watching for wallabies. Someone called off the hunt," someone said.

"Called off the hunt," Fenella echoed.

"Yeah. I was out in my section, watching for my little friends, when Rodney rang and told me to come back here. So here we are, with no idea of what's going on out there," a man told her.

"There were a lot of police cars parked around our car when we left," Fenella said.

"I saw them. I'm going to guess that one of our volunteers had a heart attack and died when he or she actually finally saw a wallaby," another voice called out.

Everyone laughed.

"So who's missing?" another voice asked. "We've all been doing this for long enough that we should be able to work out who isn't here."

"Darrell had a lot of new volunteers this time," the woman who'd said the coffee was a pound per cup replied.

Fenella studied her. Maybe forty, she had blonde hair that was caught in a casual ponytail. Her clothes looked expensive and there was no way she'd been outside in the rain thus far this morning.

"Really? Where did he find new volunteers?" someone asked.

The blonde shrugged. "Ask Fenella. She's one of them."

"He sent me a letter," Fenella replied. "It was all about the charity and the good work that it does, and it asked me to consider giving up an hour of my time for the hunt. I thought it might be interesting."

"And was it?" the blonde asked mockingly.

"It might have been, in better weather," Fenella told her. "I didn't catch your name."

The other woman smiled thinly. "I didn't give it."

"And no one else here knows who you are," someone laughed. "She's Jody Stevenson Higgins, or is it Higgins Stevenson?"

The blonde flushed. "It's Stevenson. Full stop. I didn't use Higgins when I was married to Darrell and I certainly don't use it now."

"You were married to Darrell?" Fenella asked.

"I was. It was the worst year of my life."

"I'm surprised you support his charity, then," Fenella said.

Jody shrugged. "I can't blame the wallabies for the way that man treated me, can I? Anyway, Darrell and I are still friends, of a sort. I help him with his charity and he helps me in other ways."

"And she gets to keep a very close eye on the charity's finances," a voice called. "Just in case Darrell starts pocketing any of the funds that get donated. She'd want a share of anything he did pocket, you understand."

Jody laughed. "I earned every penny I've ever received from Darrell and a good deal more. It was a very long year."

Fenella glanced at Daniel. His smile seemed to suggest that she should continue. "Rodney isn't here?" she asked.

"No, but we know he didn't have a heart attack. He's the one who rang all of us and told us to come back here," Jody told her.

"Right, so who is missing?" Fenella asked.

"Gail isn't here," a voice said.

"Gail?" Jody said scornfully. "She probably refused to leave. She's probably tied herself to a tree in protest of the cancellation. Having said that, she'd be at the top of my list of people who would probably die if they ever actually did see a wallaby."

"I can't imagine what you must be thinking of all of us," a man said. He stood up from one of the couches and walked over to Fenella. "I'm Nicholas Fitzgerald. Welcome to the Manx Wallaby Society. We truly aren't always this bad. Things are just in a bit of a mess today. I've been doing these hunts from the very beginning and we've never had one canceled, not after it had started, anyway. We're all confused and some of us are worried about what might have happened to cause the cancelation."

Nicholas had to be in his sixties, Fenella guessed. His grey hair was neatly trimmed, as was his moustache. She could see damp patches around his wrists and ankles, no doubt where his raincoat had failed to provide adequate cover while he'd been standing in the rain.

"It's nice to meet you," Fenella told him.

"We can always use new volunteers," Nicholas told her. "We lose people all the time, especially when we've had bad weather for a few months in a row."

"And we've had bad weather for several months in a row now," a woman said. She also looked to be in her sixties, with grey hair in a neat bun. Like Nicholas, her clothes were damp in spots, but otherwise she was immaculate. She grinned at Fenella.

"I'm Sara Hampton. I love wildlife and I've been doing these hunts for about a year now. I'll admit that today was a struggle, though. My first thought, when Rodney said the hunt was canceled, was that Darrell had finally come to his senses and called things off due to the weather. I should have known better, though."

"You really should have," another man who looked even older than Nicholas said. He had a handful of grey strands of hair on his head that seemed to stick out in every direction. "I'm William Faragher," he told her. "I've been hunting the wallabies for more years than I want to admit. I was doing it well before young Darrell decided to make it his pet project, anyway."

"It's nice to meet you," Fenella told him.

"But we were going to try to work out who's missing," Jody said. "Who has the list of volunteers? Kristen, please tell me that you're good for something."

The very pretty blonde who was standing behind the desk in the corner flushed. "You could at least pretend to be polite to me in front of other people," she complained.

"I can't imagine why I would," Jody shot back. "You slept with my husband."

Kristen sighed. "How many times do we have to have this conversation? I didn't sleep with Darrell when you two were married. You were already separated when I met him."

"Yeah, right, I'm going to believe that," Jody said, rolling her eyes.

"You should believe it, because it's true," Kristen told her.

"That's Kristen Warner," Sara told Fenella. "She's Darrell's most recent girlfriend."

"And thanks for that," Kristen said sharply.

Sara shrugged.

"Do you have the volunteer list?" Jody asked.

Kristen stared at her for a minute and then shook her head. "Darrell took care of everything himself this time. Rodney usually did the rota and then I simply kept track of everyone throughout the day. This time Darrell told us both that he'd deal with it all himself. I never even saw the final list."

"Is he one who changed all of the sections, too?" Nicholas asked. "My section today was far too large for one person to observe. The old sections were all just right."

"Darrell told me he wanted to try something different this time. He seemed to think that we were missing things because of gaps between sections. He spent ages going over the maps, drawing and redrawing everything," Kristen said.

"Well, he did a terrible job of it," William said. "We need to go back to the previous sections next month."

"That will up to Darrell," Kristen said.

"If he wants me to volunteer again, we'll go back to the old sections," William amended himself.

Kristen frowned. "You know how much he relies on you, William."

"Yes, I do," William replied.

"I thought the new sections worked just fine," the only person who hadn't yet introduced himself said. He stood up from his couch and crossed to where everyone was standing near the coffee machine. "I'm Harry Fields," he told Fenella as he poured himself a drink. Harry was younger than the other men. Fenella would have put him at not much more than forty. His hair was dark with only a few grey strands sprinkled through it. He was wearing expensive-looking casual clothes and Fenella couldn't detect any dampness anywhere on the man.

"Which section were you watching?" William demanded.

"I had a later shift," Harry replied. "I was due to go out at eleven. I was here with Kristen and Jody when Rodney rang to let us know that the hunt had been canceled."

"Rodney rang here, too?" Sara asked. "Where's Darrell in all of this?"

"That's a very good question," Jody said. "Where is Darrell?" She turned and looked at Kristen. "Where is Darrell?" she repeated.

Kristen shrugged. "He went out to the site. He was going to walk the sections himself to see how they were working. He texted me to tell me that because he'd left here before I got here. I haven't heard from him since."

The room fell silent and Fenella could almost feel the atmosphere darkening as everyone considered what Kristen had said.

"We're missing a bunch of volunteers, of course," Sara said after a moment. "Jake's not here."

"Jake's in Birmingham, visiting his daughter," Nicholas said. "She just had another baby."

"Another one? I thought she already had six," Sara replied.

"I believe this one is number six, actually," Nicholas told her. "It was finally a girl, after five boys, so maybe they'll stop."

Sara nodded. "What about Dave? He never misses a hunt."

"He's in Noble's," Kristen told her. "Apparently, he had a mild stroke. He's expected to make a full recovery, but it's going to take some time."

"What a shame," Sara said. "Who else is missing, though?"

"Doug?" William asked.

"Moved to Liverpool to be near his daughter. He hasn't been here in months," Sara replied.

"Betty?" someone suggested.

"She's on her honeymoon," Kristen told them.

To Fenella it seemed as if everyone gasped at once.

"Her honeymoon?" Sara repeated. "I'm sorry, but are we talking about the same woman? Betty Christian? She's been fifty-nine for the past six years and as far as I know, she's never looked at a man."

Kristen nodded. "That's Betty. She told me as much, too, about the not looking at a man, anyway. Apparently, she was at ShopFast one day and she nearly got knocked down by some guy on one of the motorized scooter things. Turns out he didn't really know how to drive it or how to grocery shop. His wife had just passed away a few weeks earlier and that was the first time he'd ventured out of his house alone since he'd lost her. According to Betty, they started talking in the bakery and by the time they'd reached the frozen foods, he'd asked her to have dinner with him. They went out every night for a week and then he proposed."

"After a week?" Sara said incredulously.

"I know, it doesn't make any sense, but that's the story Betty told me. Anyway, they got married a week later and they're on their honeymoon now. They're on a cruise around the Caribbean, which I can't imagine Betty will enjoy. Apparently, it was something her new husband always wanted to do, but his first wife wouldn't go with him," Kristen told them all.

"Perhaps, instead of just listening to the story, you should have rung Betty's doctor. It sounds to me as if she's taken leave of her senses," Sara said.

Kristen shrugged. "She told me everything over the phone when I rang to give her the date for today's hunt. I barely had time to process what she was saying before she'd hung up so that she could finish her packing. They left that same afternoon. I believe they're due back one day next week."

"It's all very odd. What's her new husband's name? Maybe the police should investigate. Maybe he only went after Betty for her money," Sara said.

"She didn't give me his name, but I truly don't think Betty has much money. He's the one paying for the cruise, anyway. She told me that much. I gather he insisted on a cabin with a balcony, even though it was more costly than the other options. She was very excited," Kristen replied.

"He's going to push her off the balcony and inherit all of her money," Sara gasped.

"Does she have any money?" Nicholas asked. "She was a schoolteacher, wasn't she? I always got the impression that she barely had enough coming in each month to pay her bills."

"Maybe that's what she wants people to think, but she's secretly hoarding a fortune," Sara replied. "I'm going to ring the police later and suggest that they investigate. Kristen should have done that the moment she finished speaking to Betty, really."

"I never once imagined," Kristen began.

"Never mind that," William interrupted. "We still haven't worked out who is missing, aside from Rodney and Darrell, of course."

♪"We know Rodney is fine, as he's the one who rang everyone," Nicholas said. "What if something has happened to Darrell?"

"To Darrell? Nothing bad ever happens to Darrell," Jody interjected. "He leads a charmed life, that man."

"If there aren't any volunteers missing, surely there weren't enough people in the Curraghs this morning to fully cover all of the sections," Fenella said.

Kristen looked around and then shrugged. "We do the best we can with the volunteers we can get. Under the old system, when we were short-handed, we could redistribute the sections, so eight sections could become seven, or even six if necessary. I'm not sure how Darrell was doing things under his new plan, though."

"And let's be honest," William added. "We've never had enough volunteers to cover the entire area for an entire day. Darrell likes to gloss over that part when he talks about the charity, but in truth, we usually only cover about half of the actual area and normally only manage about eight hours of that."

Jody laughed. "And now you should be really honest and tell everyone exactly how many wallabies have been counted over the past year," she suggested.

William flushed. "I kept telling Darrell that we're doing things all wrong. The wallabies aren't going to come anywhere near people, not if they spot them, and we've never made any effort to hide ourselves. Besides, they're nocturnal, or nearly so. We should have started our shifts at dusk and worked through the night, rather than standing around all day while the wallabies are resting."

Fenella wondered why Darrell hadn't listened to William. Maybe it had something to do with getting volunteers, though. If they had trouble finding enough for shifts in the daytime, they'd probably never manage to find people willing to stay up all night.

"I'm starting to worry about Gail," Kristen said after a moment.

"She's the only one who isn't here. I thought Rodney told me that he'd spoken to her. Even if she took her time walking out of the Curraghs, she should have been here by now."

"Why don't you ring her?" William suggested. "Maybe she decided to go home instead of coming here."

"Why would she do that? She loves coming and sitting here all day, whether we have a hunt going on or not," Jody said.

Kristen reached for the phone on the desk in front of her. Before she touched it, though, the front door swung open.

Inspector Alfred Patrick walked into the room, accompanied by two uniformed constables. His eyes seemed to miss nothing as they moved around the room.

"Good morning," he said. He glanced at his watch and sighed. "It's technically afternoon, though. Good afternoon. I appreciate the patience that you've all shown while waiting for my arrival. I'm going to need a private space where I can meet with each person in the room individually."

Jody looked at Kristen. "He can use Darrell's office, can't he?" she asked the other woman.

Kristen frowned. "Darrell won't be happy about that."

"I'd rather not use that space if there's anything else available," Alfred told them.

"There's a small conference room, too, but it's pretty tiny," Jody replied.

"It will have to do," Alfred said. "Where is it?"

Jody gave Kristen another look, but Kristen didn't move. Sighing, Jody walked to the back wall of the room and opened the single door there. From where Fenella was standing, it appeared to open into a very short corridor. Alfred and Jody disappeared through the door, leaving the others with the two constables.

"So, what's going on?" William demanded of one of them.

"I'm sorry, sir, but I can't answer any questions," he replied.

"The inspector can't hear you from in there. Just give us a hint," Harry said from his seat on the couch.

"I'm sorry, sir, but I'm not entirely certain what's happening myself," the constable said.

Fenella noticed that Daniel seemed pleased with the young man's reply. Before anyone else could say anything, Alfred returned.

"I'm going to speak to each of you individually and then allow you to leave. When you do leave, I'm going to ask you to go out through the back door and to leave without attempting to speak to anyone who is still here," he announced. "Does anyone have any questions for me before we begin?"

"What's going on?" Sara asked.

"That's a good question. I'll explain more to each of you in turn," Alfred replied. "I don't suppose there's a list of who you all are anywhere?"

"I have a list of our regular volunteers," Kristen told him. "There are a few people here who aren't on the list, though."

"I'll take whatever you have," Alfred said. "I can add people if they aren't on the list."

"This is the list of volunteers from our hunt in January," Kristen said after searching through a pile of papers for a minute. "Darrell took the February one from me when he started working on today's event. I never got it back."

"As I said, I'll work with whatever you have." Alfred took the sheet and studied it for a moment. "Right, I now have at least some of your names. This list also details how long you've been working with the charity, which might be useful information. I'm just going to start at the top of the list with William Faragher unless anyone objects."

"How long will all of this take?" Harry asked. "The others are all retired or whatever, but I have a business to run, you understand."

Alfred frowned. "You are?"

"Harry Fields."

"You aren't on the list."

"He only volunteered for the first time in February," Kristen explained. "He's a business associate of Darrell's who was kind enough to agree to help out in February and then again this month."

Harry nodded. "I told Darrell that I needed to be done by midday today, though. I have some important appointments this afternoon."

"I can start with you, then," Alfred said. "I'm going to leave a constable here with the rest of you. That doesn't mean you can't speak to one another, though."

Just that someone will be paying close attention to everything you say, Fenella added in her head. Of course, with Daniel there, that was already the case, even if it had been less obvious.

Alfred and Harry left with one of the constables while the other went and stood near the door. After a moment, Jody blew out a breath.

"This is crazy. Why won't anyone tell us what's going on?" she demanded.

"Because something awful has happened and the inspector wants to see your face as he breaks the bad news to you," Sara told her. "Someone must have been murdered in the Curraghs. That's the only thing that makes any sense at all."

"You've been watching too much telly again," Nicholas told her. "No one gets murdered on the Isle of Man."

"Lots of people have been murdered here lately," Sara countered. "And there were a cluster of murders in the late nineties, too. I wonder who's dead."

"It won't be anyone we know," William said. "We're all too smart to kill anyone in the Curraghs on one of our hunt days. That's the only time anyone is out there, after all."

"I don't know that that's entirely true," Sara said.

"It's mostly true," William countered. "Have you ever seen anyone there during a hunt who wasn't with our group?"

"Well, no," she admitted. "But maybe people who enjoy the Curraghs try to stay away on hunt days."

"Maybe. Or maybe no one besides us regularly visits," William replied. "Remember, I've been hunting wallabies for years. It was a lonely job back before Darrell got involved. The Curraghs are beautiful, but isolated. If you were smart about it, you could hide a body out there and it wouldn't ever get found."

Fenella shivered. She and Daniel had come across Darrell's body accidentally. If they hadn't found it, would it have remained undiscovered?

"Maybe someone tripped over a body that's been out there for years," Sara suggested. "Who could it have been? Who's gone missing in the past few years?"

"Maybe it's Betty," Nicholas said. "Maybe her new husband killed her and then went on their honeymoon all by himself."

"What a horrible thought," Sara said with a smile.

Alfred's return interrupted the conversation. He looked around the room and then nodded at William. "Mr. Faragher? I just have a few questions for you."

William got to his feet and followed the inspector out of the room.

"Do Rodney and Darrell take shifts, too?" Fenella asked as the idea crossed her mind.

"Darrell often fills in wherever he's needed," Kristen told her. "Rodney is usually here, managing everything remotely. This time, with Darrell doing all of the managing, Rodney decided to go out to the site. I think he was hoping he'd find that Darrell had made a mess of everything, really."

"Of course he was," Jody laughed. "Rodney's never happy unless everything is being done exactly the way that he wants it done, even if there are a dozen better ways to do something. Oh, in this case, Darrell's way probably wasn't any better, but regardless, Rodney must have been furious when Darrell took over the planning. I'm surprised he put up with it, actually."

"He didn't have much choice, really," Kristen said. "Rodney did the schedule, but we were clearly short-handed. When he came in to talk to Darrell about it, Darrell told him not to worry and that he'd make it all work. The next day, Darrell started redrawing the sections and reassigning the volunteers."

"After Rodney had already done all of the work?" Sara asked.

"Yes, well, most of the work, anyway. As I said, it was clear we didn't have enough staff to cover everything," Kristen replied.

"But then, we never do," Jody pointed out.

"Darrell is trying to find a way to achieve better coverage for a longer period," Kristen replied. "He's hoping that his new sections will be more successful."

"Except some sections are too large for one person and other sections are oddly shaped or otherwise unmanageable," Nicholas countered.

"The new sections aren't perfect," Kristen admitted, seemingly reluctantly. "I'm sure Darrell will listen to everyone's ideas before next month."

"You aren't going to reschedule this month's hunt?" Sara asked.

Kristen shrugged. "Darrell is away on business for the rest of the month. We'll have to see what he and Rodney want to do, but I suspect they'll decide to simply leave everything until April."

"But what about the consistency of our data?" Sara asked. "We've an unbroken record now for twelve months. The last thing we want is a gap in our records."

"We can always use the data from the hours and sections that were actually completed," Kristen told her. "The entire first hour was completed with some sections covered, for a start."

"Did anyone see anything?" Sara demanded.

"I don't have all of the reports yet," Kristen replied. "Which reminds me, Fenella, you haven't completed your report."

"Oh, right. I'd completely forgotten about that," Fenella replied.

Kristen took a clipboard off her desk and slid a sheet of paper onto it. She walked over and handed the clipboard and a pen to Fenella, who glanced down at the sheet and frowned.

"That's a lot of questions," Daniel whispered in her ear as she stared at the clipboard.

"No one told me about the paperwork," Fenella whispered back. "I'm going to sit down for this."

She took a seat on the nearest couch and Daniel sat down next to her. Feeling as if she was being forced to do something against her will, Fenella began to answer the questions on the sheet.

There were twenty-six questions on the front of the page and Fenella felt herself getting increasingly fed up as she worked her way through them.

"Which of the following birds did you see during your hour?" she read out to Daniel. "I don't know what any of these types of birds are, do you?"

He looked at the list and then shrugged. "Not really."

"I didn't know I needed to be a bird expert to do this," she muttered as she ticked the box next to none.

"Which bird calls did you hear during your shift?" she asked Daniel.

"No idea," he said.

She laughed. "This is insane. I can't answer any of these questions, not really."

"Darrell probably didn't warn you about the paperwork, did he?" Jody called from where she was standing. "And you probably don't know how to answer any of the questions. For what it's worth, I doubt most of the volunteers can recognize all of the footprints, bird calls, and other things that Darrell seems to think everyone should know."

"Did he, er, I mean, does he know all about such things?" Fenella asked.

"I doubt it. I believe someone from some conservation group on the island put the report together for him. That man knew everything about every plant, animal, bird, whatever on the island. I believe he thought Darrell was going to be interested in more than just wallabies," Jody told her.

"I haven't even had any questions about wallabies, yet," Fenella replied.

"Oh, that's on the back," Jody said. "I hope you inspected your section very carefully for evidence of wallaby excrement. There's an entire section about that on the back of the page."

Fenella made a face. If she'd known about the report, she never would have volunteered. She was still working on the first page of the document when Alfred returned. He glanced around the room and then took Sara away for her questioning.

Alfred got through Sara, Nicholas, and Jody before Fenella was done with the report.

"It took far too long to simply say that I didn't see a single thing," Fenella complained as she handed the sheet back to Kristen.

The younger woman nodded. "I've been trying to persuade Darrell to do a new, simplified report, but he likes this one. It's the same as the official government reports on land usage, or something. I forget exactly what he said about it. Anyway, you can complain to him as much as you like, but I can't see him changing it."

Fenella knew there was no way Darrell was going to change anything, so she simply nodded and then went and sat back down next to Daniel. He took her hand and gave it a squeeze.

"You okay?" he asked in a low voice.

"I suppose so. I'm tired and hungry and sad, all at once."

He nodded. "It shouldn't be too much longer now. Kristen is the only person who hasn't spoken to Alfred."

The inspector was back only a few minutes later. He took Kristen away for her turn, leaving Fenella and Daniel on their own with the constable.

"I need more coffee," Fenella said. She got up and poured herself a cup. "Coffee?" she asked Daniel.

He hesitated for a moment and then nodded. "I'm falling asleep sitting here," he admitted as he stood up and joined her at the coffee machine.

"Can I offer the constable coffee, or is that against the rules?" she asked him after her first sip.

"Jacobs, do you want coffee?" Daniel asked the young man.

He flushed and shook his head. "Thank you, sir, but no, sir."

Fenella looked over the selection of snacks on display. Nothing looked particularly appealing. After a moment, her hunger won out and she grabbed a chocolate covered digestive biscuit from one of the plates. She'd had them before and she knew they weren't anything terribly special, but she needed something to keep her stomach from growling.

Alfred was back before she'd finished her coffee.

"Daniel, Fenella? Let's talk," he suggested.

4

The pair followed the police inspector into the conference room. Jody had been telling the truth. The room was tiny. Alfred slid into a chair and gestured.

"Take a seat," he told them both.

The table took up nearly all of the space in the room. There were six chairs around it and Fenella sat down across from Alfred. Daniel took the seat next to her. The uniformed constable squeezed his way around the table to sit next to Alfred.

"I'm going to take your statements individually in a moment, but before I do that, I wanted to ask you what you learned while you were here," Alfred told them.

"We met everyone, but I don't know that we learned much of anything," Fenella replied.

"Take me through everything that happened after you arrived here," Alfred told her.

She glanced at Daniel. Surely, he should be the one talking to the other inspector.

"You go ahead," Daniel said. "I didn't say much, anyway."

Sighing, Fenella began, doing her best to remember everything that had been said in the time they'd spent at the office waiting for Alfred to arrive. When she was done, Daniel gave her a smile.

"You remembered more than I did," he told her.

"Thank you for all of that," Alfred said. "I'm going to take Daniel's statement next, if you don't mind?"

Fenella shrugged. "I'll go back and wait in the lobby, then, shall I?"

"Yes, please," Alfred replied.

The uniformed constable walked her back out into the other room. Fenella poured herself another cup of coffee, more out of boredom than a desire to drink more. The door swung open a moment later.

"Where is everyone?" Rodney demanded as he stomped into the room.

"The volunteers have all been sent home once they've been interviewed," the constable at the door told him.

"What about Jody and Kristen, though? They're meant to be here," Rodney replied.

The constable shook his head. "I'm not certain where anyone went," he said. "I can ask Inspector Patrick if he knows when he's finished the interview he's currently conducting."

"Never mind. I'll ring them," Rodney snapped. He walked over to the desk in the corner and picked up the phone.

"Jody? It's Rodney. Where are you?"

"I'm sure you're very upset, but we still have work to do. I'll expect you here within the hour."

He put the phone down and then picked it up again immediately. "Kristen? It's Rodney. Ring me back at the office when you get this message."

Frowning, the man dropped into the chair behind the desk. As he began to flip through the papers on the desk, the constable spoke.

"I believe the inspector would prefer it if you didn't touch anything," he said.

"Darrell is dead. There are a number of things that need doing with some urgency as a result. He had several active business concerns that will need handling and, of course, something will need to be done about the charity, as well," Rodney replied.

The interior door opened and Daniel and Alfred walked out.

"Ah, Mr. Simmons, hello," Alfred said. "I wasn't expecting to see you here."

"I told you that I was going to have to come here and start dealing with everything when you informed me that Darrell was dead," Rodney countered.

"Yes, but I thought we'd agreed that you'd leave that until tomorrow," Alfred replied.

"Then I went home and started to think," Rodney told him. "There are so many things that need to be done. Darrell had a number of different business deals upon which he was working. Those all need to be managed. Running a charity is a huge undertaking, as well. I simply couldn't sit at home and leave everything undone."

"I'm afraid I'm going to have to ask you to wait a short while before you do anything," Alfred told him. "I have one more person to interview and then I'm going to want to go through all of the papers on that desk and Mr. Higgins's office before you move anything."

Rodney sighed and then sat back in the chair. "At least if I'm here, I can answer the telephone, can't I? I'm sure people will start ringing as soon as they hear about Darrell's unfortunate accident. I want to be able to set minds at ease and assure people that everything is being managed."

"You can answer the telephone," Alfred told him. "As for managing everything, that's a matter for the advocates, not me."

Rodney frowned. "I must ring Darrell's advocate, mustn't I? He'll have Darrell's latest will. I'm sure that will help clear up things."

"I've sent someone to speak to Darrell's advocate, actually," Alfred replied. "No doubt he'll be in touch with you as soon as he's finished speaking to the police."

"Wonderful," Rodney muttered.

The door swung open and Jody walked in.

"I'm here, but I'm not happy about it," she announced as she looked around the room.

"We can't do anything until the police are done with their investigation," Rodney told her. "You may as well go home again, I suppose."

"What did Mark say about everything?" Jody asked.

"I haven't spoken to Mark yet," Rodney replied.

Jody sighed. "What do you want to bet Darrell hadn't updated his will in years?" she asked. "I'm sure Mark has been nagging him for ages to do it, but you know how Darrell was."

"Maybe he left everything to you," Rodney suggested.

Jody laughed. "That would be a lovely surprise, but I'm pretty certain our divorce would have invalidated any will that he might have made leaving things to me. I just hope he didn't leave everything to Kristen."

Rodney laughed bitterly. "He wasn't that enamored of the woman," he said, sounding slightly uncertain.

"Ms. Woods, I need to get your statement," Alfred said. "I'd appreciate it if everyone else would simply wait here until I get back."

Rodney shrugged. "We've no choice, really, have we?"

"I want to go home," Jody announced.

The phone rang before anyone could reply. Rodney picked it up. After giving a handful of monosyllabic replies, he put the receiver back down.

"Mark is on his way," he said.

"Mark?" Alfred repeated.

"Mark Masterson, Darrell's advocate," Rodney explained.

"Things might just get interesting, then," Jody said as she dropped into a chair.

"Let me know when Mr. Masterson arrives," Alfred told the constable at the door.

He nodded and then Alfred turned back to Fenella. "Let's see if we can get our conversation done before he gets here."

Fenella followed him back into the conference room and sat back down in the same chair.

"Tell me how you first heard about the Manx Wallaby Society," Alfred began.

"Darrell sent me a letter about the society and about today's hunt."

"And you thought you'd enjoy standing in a field for an hour?"

"It sounded interesting. The letter was all about how unique and special it is to have a wild population of wallabies on the island. That a breeding pair managed to escape and that they've thrived in the Curraghs fascinated me."

"What happened next?"

"There was a phone number to call for more information, so I called. The man who answered identified himself as Darrell Higgins, the charity's founder."

"Tell what you can remember about the conversation."

"I told him who I was and that I'd received his letter. He said something about being flattered that I'd taken the time to read what he'd written. Then I said that I wanted to volunteer for an hour at their next wallaby hunt. He told me I could pick any time between nine and nine, so I offered to do the first hour. I'm always up at seven because my kitten wakes me, you see."

Alfred looked as if he wanted to ask her something, but he didn't. "Continue," he said instead.

"That was about it, really. He told me to report here, to this office, at half eight today. I asked if I could bring a friend and he said the more the merrier, although we would be asked to limit our conversations while we were in the Curraghs so as not to frighten away any wallabies."

"Had you already invited Daniel to come with you?"

"No, I just asked him a few days ago. He was talking about taking a day off from work and I mentioned that I was doing the wallaby hunt today. I told him he was welcome to join me and he accepted."

"And did you get the impression that he already knew Darrell Higgins?"

"No, not at all. In fact, we talked about how he'd never met the man or heard of the charity."

Alfred nodded and made a note. "What happened this morning?"

"We drove over to the office here and I ran in to get our assignment. Darrell handed me the assignment and I went back out and told Daniel where we were going."

"And the assignment was GPS coordinates?"

"There was a map, too, but it was pretty confusing. We plugged the GPS coordinates into Daniel's phone and went from there."

"What time did you get to your assigned space?"

"It wasn't much after nine, but we were a few minutes late," Fenella admitted. "It took longer than we'd expected to walk from where we'd left the car."

"How many other people did you see as you walked to your place?"

"I didn't see anyone. There weren't any other cars parked anywhere around where Daniel left the car, either."

"What were you to do about, um, calls of nature?"

Fenella found herself blushing. "It was only an hour. That was one of the reasons why I only signed up for a single hour, really. There aren't any bathrooms out in the Curraghs. I believe the closest ones are at the Wildlife Park, but they certainly weren't walking distance from where we were stationed."

"So what happened when you or Daniel needed to go?"

"We didn't. As I said, it was only an hour. I don't know about Daniel, but I deliberately didn't drink any coffee this morning, not before we got back here after our shift."

Alfred nodded. "Did you simply stand in one place for an hour then or were you walking around your assigned section?"

"We stood in one place for the most part. I walked around a little bit to try to warm myself up, but mostly, we stood still. The idea is not to disturb the wallabies, of course."

"Did you see anyone during your hour?"

Fenella told him about Rodney's visit, leaving out what she and Daniel had been doing when the man had arrived. "Besides him, the only other person we saw was Gail, when she came to take our place."

"And after she arrived, you headed back to Daniel's car?"

"Yes, although we weren't entirely sure where we were going," Fenella explained. "We'd been following the GPS coordinates on the way in, but we hadn't bothered to note where we'd left the car. I'm afraid we wandered around for a while, trying to find our way out."

"You should have been more careful. The Curraghs are huge. You could have been lost for a long time."

"We used the map in Daniel's phone when we had a signal. Mobile reception was pretty patchy, though."

"And how many people did you see on your way back to the car?"

"None, until we found the body."

"And yet the entire area was supposed to have been under observation by a group of volunteers," Alfred said thoughtfully.

"Someone here did say that they were nearly always short of a few volunteers and that they never managed to cover the entire area for the entire day."

"Yes, I was told the same thing. Interesting."

Fenella wondered why it was interesting, but she didn't ask.

He asked her a few more questions and she did her best to answer them.

"As I said before, I don't consider you a suspect in this," Alfred said as he shut his notebook. "I know Daniel well enough to trust his judgment for one thing, and you were with him for the entire morning, anyway. He told me that you have a knack for bumping into people as you make your way around the island. If you speak to any of the other volunteers again, anywhere, please ring me immediately." He handed Fenella a business card. "My mobile number is on the back. Ring that."

She nodded. "I could simply tell Daniel if I see anyone," she suggested.

"By all means, but ring me, as well."

Alfred stood up and then waited while Fenella did the same. They'd just reached the lobby when the front door swung open.

"What a bloody mess," the man who walked into the building said loudly. He was probably forty, with dark brown hair and hazel eyes. The suit he was wearing had clearly been expensive, but he had on a pair of athletic shoes with it.

"Were you at the gym?" Rodney asked, staring at the man's feet.

"Something like that," was the reply.

"I'm Inspector Alfred Patrick. You are?" The inspector took charge.

"Mark Masterson. I was Darrell's advocate. We were dealing with a number of very important business deals, and of course, this charity was his primary concern. I'm afraid it's going to take a while to get everything sorted."

"I still need to go through things both here and at Mr. Higgins's home," Alfred told him.

"Yes, of course, finding out who killed Darrell has to be the main priority. Are you quite certain he was murdered?" Mark asked.

"At this point, we don't have an official ruling, but we're treating the case as a murder investigation. If the coroner returns a different verdict, we'll deal with that when it happens," Alfred replied.

"Who inherits?" Jody demanded.

Mark shook his head. "I'm not at liberty to discuss the contents of Darrell's will at this point."

She laughed. "Of course not. At least he had a will, then?"

Mark hesitated and then nodded slowly. "I suppose it can't hurt to divulge that he did, indeed, have a will. He'd updated it quite recently, actually."

"So Kristen might get lucky after all," Jody said thoughtfully.

Mark pressed his lips together and then looked at Alfred.

"I'm going to have a team of experts go through the office here," Alfred said. "You're welcome to stay if you have any concerns about what they might find," he told the advocate.

Mark shook his head. "I have other things to do. Darrell was my most important client, but he wasn't my only client. I'm going to have to rearrange my schedule for the next week or so to free up the time I'm going to need to deal with Darrell's untimely death."

"In that case, I'll get my people started in here immediately. I also need someone to provide access to Darrell's home," Alfred said.

"I can let you in there," Jody offered. "I still have a key."

"Really?" Alfred asked.

Jody shrugged. "Darrell and I were still friends, and I was very involved in the charity. He never asked for his key back, and I never offered to return it. I never used it, but I liked to believe that it upset Kristen that I had it."

Fenella hid a smile. Poor Kristen.

Alfred pulled Daniel to one side of the room and the pair had a whispered conversation before Daniel nodded and walked back over to Fenella.

"Time to go," he told her.

She nodded, although she wasn't in any hurry to leave. Once they left, she'd struggle to find out what was happening with the investigation.

Daniel took her arm and the pair walked back outside. The rain had stopped and the sun was doing its best to break through the thick cloud cover.

"It looks as if it might be a nice afternoon," Daniel remarked as they climbed into the car.

"I should have volunteered for the afternoon. The hunt would have been called off before we were even due to arrive."

"Unless no one else found the body," Daniel suggested.

"Surely someone would have found it. People would have been looking for Darrell, if nothing else."

"According to the map that Alfred showed me, the spot where we found Darrell's body was outside of the area the society was monitoring."

"Really? That's interesting, but I'm not sure what to make of it."

Daniel chuckled. "That's exactly how I felt about that information. I suggested to Alfred that he find out if that area was covered under the old system, before Darrell started redrawing all of the maps."

"Why did Darrell redraw the maps and change everything this month?"

"Good question. No one seems to have an answer for it, either."

"I'm sorry I dragged you into all of this," Fenella said in a low voice.

"You shouldn't be at all sorry. All of the blame lies with the killer, not with you. You were simply trying to do a good deed."

"Yeah, I won't make that mistake again."

Daniel laughed. "If the killer had been a tiny bit smarter, he or she would have covered the body in something or taken away Darrell's orange coat. Without that, I doubt we would have noticed the body."

"He'd still have been found eventually. Can't the phone company trace someone's phone if they go missing?"

"Yes, you're right. Someone would have rung the police when he didn't come back to the office all day. Eventually, the police could have traced his phone, which was in his pocket."

"So he'd have been found by the end of the day, regardless."

Daniel sighed. "Selfishly, I wish we hadn't found the body."

"But if he'd been found hours later, we still would have had to answer a lot of questions," Fenella pointed out.

"What do you want to do now?" Daniel asked, changing the subject. While they'd been talking, he'd been driving them back to Douglas. Now he stopped his car in front of Fenella's apartment building.

"I'm starving, but also weirdly not hungry," she sighed. "I still feel cold and damp, too."

"It's nearly one o'clock," Daniel said. "I really want to go home, shower, and then change into dry clothes. Why don't I collect you at five? We can go and get dinner somewhere."

"That sounds good," Fenella agreed. While she was disappointed that they weren't going to spend the afternoon together, she really wanted a long soak in her huge bathtub. Maybe, after a while, she'd start to feel warm again.

"I'll see you later," Daniel said as he leaned over and gave her a quick kiss.

"Great, um, thanks for this morning." She made a face as the words came out of her mouth.

Daniel just laughed. "I'm just hoping that Alfred finds the killer before tomorrow morning. Otherwise, I'm going to have to go and have a chat with the chief constable."

Fenella got out of the car and made her way into the huge lobby of her building. When she stopped at her mailbox, she frowned at the collection of letters she found inside.

"Charity, charity, charity," she muttered as she flipped through them on elevator. "And after today, I'm not feeling especially generous."

The elevator doors opened on the sixth floor. It only took her a minute to walk to her door and open it with her keycard.

"Merow," Katie said from a sunny spot near the window.

"Hello to you, too," Fenella replied. "I've had a terrible morning, thanks for asking. I know Shelly gave you your lunch, because I wasn't sure when I'd be back. I'm going to take a bath."

Katie stared at her for a minute and then put her head back down. Fenella reckoned that the animal was asleep in seconds. Fenella had only just arrived on the island when Katie had walked into her apartment and made herself at home. A year later, Fenella couldn't imagine life without the feisty but loving animal, even if Katie did insist on waking her early every morning.

The bathtub in the master bathroom was enormous and Fenella rarely used it. Now she filled it with hot water and bubble bath. It was tempting to grab a book, but Fenella knew from experience that reading in the bath was difficult. Inevitably, she'd end up with a wet book and sore arms from trying to keep the book above water. Instead, she switched on the radio and then slid into the tub, ready to relax.

"In local news, one of the island's most successful businessmen, Darrell Higgins, was found dead in the Ballaugh Curraghs this morning by two volunteers working with the Manx Wallaby Society. The society was Darrell's own charitable organization, set up to monitor and support the island's wild wallaby population. Monthly hunts, held by the charity, were meant to track the size and health of the wallaby group. I'm sure our two volunteers never imagined what horrors they were going to find today."

"You can say that again," Fenella muttered.

"Not again," a voice said.

Fenella jumped, splashing water everywhere.

"You found another body," Mona said from the doorway. She shook her head. "I did warn you not to volunteer, didn't I?"

"You said it would be wet and boring. If you'd told me that I'd be finding a dead man, I wouldn't have gone."

"You should have expected to find a dead man. You do so with alarming regularity."

"That isn't fair," Fenella said angrily.

Mona sighed. "At least this time you had Daniel with you, didn't you?"

"Yes, Daniel was with me the entire morning."

"So you won't be a suspect."

"I certainly hope not."

"What happened to Darrell, then?"

"I've no idea. We found him under a bush."

"Strangled, stabbed, shot? You must know something."

"There was a lot of blood, but I didn't see any murder weapon."

"Interesting."

"It wasn't," Fenella said flatly.

"But who could have wanted Darrell Higgins dead? I don't know much about him, really. He had some ex-wives, but I can't see any of them stomping around the Curraghs, not even for a chance to kill Darrell. I don't suppose he was murdered right next to the road?"

"No, we found the body some distance inside the Curraghs."

"So whoever killed him had to have walked there. That rules out the man's ex-wives, then, at least the ones that I've met."

"I only met one of them, Jody Stevenson."

Mona made a face. "I didn't realize he'd actually married her. They were together for a while after his third marriage ended, but I thought he'd grow tired of her long before she managed to get a wedding ring out of him."

"Apparently, they were married for a year."

"Which is about the sum total of the man's attention span. I don't think any of his marriages lasted much beyond a first anniversary. The same is true, of course, for his involvement in various charities over the years."

"And he'd been running the Manx Wallaby Society for about a year. Maybe he was getting ready to close it down."

"Knowing Darrell, that wouldn't surprise me. It doesn't strike me as much of a motive for murder, though."

"I wasn't suggesting it as a motive for murder. I was just thinking out loud, really."

"Where did you meet Jody?" Mona asked.

"She was at the charity's offices. Daniel and I went there after we found the body. Alfred had all of the volunteers go there when they left the Curraghs."

"So you and Daniel went along, pretending to be just regular volunteers."

"We were just regular volunteers, really."

"Yes, of course. Why was Jody there?"

"I gather she helps out with the charity. She said something about her and Darrell still being friends, even though they were divorced. She also said their marriage had been a really long year, though."

Mona frowned. "Darrell must have still been useful to her. Maybe he was paying her to work for the charity. I'm not sure why he would, but maybe she knew something that she was holding over him."

"You think she was blackmailing him into letting her work for the charity?"

"I think she was probably getting paid to do nothing much in exchange for keeping her mouth shut about Darrell's business deals," Mona corrected her. "The man was bored and lazy, but every once in a while he'd get himself involved in something, usually something controversial."

"Such as?"

"Oh, he was behind the plans to expand the airport a few years ago. Just about everyone on the island hated the idea, but he wanted to be able to bring in larger planes for his own personal satisfaction. In the end, the government decided not to expand and Darrell moved on to other things."

"What other things?"

"I've no idea. I barely knew him and I certainly didn't keep track of his business deals. You'll have to work that out for yourself."

"If it was something controversial, maybe that's where the motive for his murder comes in."

"Maybe. Or maybe it was personal. If he was single again, he had to have another woman in his life."

"He did. Her name is Kristen Warner. It seems as if she works for the charity, too."

Mona laughed. "Only Darrell would have his ex-wife and his current girlfriend work together."

"They didn't seem to care for one another."

"Of course not. I don't believe I know Kristen Warner. Is she much younger than Jody?"

"She seems younger, maybe in her early thirties, where Jody is probably forty."

"She's forty-three," Mona told her. "I knew her parents."

"Right, well, Kristen seems younger. In my opinion, Kristen is prettier, too."

"Younger, prettier, and I'm sure no more likely to actually be out hiking in the rain, not even to kill Darrell."

Fenella frowned and then nodded. "I can't see either of them taking part in the hunt. They were both working at the office when we got there, anyway."

"Did you say you met some of the other volunteers?"

"We met William Faragher. He was probably eighty and he said he's been tracking the wallabies for years."

"I know him, but not well. He didn't travel in the same social circle as Max and myself."

"Why doesn't that surprise me?"

Mona shrugged. "I'm sure he's a lovely man."

"What about Rodney Simmons?"

"Darrell's assistant. He worked for Darrell for many years. He was devoted to the man, but Darrell never truly appreciated him."

"Maybe he finally got tired of being devoted."

"Maybe. I can't see him traipsing around the Curraghs, either."

"Except he was. Darrell had redone all of the maps and assignments and Rodney was out there, trying to find everyone and make sure that things were going right."

"Really? Rodney was out in the rain? I can't picture it, but I'll believe you. I can't imagine Darrell redoing anything, either. I never saw him lift a finger to do work, not if he could get someone else to do it for him."

"Well, apparently this time he'd decided he wanted to change things and do it all himself. Rodney seemed very unhappy about it, though."

"Interesting. I shall give that some thought later. Who else did you meet?"

"Nicholas Fitzgerald."

"Sixties? Moustache? Boring."

Fenella chuckled. "He seemed very nice."

"No doubt. He is very nice. His wife passed away a few years ago and I always thought she probably died of boredom."

"Sara Hampton."

"Ah, how is Sara? She never approved of me, of course, but she was always unfailingly polite."

"She seemed nice, too."

"Yes, of course. They're all charity volunteers. Of course they're nice."

"Harry Fields didn't seem all that nice."

"Harry Fields? Forties? Dark hair? Evil eyes?"

"I don't know about evil eyes, but the rest is accurate."

"What was he doing there?"

"Kristen said he was a business associate of Darrell's who was kind enough to help out with the hunt."

"Tell Daniel to investigate exactly what he and Darrell were doing together. I'm pretty sure he'll find at least one motive for murder there. Harry Fields is a nasty man."

"Oh, dear."

"He'd have happily murdered a dozen people if he saw clear financial gain in it," Mona told her. "Actually, that's probably not totally accurate. He'd have paid someone else to murder a dozen people. I can't see him doing the dirty work himself."

"What about Gail Greer?" Fenella asked.

"Doesn't sound familiar."

"She's only been on the island for a few years. Maybe you never met her."

"Darrell and Harry must have been planning something," Mona said. "If you can find out what they were doing, you'll have your motive and probably your killer, too."

"I'm sure Alfred will be checking into their business dealings."

"Alfred?"

"Alfred Patrick. He's the police inspector in charge of the case."

Mona grinned. "He's an inspector now, is he? I rather lost track of him over the years. He stopped me for speeding once, you know."

"He mentioned it."

She laughed. "I was memorable."

"You were driving the chief constable's car."

"Yes, of course, because he'd only just bought it and Max was thinking of buying me one just the same. I took it for a spin across the mountain and then quite forgot about the speed limits in Ramsey. Alfred was quite cross when he stopped me."

"But you got away with it."

Mona waved a hand. "Max would have paid for the ticket if he'd actually given me one. I think the chief constable would have been upset, though. Alfred is in charge of the case, then?"

"Yes, he is."

"It's a shame Daniel can't simply handle it. Alfred is smart, though. And, of course, we'll be helping him. We'll have the case solved in no time."

$$\text{❀} \quad 5 \quad \text{❀}$$

"You mean, he'll have the case solved in no time," Fenella said. Mona shrugged. "Did you meet anyone else?"

"No."

"Right, then tell Daniel to focus on Darrell's business concerns. That seems the most obvious place for a motive to have arisen."

"Aside from the ex-wives."

"Well, yes, ex-wives are always suspect, aren't they? But, as I said before, none of Darrell's exes would walk through the Curraghs, especially in the rain."

"I think I'm just going to leave it all up to Daniel and Alfred."

"Of course you are," Mona said. "I wonder if Max knew any of the suspects. I must go and ask him. He may know what Darrell and Harry were working on, too. He tries to keep up with island business, you know."

The woman faded from view, leaving Fenella shaking her head. "It isn't our concern," she said loudly.

By now the water in the tub had grown cold. Fenella wrapped herself in a towel and climbed out as the water slowly emptied. Still in her towel, she headed for the bedroom to look for something to wear for her dinner with Daniel.

Along with the money and property that she'd inherited from Mona, she'd also inherited a large wardrobe full of gorgeous clothes. Nearly everything in the wardrobe had been custom made for Mona, but even though she and Fenella had very different body shapes, every piece of clothing Fenella tried on always fit her perfectly. Now she flipped through several different dresses, trying to find something that was pretty but not too fancy. Daniel hadn't said where he was taking her for dinner. She didn't want to be over or underdressed.

A blue dress caught her eye. It was somewhat lighter than navy and had a swirling skirt that almost seemed to sparkle in the light.

"Too fancy," she said regretfully as she returned it to the wardrobe. Another blue dress, in a darker shade and a simpler style, felt more appropriate. Once dressed, she twisted her hair into a simple twist and then redid her makeup.

"You'll do," she told herself as she headed for the kitchen. Katie needed her dinner before Fenella could go out. She filled the animal's food and water bowls, adding a few treats to the top of the food bowl.

"You be a good kitty while I'm out," Fenella told her.

"Meroowww," Katie replied before starting to eat.

Someone knocked on the door before Fenella could continue.

"I just wanted to make sure you were back," Shelly said when Fenella opened the door.

Shelly was a retired teacher who'd been unexpectedly widowed a few years earlier. In her grief, she'd sold the house that she and her husband had shared, retired early from teaching, and moved into the apartment next door to Fenella's Aunt Mona. According to Shelly, Mona had helped her through her worst days, encouraging the new widow to embrace her new life as she recovered from her loss.

Today Shelly was wearing a bright red sweater with red plaid trousers. On anyone else, Fenella would have hated it, but it seemed just right for Shelly, who always wore bright colors and interesting patterns.

"I'm back and I've fed Katie," Fenella assured her friend.

"It looks as if you're on your way out again."

"Daniel and I are going out for dinner."

"Oh, good. Did you have a nice time this morning, then?"

Fenella frowned. "Not at all. We stood in the rain for a pointless hour and then we found a dead body."

Shelly gasped. "Who?"

"Darrell Higgins."

Shelly shook her head. "I've been writing all day. I haven't heard any local news. What happened? Did he have a heart attack?"

Shelly was writing a romance novel in her spare time. Fenella knew that the other woman tried to spend at least a few hours each week writing.

"He was murdered," she said flatly.

"Are you okay?"

Fenella shrugged. "I'm fine. It was awful, but Daniel was with me, at least."

"What about the poor wallabies? Who will look after them now?"

"I don't know what's going to happen with the charity. His advocate and his assistant are going to have to work it out, I suppose."

"Rodney must be beside himself. He was devoted to Darrell. He'd been working for him for years and years."

"I didn't realize you knew Darrell."

"I didn't really know Darrell, but I know Rodney. He used to work with John, years ago, before he met Darrell."

"Really?"

The sound of the elevator opening interrupted the conversation. Both women turned and watched as Daniel and Tim walked toward them.

Tim Blake was Shelly's significant other. The pair had been dating for some months now and Fenella knew that Tim made Shelly happy. He and Daniel appeared to be chatting as they walked.

"And there they are," Tim said with a grin as they reached Fenella's door. "The two most beautiful women on the Isle of Man."

"Tim," Shelly laughed. "I hardly think so."

"Well, I think so," Tim told her. He pulled Shelly into a hug.

Daniel looked at Fenella. "You look stunning," he said.

"Thanks."

"Where are you off to tonight?" Tim asked.

"Someone told me about a nice place in Laxey. I thought it might be worth trying," Daniel replied.

Tim named a restaurant that Fenella had heard of but not tried.

Daniel nodded. "I've been told the food is excellent."

"It is," Tim agreed.

"I hope you have a booking," Shelly interjected. "It's always busy."

"I did make a booking," Daniel replied. He glanced at his watch. "And we'd better hurry if we're going to make it."

Fenella put on her shoes and grabbed her handbag while Daniel and the others chatted at the door. She gave Shelly a quick hug before she took Daniel's arm and let him lead her to the elevators.

"What are they doing tonight?" she asked him as the elevator began its descent.

"Tim made a booking at that little place on the promenade."

Fenella nodded. "It's Shelly's favorite."

"I told them we might see them at the pub later, though."

"I'd like that," Fenella said happily. While there were a number of pubs all along the Douglas promenade, she knew which one Daniel meant. The Tale and Tail was unique and one of her favorite places on the island.

The drive into Laxey didn't take long. Daniel found a spot in the restaurant's small parking lot.

"It looks busy," Fenella said as they walked toward to the door.

"I'm told it's always busy," Daniel replied. "Apparently, the food is that good."

Inside the small building, there seemed to be people waiting everywhere. Daniel frowned. "Why don't you wait here?" he suggested before he pushed his way through the dozens of people who were simply standing around. He was back a moment later.

"Our table is ready," he told Fenella, sounding slightly surprised.

"Why is our table ready when all these people are waiting?" she whispered as they followed the host to a table in the back corner of the room.

"Apparently, none of them made bookings," Daniel told her.

"I hope this is satisfactory," the host said as he held Fenella's chair for her.

"It's perfect," she told him as she slid into the seat.

They took menus from the man and then watched as he rushed away.

"Why would you come here without a reservation?" Fenella asked after a moment.

Daniel shrugged. "Maybe not everyone plans ahead."

She opened her menu and instantly got lost in the delicious sounding descriptions. After several minutes, with her stomach rumbling and her mouth watering, she shut her menu. "I can't possibly decide," she told Daniel.

"I was just thinking the same thing," he told her. "It all sounds incredible."

"Good evening. Before you make any decisions, let me tell you about today's specials," the waiter said from Fenella's side.

"Oh, dear, not more choices," she sighed.

The specials all sounded wonderful, too, leaving Fenella even more uncertain.

"I've narrowed it down to two," Daniel told her after the waiter had taken their request for soft drinks.

"Which two?"

"The chicken from today's specials and the steak on the menu."

"Those are two of the more tempting dishes for me, too. Why don't you get one and I'll get the other and we can share?"

"Are you sure?"

"While there are a dozen other things I want to try, those two are both really appealing. This way I'll get to try two things, anyway."

When the waiter returned with their drinks, they ordered. As they settled back in their chairs, Daniel took her hand.

"Are you okay?" he asked.

She shrugged. "I've been better. Finding dead bodies is never my favorite activity."

He nodded. "Believe it or not, in spite of my job, I don't often find dead bodies. Today was, well, unnerving."

"That's a good word for it."

"It should go without saying that I don't want you involved in the investigation."

"I never try to get involved."

Daniel sighed. "I know that, but you always seem to find yourself right at the center of everything, anyway."

"It's a small island."

"And you have a knack for running into my suspects wherever you go."

"It isn't intentional."

"Anyway, if you do see any of the, er, witnesses, you must let me know immediately."

"Alfred said much the same thing."

"Of course, it's his case, not mine. I'm not worried about the case. I'm worried about you."

"Me? Why?"

"I always worry that someone is going to think that you know things that you don't. Murder investigations are complicated and someone killed Darrell while we were not that far away, simply standing in a field. What if the killer starts to worry that we saw something we shouldn't have seen?"

"Then you'll be in as much danger as I am."

"I can take care of myself."

"And so can I."

Daniel looked as if he wanted to object, but the waiter brought their appetizers and provided a helpful diversion.

"Delicious," Fenella said after her first bite. "Try mine."

"If you'll try mine," he replied.

They ate in silence for several minutes. Fenella was lost in thought, wondering if she and Daniel needed to worry about the killer. "Darrell had to have been killed after I spoke to him this morning," she said thoughtfully.

"And as far as I know, you were the last person to see him alive."

Fenella shuddered. "Aside from his killer, of course."

"Of course. I shouldn't repeat any of this, but according to Rodney, when he arrived at the office just before nine, Darrell had gone. He'd left a note for Rodney to say that he was heading to the Curraghs and that he'd see him later. Once Kristen and Jody arrived at the office, Rodney followed Darrell to the Curraghs."

"Why?"

"Why what?"

"Why did Rodney head to the Curraghs? I'm sure someone told me that he usually managed things from the office."

Daniel shrugged. "Maybe we should talk about something else. What's new in your life?"

Fenella thought for a minute. "I've been taking a class in reading old documents. You know that, though. We read a fascinating document from the Civil War period the other night."

"Really? I suppose I didn't realize the museum's archives went back that far."

"They go back even further than that. They have tons of seventeenth century papers, so many that some of them aren't even indexed. Marjorie is hoping I'll do some indexing for her, actually."

Marjorie Stevens was the Manx Museum's librarian and archivist. She was teaching the class that Fenella was taking and she was eager to get Fenella involved in researching the history of the island. Fenella was fascinated by the documents they were reading in class, but she was also enjoying living life without any responsibilities. Agreeing to work with Marjorie would mean having to behave like an adult again, something Fenella wasn't sure she was ready to do just yet.

She and Daniel chatted about some of the documents she'd read in her class before their main courses arrived. The food was every bit as delicious as they'd been told and they enjoyed both meals.

"I'll just get you the pudding menu," the waiter said as he cleared away their empty dishes.

"I'm so full," Fenella protested.

"We can look," Daniel suggested.

Of course, once she'd read the descriptions, she couldn't say no. "The chocolate gateau," she said when the waiter returned.

"Raspberry meringue," Daniel told him.

"Delicious," Fenella sighed. "Everything has been delicious."

"I'm glad to hear that," the waiter said.

"We'll have to come back again soon," Daniel said as he and Fenella got to their feet.

"Yes, please," she said happily.

As they headed for the door, her eyes were drawn to a couple that seemed to be having a very intense conversation at a table near the door. The man said something and the woman began to laugh loudly. Fenella took another step and then stopped as she recognized the female half of the couple.

"Kristen doesn't seem as sad as I thought she might be," she whispered to Daniel.

He looked over at the couple and frowned. "Indeed," he replied as Kristen laughed again.

"I feel as if I should offer my condolences," Fenella told Daniel.

"I don't think you should interrupt," he said firmly.

She nodded reluctantly. "I'm just going to freshen up before we drive home," she said, nodding toward the sign that pointed to the restrooms.

Daniel shrugged. "I'll wait in the car. It's too crowded in here."

Fenella crossed to the small door in the corner and pushed it open. There was a small area with comfortable looking couches and chairs arranged in front of a row of mirrors between her and the stalls. She quickly took care of business and then sat down on one of the couches to touch up her lipstick. Of course, the lipstick was lost somewhere in the bottom of her bag. She'd just found it when the door swung open.

"Oh, oh, it's, I mean, we met earlier today, didn't we?" Kristen said, frowning at Fenella.

"Yes, we did. I was a new volunteer at the wallaby hunt," Fenella replied. "It's Fenella Woods."

"Yes, of course. I would have remembered eventually. I'm Kristen Warner."

"Yes, I remember. You were Darrell's girlfriend. I'm very sorry for your loss."

Kristen stared at her for a moment and then burst into tears. Fenella stood up and pulled the other woman into a hug. "I'm sorry. I didn't mean to upset you," she said quickly.

"It's not your fault. I'm working so hard at pretending that I'm okay that I simply couldn't take it anymore," Kristen told her. "I've made a huge mess of everything, really."

"Is there anything I can do to help?"

"Can you go out there and tell the man I was with that I'm ill? I'll get a taxi home. I don't want to see him again."

"I suppose so," Fenella said doubtfully.

Kristen sighed. "It's my own fault, of course. Darrell and I were fighting and I thought if I started seeing other men that he'd realize how much I meant to him. Except he never found out about the other men. He went and died instead and now I'm stuck on a blind date with some guy I met online. I simply don't know how to tell him that I lied about being available, but now I truly am available because the man I love is dead."

"I'll get rid of him for you," Fenella said. "Do you think you'll want to see him again, maybe once you've had a chance to recover, or do you want me to get rid of him for good?"

"I don't know. I can't think straight. He seems nice enough and he has a good job, too. I simply don't know what I want to do."

"I'll tell him that you're ill and leave it at that," Fenella said. "Are you going to stay here?"

"Yes, until I know the coast is clear."

Fenella walked back out into the dining room. The man Kristen had been with was watching the bathroom door with undisguised interest. She walked over and sat down in Kristen's chair. "I'm sorry, but Kristen asked me to come out and apologize to you. She's not feeling at all well. She said to tell you that she'll get a taxi home, but not until she's feeling a bit better."

"That's crazy. I'll wait for her," he replied, frowning. He was handsome in a bland way and Fenella thought he was probably too nice for Kristen.

"I think she'd rather you didn't. She's not looking her best right now."

"I don't care how she looks. What sort of man would leave a sick woman on her own?"

"She isn't on her own. I'm going to make sure that she gets home safely. We're old friends." As of this morning, Fenella added silently.

He continued to protest for another minute, but Fenella refused to agree to anything other than his leaving Kristen with her. Eventually, he sighed and got to his feet. "This isn't just some way for her to get rid of me, is it? I thought things were going really well between us."

"She's not well. If she didn't want to see you again, she would have simply told you that to your face."

The man flushed. "Tell her to ring me when she's feeling better, then," he said before he turned and left the restaurant.

Daniel walked back in before Fenella could get to her feet.

"What's going on?" he demanded.

"Kristen came into the bathroom while I was in there. She asked me to get rid of her date for her."

Fenella could almost see Daniel counting to ten in his head before he spoke again. "And have you managed it?"

"He just left. I need to let Kristen know that she can come out now. She's going to get a taxi home."

"We can take her home," Daniel said flatly.

Fenella was going to object, but there was a little bit of her that was worried about Kristen. "I'll go and get her," she muttered as she headed back to the bathroom.

"He's gone?" Kristen asked.

"Yes. Daniel and I will take you home."

"Are you sure? I don't want to be a bother."

Too late, Fenella thought. "Let's go," she said instead.

"Thank you so much," Kristen told Daniel as they joined him in the restaurant. "I thought I was okay, that I was dealing with Darrell's death, you know? And then it all hit me and I couldn't face the man I was having dinner with again. He doesn't know about Darrell, of course."

Fenella was sure that Daniel had dozens of questions he wanted to ask, but he didn't say a word, he simply led the pair of them out to his car.

"Where do you live?" he asked Kristen once they were all in the car.

"I have a flat in Onchan," she replied, giving him the address.

"Are you going to be okay?" Fenella asked her.

"I don't even know," she replied. "I'm going to go home and go to bed. I'm sure I'll feel better in the morning. Or maybe I won't. What are you doing tomorrow?"

"Me? I'm not sure what you mean," Fenella stammered.

"Will you meet me for coffee?" Kristen asked. "I feel as if I'm going to need someone to talk to and I don't have many friends on the island." She laughed. "Who am I kidding? I don't have any friends on the island, and right now I need a friend."

"We can have coffee," Fenella said hesitantly.

Kristen named a small coffee shop in Onchan. "I can walk there from my flat," she explained. "It's usually pretty quiet, so if I end up sobbing into my cup, no one will notice."

"Ten o'clock?" Fenella suggested.

"Make it eleven. I'll probably lie in."

A few minutes later, Daniel pulled into the parking lot for the large building that Kristen called home. "I'll just walk you to your door," he said.

Fenella sat in the car and watched the street while she waited. A dozen cars went by, everyone seemingly hurrying one way or the other.

"It wasn't enough that you spoke to her, now you're having coffee with her tomorrow," Daniel said as he restarted the car.

"She suggested it," Fenella replied defensively.

"I know. What I don't know is how you did it."

"I didn't do anything. All I wanted to do was use the bathroom. I didn't think she'd follow me. I certainly didn't think she'd ask for my help, and I really didn't expect her to invite me to get coffee tomorrow."

Daniel sighed. "I'm sorry I'm a bit out of sorts. I was looking forward to spending the day with you today and it hasn't exactly gone to plan."

"I'd hate to think that you'd plan to find a dead body."

Daniel chuckled. "I'm sorry. Dinner was lovely, but spending time with Kristen wasn't exactly what I had in mind."

"I didn't plan it," Fenella reminded him.

"I know. It isn't your fault, it's just, well, unfortunate. Whatever, let's go to the pub and have a drink."

"That sounds like the best idea of the day."

He parked his car on the promenade in front of her apartment building and the pair walked to the Tale and Tail. No matter how many times she went there, Fenella always found herself stopping right inside the door to admire the room. It had once been the library in a huge seaside mansion. The new owners had turned the mansion into a luxury hotel, but had left the library largely untouched, only adding a bar to the middle of the room. They'd kept all of the books on the shelves. The addition of dozens of cat beds had given the pub the second half of its name. Rescued cats lounged all around the space, some in beds, others on shelves, and others on the various couches and chairs on the upper level.

Daniel got a soft drink for himself and a glass of wine for Fenella before they climbed the winding staircase and found an empty couch with a table in front of it. Fenella sank down and sighed deeply. "What a day," she said as she took a sip of her drink.

"It's been a long one," Daniel said. "I'm really going to have to start looking at flats on the promenade. It would be nice to not have to drive home from here."

"You could have one drink."

"I could, but I'd rather not. After the day we had, I'm afraid one might lead to many more. I have to work in the morning."

Fenella nodded. "Will you be doing anything to help with the investigation into Darrell's death?"

"Officially, I'm a witness, so I can't be involved in the investigation. I believe Alfred is hoping I might be able to offer some insider knowledge, but I don't really have any."

"Maybe I'll learn something tomorrow from Kristen."

"Maybe I'll be at the next table, keeping an eye on you."

"Kristen isn't going to talk to me if you're at the next table."

"She also isn't going to stab you to death if I'm at the next table."

"She isn't going to stab me, whether you're there or not. You don't think she killed Darrell, do you?"

"She's a suspect. That's enough to worry me."

"You're worrying unnecessarily. We'll be in a public place."

Daniel nodded, but he didn't look convinced. "Just don't be surprised if you recognize someone in the coffee shop tomorrow."

Fenella swallowed a sigh. Part of her was flattered that Daniel was worried about her, but part of her found it annoying.

"Are you actually looking for a flat, then?" she asked.

He smiled. "I should be, but I haven't done anything more than grab a brochure or two from one of the estate agents. I need to find out what my house is worth before I find the perfect flat and then discover that I can't afford it."

"Your house is large and modern. It should be worth a lot, considering the price of houses on the island."

"I hope so. I still have a mortgage to pay off, but I'm hoping a flat will be less expensive."

"You want to live right on the promenade?"

"In a perfect world, but I don't know that I can afford that."

"If anything comes up in my building, I'll let you know."

"I'm pretty sure I can't afford your building."

Fenella frowned. It was time to change the subject before things got awkward. "I enjoyed meeting your sister last month. How is she?"

Daniel blinked at her and then chuckled. "Yes, talking about money is difficult, isn't it? Deborah said something about my ex-wife, too, didn't she?"

"Maybe."

"I'm sure in Deborah's eyes it was money that came between Jane and me, but it wasn't that simple."

"Deborah said that your ex inherited some money and decided she wanted to travel the world."

"That's part of it, anyway," Daniel said with a sigh. "I really could use a drink if we're going to have this conversation."

"So have a drink. You can always sleep in my spare room if you can't drive home."

Daniel took her hand and gave it a squeeze. "That's very tempting, but when I stay with you, I don't want to sleep in the spare room."

Fenella felt herself blush. "So what should we talk about?" she asked awkwardly.

"Jane and I were having problems long before she inherited any money. She hated my job. She hated the hours, and the dangers, and that I always saw the very worst in everyone. When I met her, I wasn't an inspector yet, and she was right to be worried about the things I was doing. It wasn't long after I finally made inspector that she inherited that money."

"Which should have been good news for both of you."

"She wanted me to take a year off to travel. I'd worked really hard to get to inspector. I wasn't ready to risk that, not right then, anyway. I thought we should invest the money, maybe buy a house. We were just renting. I wanted to start a family, too, but to Jane the money represented freedom. It wasn't enough to live on forever, or even close to it, but it was enough to pay for a yearlong trip around the world. To me, that seemed a foolish way to use the money. After the year, we would have had to come back and start over again, renting a new flat and going back to work."

"And you couldn't find a middle ground?"

"I don't think we really tried. As I said, we'd been having trouble, anyway. I wanted children and Jane didn't. I wanted to buy a house, but Jane was happy renting. There were many little issues that probably would have driven us apart eventually, regardless of the money. The money was just the thing that finally meant we had to make a decision regarding whether we were going to stay together or not. Jane decided she wanted to travel more than she wanted to stay married to me."

"I'm sorry."

He shrugged. "I'm not. It was the right decision. We weren't making each other happy anymore, but neither of us was unhappy enough to end things. We were just going through the motions because that was easier than dealing with ending things. We parted friends and I still care for her, although I doubt I'll ever see her again."

"Where is she now?"

"She traveled all over the world and now she's settled in London. We're friends on social media, so I know that much, but I don't know much more. There were men in her photos over the year she was traveling, but never the same one for more than a few days."

"And you aren't curious?"

He looked at her for a moment and then shrugged. "Not really. It's been long enough now that I can't quite remember what it was like, living with her. As I said, we'd drifted apart, but neither of us wanted to admit it. We're better apart. I'm happier here than I ever was across. And you're here, too," he added, squeezing her hand again.

Fenella blushed. "I can't give you children," she blurted out. Her one accidental pregnancy had resulted in a miscarriage that had left her unable to have children. As she was forty-nine, it was probably too late for her to have children, anyway. Daniel was a few years younger and, of course, could potentially father children for many years to come.

Daniel nodded. "You told me that before. The older I get, the less tempted I am by the idea of having them, though. Maybe I'm just getting increasingly selfish. I don't know. Let's just say that I'm not prepared to end things between us over the matter. You've already become rather important to me and I want to see where things go between us."

"Are you sure?"

"Quite sure."

Fenella wanted to argue, but she really hoped that Daniel meant what he was saying. There was a part of her that was still sad and disappointed that she couldn't have children of her own. She really didn't want the issue to drive her and Daniel apart. She finished her drink and then looked at her watch.

"It's getting late," Daniel said, putting her thoughts into words. "It's been a long and difficult day. I should get you home."

❦ 6 ❦

They took the elevator back down to the ground floor. Daniel held her hand all the way back to her apartment.

"Invite me in," he suggested as she opened her door.

"For coffee?"

"For whatever."

She turned and faced him. "I don't think we're ready for whatever."

He opened his mouth and then shut it again. "You're probably right," he said eventually. "It would improve on what's been a horrible day, though."

"Or make things worse," she suggested.

"I love your optimism," he teased.

She laughed. "I want our first time to be special. I'm not ready yet."

"You'll let me know when you are, right?"

"You'll be the first to know."

The kiss almost changed her mind. When Daniel finally lifted his head, he grinned at her. "I hope I'm not the only one who feels the chemistry between us."

"You aren't," she said, feeling as if she was struggling to catch her breath.

"Meerroww," Katie complained.

"Someone else wants your attention," Daniel said.

Saved by the kitten, Fenella thought as Katie's demands stopped her from dragging Daniel into her apartment and then into her bed.

"Maybe you should come home with me," Daniel whispered.

"Merreww," Katie said angrily.

"Another time," Fenella replied.

"Soon?"

Fenella flushed. "I don't mean to be difficult."

"I know. You aren't being difficult. You're being sensible. I need sleep anyway, and I'm sure if we spent the night together, neither of us would get any sleep."

This time the kiss was short, but full of passion. Daniel lifted his head and winked at her. "Sleep well," he said softly before he turned and walked away.

"Don't go," she said in a whisper as the elevator doors shut behind him.

"I thought he was going to stay," Mona said as Fenella locked the apartment door.

"I'm not ready for him to stay."

"The poor man."

"Oh, don't. It's been an awful enough day."

"I had a chat with Max about Darrell."

"And? What did he have to say about the man?"

"He didn't care for him. He said Darrell couldn't be trusted. He agreed with me that whoever killed him must have done so because of whatever Darrell and Harry were cooking up between them. Max didn't care for Harry, either."

"Great. Tell Max thanks for the information."

"I will, although he doesn't know who you are, of course. He isn't aware that he's dead and he certainly doesn't know that I'm dead. There's no way I can explain to him why you're now living here."

"Maybe you could just tell him that I'm visiting?"

"It's not worth the effort. Max is happiest when he thinks every-thing is exactly as he remembers it, anyway."

A dozen questions sprang into Fenella's head, but she yawned before she could ask any of them. That seemed to suggest that she would be better off simply going to bed. "Good night," she told her aunt before she headed into the master bedroom. Katie was already in her place in the exact center of the bed.

Fenella crawled into bed and snuggled down. It had been an incredibly long and emotionally draining day. She just had to hope that she wouldn't have any nightmares. What felt like only a few minutes later, Katie began to tap on her nose.

"It can't be seven," Fenella moaned as she opened one eye to squint at the clock. It was exactly seven and Katie wanted her breakfast.

"They make containers with timers that open up at set times," she told the kitten as she poured her food into a bowl. "Would you like that? I could set the timer for seven and every morning your food would be magically be available."

Katie looked up at her and then firmly shook her head. Fenella nodded. "I didn't think you'd like the idea. Anyway, if you didn't get me up at seven, I'd probably just stay in bed all day. We can't have that, can we?"

Fenella took a shower and got dressed before she got herself some breakfast. After a bowl of cereal and some toast, she decided to take a walk on the promenade. "It looks pleasant enough out there," she told Katie. "Though it's probably colder than it looks."

She grabbed a jacket and headed out. As soon as she'd exited her building, she pulled the jacket on. It was quite a bit colder outside than it had looked from her apartment. The sun was shining, but it didn't seem to be doing anything to warm up the day. Shivering slightly, Fenella set out at a rapid pace, determined to warm herself up with the effort. An hour later, she was back in her apartment, still feeling slightly chilled.

The pot of coffee that she'd brewed with her breakfast was still half full. She poured herself another cup and then sat down to enjoy her stunning views of the promenade and the sea. When the phone rang, she very nearly didn't bother answering it.

"Hello?"

"Ah, Maggie, my dear, hello," a familiar voice said.

Fenella frowned. There was only one person in the world who called her Maggie. Jack Dawson had been the man in her life for over ten years. He was about ten years older than she was and he was a professor at the university where she'd studied and then worked. For a long time he'd seemed unwilling to believe that their relationship was finished, but a recent trip to the island had seen Jack changing in many ways. Fenella could only hope that he would be happier now that he'd started traveling and experiencing more of what life had to offer.

"Hello, Jack," she said after a moment. "How are you?"

"I'm very well, thank you. How are you?"

"I'm fine, thanks."

"I do hope you haven't found any dead bodies lately."

Fenella swallowed a sigh. "Let's just talk about you, shall we?"

"Seriously? My dear Maggie, what is going on over there? Every time I call, you've found another murder victim. I don't suppose this particular body died of natural causes?"

"I don't believe so, no. But how was Miami?"

"Oh, not at all suitable, really. It was incredibly hot and I saw a great many people running around in not very much clothing. I don't think I'd want to live there, although it was interesting to visit."

"Are you looking at any other jobs, then?" Jack had been working at the same university for his entire career. After his visit to the island, he'd started applying for jobs elsewhere. Thus far, he'd visited Las Vegas and Miami for interviews.

"I have an interview next month in Pittsburgh."

"Pittsburgh? That isn't very far away, anyway."

"No, I can drive to this one. I don't really care for flying."

"You've been doing rather a lot of it lately."

"Yes, but only out of necessity. I couldn't very well drive to Las Vegas, could I? It would have taken ages. Miami was too far, as well, but at least it is in the same time zone. Las Vegas wasn't, and the time change confused me for days, both there and when I got home again."

"You did seem to suffer with jet lag when you came here."

"Oh, going there was much worse than Las Vegas. Anyway, I shall simply be driving myself to Pittsburgh for the interview. They're putting me up in a hotel for a few days so I can see some of the sights of the city before I come home again."

"Perhaps you'll like Pittsburgh more than Buffalo."

"Perhaps, although I believe I'd find it difficult to support their sports teams. I don't really follow sports, of course, but I've always had a fondness for our teams here in Buffalo. They never seem to win anything, though, and I believe the Pittsburgh teams are generally more successful."

"If you like the city, the university, and the job, then maybe the sports teams won't matter so much."

"Did you know that there's a city outside of Pittsburgh called Mars?"

"I did know that. It isn't just outside of Pittsburgh, though. It's a bit of a drive away."

"I was thinking that I'd quite like to live in Mars. It would be an interesting address to give people, wouldn't it?"

Fenella laughed. "I suppose so, but the drive back and forth into the city would probably get annoying. Where is the university itself?"

"In the city, so you're probably right," Jack sighed. "I suppose I shouldn't plan on buying a house in Mars."

"See what you think of the city and the university before you start house hunting."

"Yes, of course. I may simply decide to stay here. Everything is familiar here, which is both wonderful and frustrating. But I'm sure you have other things to do besides talk to me. I simply wanted to hear your voice today. I do still miss you, I hope you know that."

"I miss you, as well," Fenella told him. I just know that we're better apart, she added silently.

"It was nice speaking with you. Do take care of yourself. Try to stop finding dead bodies."

Fenella didn't get a chance to reply before Jack disconnected. She put the phone down and then frowned at it. "I don't find them on purpose," she said, startling Katie.

Still thinking about Jack and how much he'd changed since his island visit, Fenella found a book to curl up with until it was time to head to Onchan. The drive was a short one, especially in Mona's fancy red convertible. Fenella always felt as if she arrived everywhere far too quickly when she drove Mona's wonderful car. She parked in the small parking lot for the coffee shop and then walked to the door.

There was no sign of Kristen inside the tiny building. Fenella stood in the doorway, wondering if she should get a table or wait outside. A cold breeze helped her make up her mind.

"Just you today, love?" a voice called as Fenella walked inside.

"I'm meeting a friend," Fenella replied, smiling at the motherly-looking woman in the white apron who was wiping down tables across the room.

"A friend or a blind date?" the woman asked.

"A friend," Fenella said, feeling surprised at the question.

"I don't mean to be rude," the other woman laughed, "but we seem to get a lot of blind dates here for some reason. I think it's because we're a bit out of the way and we're nearly always quiet. I could tell you some stories, I could."

"I'd love to hear them."

"Well, just until your friend turns up, then. You can sit anywhere, by the way."

Fenella chose a table in the corner, sitting so she could watch the door for Kristen's arrival.

"Coffee or tea?" she was asked.

"Coffee."

The other woman disappeared behind a door. She emerged a moment later with two steaming cups in her hands. "I'm Gloria," the woman said as she dropped into the chair opposite Fenella. "It's my break time. Okay, it isn't really, but it's my coffee shop, so I can take a break whenever I want."

Fenella laughed. "It's very nice to meet you, Gloria. I'm Fenella."

"Oh, aye, I know who you are. You're Mona Kelly's niece, the lucky one who inherited her fortune. You've been in the papers nearly every month since you arrived on the island. Finding all those dead people must be awfully sad, but you do get to spend a great deal of time with the incredibly handsome Daniel Robinson, which probably makes it all worthwhile, doesn't it?"

Fenella knew she was blushing. "Daniel is very nice," she said desperately.

"Oh, he is at that. He comes in once in a while for some cake and conversation. I've been able to help him out with one or two things since he's been on the island. I see and hear a great deal here, you understand. People come in to talk about all manner of things and they don't stop talking just because the waitress is delivering their cake, do they? If you were planning to break into someone's house and steal something valuable, you'd be wise to do your planning at home and not in a public place, that's for sure."

"I'll keep that in mind."

Gloria laughed. "Oh, I'm not worried about you. You won't be planning on breaking any laws. Not when you're involved with a police inspector. Anyway, I was going to tell you about blind dates, not criminals. I save those stories for the police inspectors."

"Very sensible."

"I suppose this is a good place for a blind date," Gloria said, looking around the room. "I mean, there isn't anyone here right now, so you'd have some privacy, but you'd still be in a public place. It's just about perfect, really."

"It does seem ideal," Fenella agreed as she glanced around the otherwise empty room. Daniel had said that he was going to have someone from the police at the coffee shop when she met with Kristen. Had he forgotten?

"It would be a real shame if you made your plans to meet someone here and then your husband also made plans to meet someone here at the same time, wouldn't it?"

Fenella stared at her. "That happened?"

"Oh, aye, twice. Two different couples, too. The first couple lived nearby and they used to come in together sometimes. They split up after she walked in and found him here with another woman. It was just too bad that the man she was meeting arrived while she was screaming at her husband. He interrupted and then, after more yelling, he and the other woman left together."

Fenella laughed. "Did they end up together?"

"They went out for a few weeks, but it didn't last. Anyway, that was the first time it happened, and then it happened again about a year later. This time I didn't know either of the pair. I think they both chose here because it was far from where they lived on the island. Anyway, he was here, cozying up with a pretty blonde when the wife walked in on the arm of some other guy. He spotted her and started yelling and carrying on. She burst into tears and ran out. The guy she'd come in with followed her and the husband stayed here and finished his coffee. I still wonder what ever happened to that pair."

"I'm curious now, too."

"I didn't get any names, of course. If I had, I probably would have watched the local paper for the divorce announcement."

"Maybe they stayed together."

"I hope not. If you're looking to cheat, you aren't in a good relationship. And if he's looking to cheat, you need a new man, anyway."

Fenella nodded as the door to the coffee shop swung open. She smiled as she recognized Constable Howard Corlett. She'd met him within days of her arrival on the island, when he'd responded to her emergency call after she'd found her first body.

"Constable Corlett, what a lovely surprise," Gloria said, getting to her feet. "Coffee with cream and one sugar?"

"Yes, please," the constable replied. He nodded at Fenella and then took a chair at a table some distance from hers. If the place stayed as empty as it was currently, he would probably still be able to hear her conversation with Kristen from where he was sitting.

Gloria was back with the constable's drink when the door opened again and Kristen rushed inside.

"I'm late," she announced as she dropped into the chair across from Fenella. "I overslept. It's the first time in ages that I didn't have to worry about the bloody wallabies before breakfast."

"You don't care for wallabies?"

Kristen shrugged. "I don't mind them, but they aren't my favorite animals or anything like that. I've only been working for the Wallaby Society because of Darrell, you see. I went after the job and the man at the same time."

"How long have you been working there, then?"

"Six months or so. I was hired about the same time as Darrell and Jody started having problems. Not that there's any connection, of course. They were already separated before I ever slept with Darrell."

Fenella didn't question the statement. "So you took the job simply to be closer to Darrell?"

"I'd met him at a party, you see. It was in Manchester. That's where I was living. Anyway, I met Darrell and I thought he was incredible. He was handsome and smart and funny and, well, let's be honest, rich. When I found that he lived over here, I decided it might be an interesting place to live. I applied for several different jobs, but the one I really wanted was with the Manx Wallaby Society so I could work with Darrell. Lucky for me, he wanted to work with me, too."

"I'm sure," Fenella murmured.

"Coffee or tea?" Gloria asked Kristen.

"Coffee, black," Kristen replied.

"Cakes or biscuits or anything for either of you?"

"What cakes do you have?" Fenella had to ask.

Gloria rattled off a list of delicious sounding cakes and pies.

"Chocolate gateau," Fenella said when Gloria was done.

Kristen made a face. "I don't eat sweets," she told them both firmly.

Gloria shrugged. "Life's too short," she said before walking away.

"So you applied for the job with Darrell, just so that you could work with him?" Fenella asked, determined to get the conversation back on track.

"Yeah, mostly. I mean, I didn't know anything about wallabies, but they were important to Darrell, so I learned all about them. I can tell you a dozen different fascinating facts about the little darlings, if you're interested."

"Not really."

"Yeah, me, either, but Darrell seemed to like them. Anyway, I got the job and then I got Darrell, too."

"I'm sorry for your loss."

Kristen shrugged. "We were having problems. I told you that last night, right? That's why I was out with another man. If I'm honest, I made plans with Jake, Jack, John, whatever his name was, the guy from last night, anyway. I made plans with him in the hopes that Darrell would find out and get upset. We'd never agreed that we wouldn't see other people, you understand."

"Was Darrell seeing anyone else?"

"I've no idea. I doubt it, because he didn't have much spare time, but he may have been. He wasn't looking for anything serious with me. After he and Jody split up, he wasn't eager to get married again, that was for certain. But I wanted something more. I was crazy about him." Kristen stopped and swiped at her eyes. It seemed more of a gesture than a necessity to Fenella.

"Did you enjoy working for the charity?"

"It was a job and not a very demanding one, really. I opened the post, but Darrell or Rodney actually dealt with it. I answered the phones, but no one ever rang, aside from when we were getting ready for a hunt. Hunt days were usually pretty busy, but even then, Rodney did most of the work, well, Rodney and Jody."

"Why is she so involved in the charity?"

"I ask myself that question every single day. She used to work for Darrell, not for the charity, but in his office. That was how they met. Anyway, I gather that after they got married, she started helping out with the charity and quit her job. When they split up, she kept on helping, even though Darrell didn't really want her there."

"He didn't?"

"Oh, he would never turn away a willing volunteer, not even his ex-wife, but it made things awkward for him and for us. I'm sure he would have been happier if she'd stopped, but he wasn't going to tell her to go."

"So what did she do for the charity?"

"Mostly, she worked on hunt days. She made the coffee and bought all the snacks and things that the volunteers ate between shifts. She used to help out with the paperwork, too. Because of all the various forms that Darrell used to have everyone fill out, there was always a lot of paperwork to do after every hunt."

"But she wasn't getting paid?"

"She got a huge settlement from Darrell when their marriage ended. I'm not sure why she got as much as she did, but it was enough that she didn't need to work. I think it amused her to spend her time at the charity office, just sitting around, reminding Darrell of his very expensive mistake."

"They were only married for a year, right? That doesn't seem long enough to warrant a huge payout."

"She didn't deserve much of anything, if you ask me. Darrell bought her a lot of very expensive gifts when they were together. She should have taken them and gone quietly."

"You don't know why she got her settlement then?"

"She has to know where the bodies are buried, if you'll pardon the expression. I mean, she must have known something about Darrell that he didn't want anyone to know. I'm not suggesting that she blackmailed him into anything, just that he'd felt it would be smart to treat her well."

"Darrell had secrets, then?"

"Everyone has secrets. Darrell was rich and successful. He probably had a great many more than most people."

"Any idea what his secrets might have been about?"

"They must have had something to do with his business interests. I can't imagine anyone killing him over wallabies, can you?" Kristen laughed.

Gloria delivered Kristen's coffee and Fenella's cake. "Is there anything else right now?" she asked.

"No, thanks, this looks great," Fenella told her.

As Gloria walked away, she took a bite of cake. "Fabulous," she said after she'd swallowed.

"Sugar, white flour, fat, nothing good," Kristen said.

"And worth every bite."

Kristen made a face. "Anyway, I'm sure Darrell had secrets. Someone killed him, after all."

"But you don't know any of his secrets."

"I might," Kristen said with a smug smile.

"If you do, I suggest you tell them to the police. Darrell was murdered, after all."

"Yeah, and now I'm all alone and probably out of a job. If I can parlay Darrell's secrets into a new job, well, I have to use what I have."

"That could be dangerous."

"I'll be fine."

"What sort of job are you looking for?"

"I thought I'd go and see Harry Fields. He and Darrell were working on several things together. Maybe he could put me to work."

"I don't know anything about him."

"He's more intense than Darrell. Darrell's business interests were something of a hobby to him. He didn't take it all that seriously. The charity meant more to him than his company, even though he lived off the money the company generated."

"That doesn't seem smart."

"Oh, he had loads of money in the bank. If his company had gone under, he'd have been fine. His parents were super wealthy and they set up all sorts of trusts and funds and whatever for Darrell. Even if he'd tried, he couldn't have spent everything."

"Perhaps his parents were wise."

"Probably. When he was younger, he was a bit wild and I was told he blew through several million pounds in a year or two. That was when his parents started setting up trusts and other things that could restrict his access to his money. I think some of it was also put into place after his first divorce. His first wife got a huge amount of money, you know."

"I didn't know."

"His second wife didn't do nearly as well, thanks to all the things his parents had put into place by the time she came along. Jody was smart enough to get involved with him once his company was making money on its own. She didn't get any of Darrell's inheritance, just a large piece of what he'd made himself over the last several years."

"And you think you'd enjoy working for Harry?"

"Oh, no. I hate working, full stop, but needs must. The job with Darrell was great because it wasn't much work. I expect Harry will actually want me to do things, but I believe he's between girlfriends at the moment, so I may have a chance there."

Fenella took a bite of cake to stop herself from lecturing the girl. Kristen was old enough to make her own choices in life, even if Fenella didn't agree with them.

"Anyway, I just have to hope that Harry didn't kill Darrell, don't I? He was at the office around ten. Do you know when Darrell died?"

"I'm sorry, but I don't."

Kristen frowned. "I truly can't see Harry actually killing anyone. He wouldn't get his hands dirty, you know? I suppose it's possible to find contract killers on the island, though. There must be one or two, mustn't there?"

"I certainly hope not."

"Harry has lots of contacts. I'm sure he'd know where to find a killer for hire if he needed one. That's better than him killing Darrell himself, but I'd still rather he wasn't involved, if I'm going to start seeing him."

"You think Harry had a motive?"

"I'm sure he must have done. He and Darrell used to argue all the time. Harry didn't think Darrell took his business seriously, which he didn't. Harry also hated the charity and the amount of time and effort that Darrell put into it. Harry used to come to the office and shout at Darrell every week."

"And that's a motive for murder?"

"Maybe, or maybe not," Kristen said, frowning. "But they might have fought about other things, too."

"Who else had a motive for killing Darrell?" Fenella asked.

Kristen chuckled. "I'm going to say Jody, just because we hate one another."

"But she'd already had a big financial settlement from him. Why would she want him dead?"

"Maybe he knew her secrets, too. I'm sure she has some. Knowing Darrell, maybe he hired someone to investigate her. I'm sure he wanted to get out from under whatever hold she had on him."

"That makes sense," Fenella said slowly, wondering if it really did.

"I thought so," Kristen beamed.

"Can you think of anyone else who might have wanted Darrell dead?"

"Not really. I mean, all the charity volunteers were in the right place at the right time to kill him, weren't they? But I can't see any reason why any of them would have actually done it. They all loved him and the charity and the bloody wallabies, too."

"How often did anyone actually see a wallaby?"

"In the last six months, there was one sighting."

"One? In six months?"

"The little darlings are nocturnal. We were wasting our time trying to find them in the daytime."

"So why bother?"

"Because Darrell was obsessed, but lazy. He hated the idea of sitting up all night watching for them. Anyway, Sara saw one back in January, or at least, she thought she did."

"She thought she did?"

"She took a photo, but it was pretty blurry. It could have been anything, really."

"That's an interesting point. Why not set up cameras to record overnight if wallabies are nocturnal?"

"Darrell was considering it. He'd requested quotes from a few different companies for cameras and all sorts of equipment, but he wasn't sure he'd be able to get permission to put anything in the Curraghs. It's all protected wetlands, you see. People are allowed there, but fancy electronics are a different matter."

"There aren't any issues with any of the volunteers?"

"Oh, Sara and Gail dislike one another, but that's down to personalities, nothing else. William can be a bit difficult, too, but he's old enough to feel as if he doesn't have to always be polite."

"And Harry started volunteering last month?"

"Yeah, and no one likes him, but they would never say anything because he's Darrell's friend."

"No one likes him?"

"He's a busy businessman who comes and does a single shift once in a while. The others are all retired and they all give a lot of time and effort to the charity. It caused some issues in February. Some of the volunteers were unhappy with how little time Harry actually spent in the Curraghs."

And I only did a single hour, Fenella thought. No doubt the volunteers weren't fond of me, either.

Suddenly, Kristen looked at her watch. "Is that the time?" she demanded. "I'm having lunch with a friend. I really must dash. It was lovely talking with you. Keep in touch."

The woman was gone before Fenella could reply. She'd dropped a two-pound coin on the table as she'd rushed away. Presumably, that was meant to cover her coffee.

"Your friend had to go?" Gloria asked a moment later.

"Yes, she did."

Gloria handed her the bill and Fenella gave her payment with a large tip. "Thank you. The cake was delicious."

"I'm glad you enjoyed it. I hope you'll be back again soon."

Vowing to make a point of coming back before long, Fenella headed for the door. Constable Corlett caught her arm as she walked out of the building.

"Ring Daniel and tell him everything that was said," he told her.

"I will. I'll ring Alfred, too."

The constable nodded. "That's a good idea. He'll want to know what Kristen had to say, as well."

"Did you hear the entire conversation?"

"I think so."

"What did she want?"

The constable looked surprised by the question. "I've no idea," he said after a moment.

"That makes two of us," Fenella said thoughtfully as she headed back to Mona's car.

7

It was a lovely day for a long drive, Fenella decided as she slid behind the steering wheel. If she'd driven her sensible car, she knew she would have headed straight home, but Mona's car was really fun to drive. She pulled out of the parking lot and turned left. For an hour, she drove around the island, making random turns as needed and simply enjoying the warmer weather and the sunshine. When she finally pulled back into the garage under her apartment building, she realized she probably should have called Daniel before she'd gone for her drive.

No doubt he was waiting to hear about her conversation with Kristen, even though Constable Corlett could have told him everything that was said.

"Howard gave me a full report as soon as he got back to the station," he told Fenella when he answered his phone. "I'd like you to take me through the conversation, though, if you don't mind."

She did her best to repeat everything that Kristen had said. When she was finished, she asked him the same thing she'd asked the constable. "What did she want?"

"I don't know. Maybe she just needed someone to talk to."

"Maybe."

"If she contacts you again, please let me know."

"Of course I will. I doubt I'll see her again, though. I probably won't see anyone from the Wallaby Society again. I certainly don't plan to volunteer for their next hunt."

Daniel chuckled. "If we don't have the case solved by the time the next hunt rolls around, I might be tempted to volunteer, just so I can talk to all of the volunteers again. I'm really hoping Alfred finds the killer soon, though."

"Do I need to call him and tell him about my conversation with Kristen?"

"You should. He'll be writing the official report of the conversation. I just took notes for my own information."

"Did Constable Corlett talk to him already?"

"He did."

"I'll call him now, then. He might not be as understanding as you were about my long drive home."

"Just tell him you were driving Mona's car. He'll understand. Everyone knows what a great little car she had."

Fenella put the phone down and shook her head. "It is a great car, but I'm not sure I want the whole island talking about it."

"Merrow," Katie replied.

The receptionist at the Ramsey station put her through to Alfred.

"Ah, yes, I was expecting you to ring. I already spoke to Howard Corlett, but if you could repeat the entire conversation for me, I'd appreciate it."

Fenella swallowed a sigh and then began. She was about halfway through the recitation when Mona appeared. Her aunt sat down next to her, clearly listening closely to what Fenella was telling the inspector.

"What did she want?" Fenella asked Alfred when she was done.

"Perhaps she simply needed a friend. She hasn't been on the island for long and I got the impression from her that she doesn't know many people here yet. I believe her focus was on Darrell, which means she may be feeling quite alone, really."

"Maybe."

"Thanks for ringing. If you see anyone else associated with the case, please let me know."

"I will," Fenella promised before she put the phone down.

"Clearly, Kristen is aware that you often help the police solve murders," Mona said. "I'm sure she wanted to do everything she could to convince you that she shouldn't be a suspect."

"Well, she didn't manage to convince me of anything. I don't know what her motive would have been, but she's still on my list of suspects."

☙ "Maybe Darrell had ended things with her."

"Maybe. Although, she was still working for the charity."

"You only think that because she was there after you found the body. Maybe he'd ended things both personally and professionally and she followed him to the Curraghs, killed him, and then went back to the office and acted as if nothing had happened."

"I suppose that's a possibility. I'm not sure she'd have had time to do all of that, though."

"She's been working for the charity for months now. I'm sure she knows the Curraghs a good deal better than you and Daniel do. It probably wouldn't have taken her long to drive over, find Darrell, kill him, and then get back to the office."

"I should ask Daniel about the timing, actually. I know Darrell was still alive just before nine, because that's when I spoke to him. We found the body not long after ten, which means the killer didn't have much time."

"Any of the volunteers could have done it," Mona told her. "All he or she had to do was follow Darrell from the office to the Curraghs. Whoever killed him may have even walked through the wetlands with Darrell, chatting away until he or she pulled out the knife."

"What makes you think he was stabbed?"

"I thought you said he was stabbed," Mona countered.

"I never said that. I'm not sure how he was killed, actually. I just know there was a lot of blood."

"So he was stabbed."

"Or shot."

"Someone would have heard the gunshot."

♣ "Maybe someone did, without realizing what the sound actually was."

"At least Kristen agrees with me that the murder had something to do with Darrell's business."

"I'm sure she wants to believe that, rather than worrying that it was anything to do with the charity. She's very involved in the charity, after all."

"But no one would kill a man over a few wallabies," Mona said.

"People get murdered for all sorts of odd reasons."

"So you think one of the volunteers killed him?"

"I didn't say that. I suppose, if I had to pick, I'd pick Harry as the killer. I didn't like him and I'm not sure why he'd volunteered with the charity."

"He'll have been doing it as a favor to Darrell, and I'm sure he was expecting to get something back in exchange for his time."

"Like what?"

"A bigger cut of whatever deal they were working on or some such thing."

"Is that a motive for murder?"

"Maybe. If I were Daniel, I'd be taking a very close look at Harry."

"It isn't Daniel's case. I'm sure Alfred is taking a very close look at everyone, anyway."

"You should ring him."

"I just spoke to him."

"Not Alfred, Harry."

"Why would I call Harry?"

"You could tell him that you have some money you want to invest. He'd probably love to hear that."

"Except it isn't true. Doncan handles all of my investments."

"But Harry doesn't need to know that. You could ask him about what he and Darrell were working on and see if you can't work out why he might have wanted Darrell dead."

"I'm not calling him."

Mona frowned. "Then you should go out."

"Go out?"

"You always run into people involved in cases when you're out and about on the island. Go somewhere."

Fenella shook her head. "I bought a few new books the other day and I haven't had time to read them. I'm going to curl up and forget all about Darrell Higgins and wallabies."

She'd only been reading for a short while when her phone rang.

"Fenella, darling, how are you?" Donald Donaldson's voice came down the line."

"I'm fine. How are you?"

"Oh, I'm fine, thank you."

"And how is Phoebe?"

"She's been battling the flu, which is setting her back. It's very frustrating. She needs to get out once in a while, but every time she goes out, she's at risk of being exposed to goodness knows what. Now she's confined to her room until she's recovered, but she hates it there."

"I'm sorry."

"I've been fighting a bit of flu myself, which hasn't helped my mood."

"I hope you feel better soon."

"I'm already feeling better than I did a few days ago. Anyway, with Phoebe stuck in the flat, I thought it might be the perfect time to come across for a few days. I'd love to buy you dinner later this week if you're free."

"Dinner?" Fenella repeated dumbly. "What about Betty?" she asked. The last she'd heard, Donald and the nurse were getting closer.

He chuckled. "She's still very much a part of my life. She's brilliant with Phoebe and we're, well, I'm not sure what we are, but it's good. She doesn't mind if I have friends, though, not even if they're female friends. I'd like to think that we're friends."

"Of course we are. The invitation just took me by surprise."

"Is that a no, then?"

"I don't know what it is."

"How's Daniel?"

Fenella felt herself blush. "We did some volunteer work together for the Manx Wallaby Society. We, um, found a dead body in the Curraghs."

"You found Darrell? I don't know why that simply never occurred to me. I suppose because I didn't know you were involved with the Wallaby Society."

"This was my first time volunteering for a hunt. It sounded like a good idea when I got the letter from Darrell."

Donald laughed. "He could be very persuasive when it came to his projects. After a while, once I'd realized that he changed projects annually, I became more immune to his demands. I did write a large check to the Wallaby Society last year, though. Darrell asked me in person to donate either time or money and money was easier."

"I should have done the same."

"Darrell was always looking for people to join his hunts. It always sounded awful to me, standing around in a field for hours on end, hoping to see a wallaby."

"It was pretty awful. It was cold and it rained the entire hour we were there."

"Maybe he would have recruited more volunteers if he'd canceled when it rained."

"Or maybe he'd never get to have a hunt. I think it rains just about every day in the winter and spring, doesn't it?"

"It can feel that way, anyway. When did you meet Darrell?"

"I only met him when I went to get our assignment for the hunt. He sent me a letter, asking me to volunteer. I called and spoke to him on the phone about a week ago, but the first time I met him was the morning of the hunt."

"I'm certain I must have introduced you to him at some charity event or another."

"You may have. I'm terrible at remembering people."

"I was shocked when I heard that he'd been murdered."

"Did you know him well?"

There was a long pause before Donald spoke again. "Not well," he said.

"What aren't you saying?"

He chuckled. "I may as well tell you the whole story. No doubt you'll share it with Daniel and then he'll want to talk to me, too, even though I know nothing about the man's murder."

"There's a story?"

"It isn't much of a story, really, but it may help provide some background on Darrell, anyway. He was, I don't know, maybe twenty years younger than I am. We were in the same social circle, although he was a good deal more social than I am. By that I mean that he used to go to every party, charity event, and social gathering that everyone held. I had a business to run, so I only went to the things that I felt I needed to attend. Darrell was always there, from a young age."

"How old was he when his parents died?"

"They didn't pass away that long ago, but they left the island when Darrell was still in his twenties. His father retired and he gave control of the business over to Darrell and a board of directors. The board did nearly all of the work, while Darrell simply enjoyed a generous income. He'd already fallen into the habit of adopting a good cause and throwing a lot of his time and effort into supporting it before his parents left the island."

"Maybe he should have been given more responsibilities to do with the business."

"Darrell was a nice enough person, but he didn't have his father's drive. If I were being unkind, I'd suggest that he was lazy. He worked hard on his various pet projects, but they never held his interest for long. Honestly, I don't know that he actually worked that hard, really. He tended to learn about whatever charity it was and to talk about it a lot, but how much actual work he did with the various organizations I don't know. I do know that he was generous financially, though, until he found a new project to support."

"How frustrating for the charities."

"I'm sure it was, at least for the first few. Once it became clear that he was never going to stick around, I think the charities he did support were simply grateful for whatever they could get while they were on his radar."

"I suppose that makes sense."

"Anyway, Darrell and I did a few business deals together, but I mostly worked with someone from the board of directors at his company, rather than with him. The last project which we worked on together, I actually worked with Rodney Simmons. Darrell got lucky when he found Rodney. The man is brilliant and, for whatever reason, he was devoted to Darrell."

"I've met him, too."

"No doubt he organized everything for the hunt."

"Actually, he didn't. Apparently, Darrell decided to do all of the work himself this time. He'd reconfigured all of the sections within the Curraghs and assigned all of the volunteers himself."

"Darrell did? That's odd. Every time I've dealt with him, he's always been more than happy to let other people do all of the work. I wonder if he and Rodney had a falling out over something."

"What might they have argued about?"

"I've no idea. As I said, from what I saw, Rodney was devoted to Darrell, and Darrell relied on Rodney for a great deal. I suppose they might have argued about anything, really."

"Money or love seems to be the most common motives for murder."

"I'm sure Darrell was compensating Rodney generously. I can't see them fighting over money."

"Could they have fought over a woman?"

"I doubt it. Rodney never seemed interested in anyone of either gender when I spoke to him. Darrell went through women at about the same pace as he went through pet projects. Most of his relationships didn't last longer than a year, and many were shorter."

"Did you ever meet Jody Stevenson? She was his last wife."

Donald chuckled. "I know Jody. She's made a career out of pursuing wealthy men. We had dinner together a few times when I was between marriages, but it wasn't anything serious."

"She's still working for the charity, even though she and Darrell were divorced."

"I'm going to suggest that Darrell was just about done with the Manx Wallaby Society. What you're telling me suggests that he was getting bored and getting ready to either shut it down or find someone else to run it."

"But he'd taken charge of things himself."

"Exactly, because he was bored with how things were usually done. He probably thought it would be fun to play around with all of

Rodney's hard work. He'd never have done anything similar with the things that Rodney did for his business, not when there was real money at stake, but he could play with the charity all he wanted."

"His current girlfriend, Kristen Warner, works for the charity, too."

Donald laughed. "I'm sure Darrell found that very amusing, having both women work there. Again, though, to me it suggests that he was getting ready to close it down. No doubt he was planning to get rid of Kristen, too."

"Would he have simply shut the charity down?"

"Probably. When he got bored with something, he tended to drop it pretty quickly. Usually he'd do one more thing, seemingly to try to renew his interest. He'd have the charity throw a huge party or he'd offer a big financial incentive for some challenge for them. Then, when that last thing finished, he'd move on immediately. As this was his own charity, though, I'm not sure what he would have done. It's possible he was trying to interest someone else in taking over."

"Couldn't he have simply kept funding it without remaining involved in the day to day operations?"

"He could have, but once he'd lost interest in something, he didn't generally continue to offer financial support, either. Again, this was his own charity, so he might have treated it differently. I can only tell you what he typically did in the past."

"What about the wallabies? I thought he really cared about them."

"I'm sure he did, for twelve months, in the same way that he cared deeply about lung cancer, sick children, and dozens of other things. He cares right up until he decides he's lost interest."

"Maybe he was trying to get Harry to take over."

"Harry?"

"Harry Fields. He was another of the volunteers. Apparently, he was a business associate of Darrell's."

"Was he now? That's interesting. I can assure you that Harry Fields wasn't going to be taking over the Wallaby Society. That man only does things that add directly to his own bottom line."

"He'd volunteered to spend an hour on the hunt."

"To get something from Darrell, no doubt. I know Harry. This is the first time I've ever heard of him volunteering for anything. He's the only person I know who doesn't support any of the island's charities, actually."

"Really?"

"Like I said before, he's all about adding to his own bank balance and nothing more."

"Could he and Darrell have had a fight?"

"They probably had several if they were working together. I'm surprised that they were, though. I wouldn't have thought that Harry would have the patience to deal with Darrell. I wonder what they were planning."

"Maybe you could find out," Fenella suggested.

"I could ask a few people. I can tell you this much, though. If Harry did eliminate Darrell, he didn't do the dirty work himself and whoever did actually kill the man will be long gone from the island by now."

"Oh, dear."

"Harry doesn't like to spend money, but when he does buy something, he always gets the very best."

"Even killers."

"Especially killers."

"Can you think of anyone else who might have had a motive for killing Darrell?"

"I suggest you tell Daniel to focus on Harry and their business dealings. There may well be something slightly dodgy there."

"Daniel isn't investigating. An inspector called Alfred Patrick is in charge."

"I know Alfred. Not well, but we've met on a couple of occasions. He's smart, but he doesn't have much of an imagination. Tell him he needs to find out what Darrell and Harry were doing."

"I will. I'm sure he'll want me to repeat every word of our conversation."

"Every word? In that case, I won't tell you how much I miss you and how much I'd really like to see you later this week."

"Why don't you call me when you're actually on the island? Being in the middle of a murder investigation makes it difficult for me to make plans."

"I'll ring you. Take care of yourself."

"Thanks, you too."

Fenella put down the phone and then frowned at it. Now she needed to call both Daniel and Alfred again. She wasn't looking forward to telling Daniel that Donald had asked her to have dinner with him, even if, as Donald had said, they were just friends.

"We're already looking into Darrell's business interests," Daniel told her after she'd repeated her conversation with Donald to him. "I'm more concerned right now with whether or not he was considering closing down the charity."

"That's something that might have upset his dedicated volunteers," Fenella suggested.

"As motives for murder go, it seems tenuous, but it's worth considering."

"Do I have to call Alfred, too?"

"I'll ring him and tell him about the conversation. As Donald isn't a suspect, I don't think you need to ring Alfred this time."

"Oh, good. I'm glad I called you first, then."

"I'm always happy to speak to you. I was planning to ring you later to see if you were free for dinner, but something has come up here and I'm not going to get away."

"I'm in the middle of an excellent book. I'm going to stay right here until I finish it anyway."

Daniel laughed. "I suppose I can't compete with a good book."

"More men should realize the truth in that."

"I'll talk to you tomorrow. I've been hearing rumors about a memorial service for Darrell. If I find out any more information, I'll let you know."

"A memorial service? I suppose we'd have to attend."

"I'm planning to attend. I'd assumed that you'd want to come along."

"I suppose I do. Call me when you have more information," Fenella said. After she put the phone down, she sat and stared at the sea for several minutes.

"Are you okay?" Mona asked eventually.

"I'm just trying to decide if I want to go to Darrell's memorial service or not."

"Of course you do. It will be your best chance to see all of the suspects in one place."

Except I'm not interested in solving the murder, I really just want a simple life, Fenella thought.

"You'd get bored," Mona told her before she faded away.

"And now she's reading my mind," Fenella complained to Katie.

The cat looked at her for a moment and then yawned. She climbed onto a nearby chair and curled up for a nap.

"I wonder if I can come back as a cat," Fenella muttered as she crossed the room, back to the table where she'd left her book. She was happily lost in its pages a minute later.

"There's no food in my flat," Shelly told her several hours later. She'd knocked on Fenella's door as Fenella had been staring into her own rather empty refrigerator.

"There isn't much here, either. Should we go out somewhere?"

"Yes, please. I spent the day writing and I'm longing to talk to a real person."

"I spent the day reading and I'm so cross that I can't even see straight," Fenella countered.

"Cross?"

"I'm not at all happy with the way the author ended the book. I loved the entire story, every word of it, right up until the very last page. Then it all went terribly wrong."

"Oh, dear. Now I'm worried about my ending."

"Have you finished?"

"Oh, no, but I think I know how it's going to end."

"It's a romance, though, so it should end with everyone living happily ever after."

"And it will, I think."

Fenella shook her head. "Let's talk over dinner. I'm starving."

They walked to the Chinese restaurant that was close to their apartment building. Fenella ordered far more food than she thought she could eat and then ate every single bite.

"I need a long walk now," she said as they emerged from the restaurant a short while later.

"Me, too. Let's walk all the way to the end."

The warm day had given way to a cool evening. Fenella pulled her coat more tightly around herself as they made their way along the promenade.

"How is the book coming?" she asked Shelly after a while.

"Slowly, but it does seem to be coming together. I'm having great fun making my main character suffer a bit, because I know it's all going to work out in the end."

"Romance heroines have to suffer for love, don't they? I mean, romance novels would be a pretty boring story if the main characters just met and fell in love without any problems, wouldn't they?"

"They would, although it would be more realistic, wouldn't it? Most real people don't have to overcome obstacles in order to be with the person they love."

Fenella shrugged. "I read to escape from real life."

"That's because your real life has been a series of murder mysteries."

"Sadly, that's very true. If only there was some all-knowing author out there writing this right now. I'm sure he or she would already know who killed Darrell."

"Don't most murder mysteries have a second victim? Who do you think will be the next to die?"

Fenella stopped in her tracks and stared at her friend. "What a horrible thought," she said eventually.

Shelly shook her head. "I was just teasing. I'm sorry. I didn't mean to make light of murder."

"I hope there isn't a second victim. I don't think the police have worked out a motive for the first murder yet."

"Money, love, sex, aren't those the most common motives?"

"Yes, and Darrell was rich, so money may well have played a part."

"He had a handful of ex-wives, too, so love or maybe sex might be in there, too."

"I talked to Donald today. He seemed to think that Darrell was probably getting ready to close down the charity. He thought Darrell was probably getting bored with it."

"Everything I've ever heard about Darrell suggests that Donald is right. From what I've heard, his attention span wasn't much longer than a year and he started the charity about a year ago, right?"

"That's right. You don't think any of his volunteers would have killed him if they'd found out that he was closing the charity, do you?"

"It seems an odd motive for murder, but from what you said, a lot of them are really concerned about the wallabies."

"Surely, though, anyone who was that upset could simply have taken over the charity themselves. Killing Darrell doesn't help anything, as now someone else will have to take over the charity, right?"

"Maybe Darrell left a fortune to the charity, but the killer knew that he'd be changing his will soon to reflect some new interest."

"There's a thought."

"His advocate will know whether Darrell changed his will annually as he changed his mind about what charity to support or not."

"I don't suppose you know Mark Masterson well enough to ask him about Darrell's will?"

Shelly laughed. "I taught him how to read, but I doubt he'd break client confidentially rules for me."

"You taught him how to read?"

"Yes, although he caught on very quickly. He raced through several reading levels in the year that I had him. He wasn't as good at maths, although he tried hard."

Fenella wondered if she needed to report this conversation to Daniel. Nothing Shelly had said seemed at all relevant, but it would give her an excuse to call Daniel, anyway.

"Let's go to the pub on the way home," Shelly suggested when they'd reached the end of the promenade.

Fenella looked at the long stretch of pavement in front of them. "That sounds like a great idea," she said tiredly. "Where's Tim tonight?" she asked as they strolled toward the Tale and Tail.

"He's packing his bags for a week away, actually. We're going to have lunch together tomorrow before he takes a late flight to London."

"And he'll be gone for a week?"

"Yes."

"Are you okay?"

Shelly shrugged. "I'm going to miss him, but there's a part of me that's not sorry that he's going, if that makes sense. I like Tim a lot. I may even be falling in love with him, which is terrifying. There's a part of me that feels as if I'm being disloyal to John, though. I promised John forever once."

"You promised to love him until death separated you. That isn't the same as forever. I know you'd bring him back if you could, but you must know that he'd want you to be happy without him."

"I know he'd want me to be happy, but I can't help but feel that he'd rather I was happy on my own," Shelly said with a sigh. "I never really considered what would happen if I were left alone. I think I just assumed that John and I would die of old age together when we were in our nineties."

"What would you have wanted him to do if you'd died first?"

"Mourn forever," she said quickly. Then she laughed. "Not really. I'd want him to feel terrible and to feel as if he'd never recover, but I suppose I'd want him to be happy, too. And if he found someone else who made him happy, I'd want him to be with her. I'd just prefer it if he was ever so slightly less happy with his second wife."

Fenella laughed. "There you are then. As long as you're slightly less happy with Tim than you were with John, you shouldn't feel guilty."

"But what if Tim makes me happier than John did?" Shelly asked, a single tear sliding down her face.

"You can't compare your life with John with your life with Tim. You and John fell in love when you were only nineteen. You grew up together. Your relationship with Tim is completely different. Tim doesn't make you happier, he simply makes you happy in a different way."

"You're very wise."

"I'm doing my best," Fenella told her, hoping she'd found the right words to console her friend.

"And now I need a drink," Shelly said with a grin.

Fenella pulled open the door to the pub and then followed Shelly into the building. They got glasses of wine from their favorite bartender and then climbed the spiral stairs to the upper level.

"At least it's quiet tonight," Shelly said as they headed for a table in a corner.

"Ah, Ms. Woods. I was told you frequented this pub. I'm delighted to discover that my sources were correct."

Fenella forced a smile onto her face as she stared at Harry Fields. Had the man been looking for her?

"I hope you can spare me a few minutes of your valuable time," Harry continued. "I'll get the next round when you're ready."

❧ 8 ❧

Fenella had only been planning on having a single drink, but as Harry joined her and Shelly at a table, she thought maybe a second one would be needed. She took a sip of her wine as Harry introduced himself to her friend.

"It's a great pleasure to meet you, Mrs. Quirk," he said.

"Please, call me Shelly. I know you recently lost a friend. I'm sorry."

Harry looked surprised and then nodded. "Thank you for that. I'm not sure I deserve it, though. Darrell and I were business associates, but perhaps not friends."

"It's always upsetting to lose someone you know," Shelly replied. "Especially under such horrific circumstances."

"I can't argue with that," Harry said. "I still keep thinking the police are going to tell us all that they made a mistake. Darrell can't possibly have been murdered. Murders are for books and big cities. Things like that don't happen on the Isle of Man."

"Unfortunately, they happen everywhere," Shelly said.

Harry shrugged. "I've never known anyone who was murdered before. Actually, that isn't exactly true. I knew Alan Collins and Mark Potter, but not well. You found both of them, didn't you?" he asked Fenella.

"Sadly, yes," she said.

"Let's talk about something more pleasant," he said. "Everyone on the island knows that you inherited Mona Kelly's fortune. I have some investment ideas that I'd love to share with you."

"Doncan Quayle handles all of my investments. You'd have to talk to him."

Harry nodded. "Sure, of course, but you must have some funds of your own, small pots of money with which you might be interested in doing something more exciting."

"I'm quite happy with Doncan."

"Oh, he's a very smart man, but he's incredibly cautious when it comes to money. What if I told you that I could double an investment in a year?"

"I'd tell you to talk to Doncan."

"Give me fifty thousand pounds this week and I'll give you back a hundred thousand in a year."

"What were you and Darrell working on together?"

Harry blinked at her. "Would you like a piece of that? What have you heard?"

"I haven't heard anything. I was simply curious what you were doing with Darrell. Someone told me that you never do anything that won't make you money. Why volunteer with Darrell's charity, then?"

"I would ask who's been talking about me, but I suspect just about everyone I know would say that same thing. I don't often get involved with charities, either financially or with my time. Unlike Darrell, I didn't inherit a fortune. I've had to work hard to earn every penny I have. I keep working hard to keep my bank balance growing. I'm planning to retire when I turn fifty. Then I'll travel and get involved with charities and whatever else I want to do."

"But you helped with Darrell's hunts."

"An hour once a month wasn't much," Harry said, waving his hand. "Darrell and I had a project we were working on together. It was important to me, so it was worth a bit of my time to make him happy. My spending an hour each month watching for wallabies made him happy."

"Was he getting bored with the charity?"

"I've no idea. We didn't really discuss it. When we first began working together, he mentioned that he needed some additional volunteers for his next hunt. I agreed to take an hour shift and then we got back to business. When the next hunt was in the planning stages, he asked me if he could put me on the schedule for another hour and I agreed. That was the sum total of our conversations about his charity, I believe."

"Are you interested in wallabies?"

Harry laughed. "Not in the slightest. I think they're pests, really. I mean, they're cute enough, but they aren't contributing anything to the island, are they? I suppose they aren't causing any harm, either, but I couldn't really understand Darrell's obsession with the beasts."

"What animals do you like?" Shelly asked.

Harry stared at her for a full minute. "I had a dog when I was a child," he said eventually.

"Did Darrell know that you weren't interested in wallabies?" Fenella wondered.

"As I said, we never talked about his charity. I offered to help because he needed more people, not out of some fascination with small marsupials. I'm sure Darrell knew that, although we didn't discuss it specifically."

"At least you know they're marsupials," Fenella said.

"I did learn that much from spending a morning or two at the office with Kristen and Jody."

"What do you think of them?"

"Kristen is beautiful, but heartless. She chased after Darrell because he had a lot of money and for no other reason. He was getting ready to move on from her, but I don't believe she knew it yet. Jody is another matter. She's much smarter than Kristen. She was smart enough to get a wedding ring out of Darrell, anyway."

"I understand she got a large settlement when they divorced, too," Fenella said.

"I believe you're right about that. I didn't know Darrell well when he and Jody were together, but I did hear that he gave her a small fortune when they split."

"Why?"

"Why? Perhaps he thought she deserved it after putting up with him for a year. Maybe they agreed to something before they married. Maybe he was simply desperate to get away from her, so he gave her everything she demanded."

"Maybe she knows where the bodies are buried," Shelly suggested.

Harry smiled thinly. "You're implying that Darrell was doing something illegal or immoral."

Shelly shrugged.

"I hope you aren't including me in that suggestion, anyway. Darrell isn't here to defend himself, but presumably, he's beyond caring, as well. I care deeply, however."

"Surely everyone has secrets," Shelly said.

"I don't have secrets that I would either pay or kill to protect," Harry said steadily.

"But did Darrell?" Shelly asked.

"I'm afraid I didn't know him well enough to answer that question. And I believe I've answered enough of your nosy questions, too, both of you. I came here to ask Fenella if she was interested in making some serious money with a small investment. I didn't expect to get inundated with rude questions."

"We were simply making conversation," Fenella said. "I'm sorry if we seemed rude."

He shrugged. "I'm sure you're used to asking people all manner of things when you're tied up in your murder investigations. This is all new to me, though."

"Who do you think killed Darrell?" Fenella had to ask.

"I wish I knew. I still can't quite believe that he's gone. I keep thinking that he's going to ring me, that it was all just a mistake, or at the very least, that he simply had a heart attack or something. The coroner hasn't given a verdict yet. It still could have been natural causes. While that would be sad, it would be less upsetting."

"You must have some suspicions," Fenella suggested.

Harry looked at her for a minute and then slowly shook his head. "I truly don't. I can't imagine anyone killing another human being. Darrell had his faults, but he was basically a good person. I can't imagine why anyone would have wanted to hurt him, let alone kill him."

"And yet someone did."

"Yes, well, until we have an official verdict, I'm going to hold onto hope that he died of natural causes. If not, maybe it was simply a tragic accident. Maybe he slipped and fell, hitting his head on a rock or something. It was raining, after all. The ground was wet and probably slippery in spots. He could have slipped or tripped over something."

Fenella didn't bother to reply. She knew that Darrell had been murdered, but she could understand the man wanting to believe otherwise. Of course, the whole conversation might just be him trying to hide the fact that he'd murdered Darrell, or paid someone to do it for him.

"Anyway," Harry said, smiling brightly, "I really do want to talk about investments with you. We can even include your advocate, if you insist. Let's make an appointment for next week, shall we?"

"I'm afraid I've no idea what Doncan's schedule looks like for next week. You should call him and make an appointment with him directly. I don't even need to be there, as he truly does handle all of my investments himself," Fenella replied.

"I'm sure you have some input, though, and if you don't, you should. This is your money we're talking about, after all. You should be watching every penny yourself," Harry told her.

"I trust Doncan. He did a good job for Mona, after all."

"I'm sure he's doing a fine job, but he could be doing a good deal more. As I understand it, you have enough money that you could afford to try a few riskier strategies with some of your funds."

"As I said, you'll have to talk to Doncan," Fenella said firmly. "Did Darrell have enough money to try riskier strategies, then?"

Harry frowned. "I don't want to talk about Darrell anymore."

"And I don't want to talk about investing with you anymore," Fenella shot back.

After an awkward moment, Harry laughed. "Touché. What shall we talk about, then?"

"Do you have any idea what's going to happen to the Wallaby Society now?" Fenella asked.

"None at all. I haven't given the matter a single thought. It was Darrell's project. I suspect it will be shut down, however that works for charities."

"What a shame," Shelly said.

"Perhaps some of the more enthusiastic volunteers will start a new charity to fill the void after the society shuts down," Harry said. "I can see William doing it, or maybe Gail. The problem is, those two don't get along at all. Neither of them will want to work with the other, even though they're the two most dedicated of the volunteers."

"Why don't they get along?" Fenella asked.

Harry shrugged. "I don't really know. William has been working with the wallabies for years and years, long before Darrell took an interest. I believe he had some issues with Darrell when Darrell first set up the charity, but Darrell finally won him over after a while. Gail, on the other hand, moved to the island specifically for the wallabies, which is a crazy notion, if you ask me."

"It is a rather odd reason to decide to move somewhere," Shelly said.

"She's a bit obsessed with wallabies, in an odd way," Harry continued. "I didn't much care for her, either, if I'm honest."

"What about the other volunteers? Do they all get along?" Fenella wondered.

"As I've only spent a short amount of time with them all, I'd have to say most of them seem to get along reasonably well. I've already mentioned the tension between Gail and William, but the others all seemed friendly enough. No one really cares for Jody, but she's good at organizing things, anyway. I think some of the volunteers were upset when Darrell brought Kristen in to manage the office, but it was a necessary change. Prior to that, the volunteers used to take turns helping out in the office, but with varying degrees of success."

Fenella finished her drink and put her glass down on the table. Shelly followed suit. "Ready to go?" she asked Fenella.

"I think so," Fenella replied.

"I'm happy to get a round in if you want another," Harry said.

Fenella took a long look at her watch and then shook her head. "I need to get my kitten her bedtime snack," she lied. "She'll be very cross if I miss it."

"Let me give you my card," Harry replied. He reached into a pocket and pulled out a silver card case. After scribbling something on the back of a card, he handed it to Fenella. "I wrote my mobile number on the back," he explained. "Ring me and we'll talk. As I said, involve your advocate if you must, but give me a chance."

"Thanks," Fenella said, dropping the card into her handbag. "Good night."

"Are you going to be at the memorial service for Darrell?" Harry asked as Fenella and Shelly got to their feet.

"When is it?" Fenella asked.

"Day after tomorrow," he told her. "At the church in Lonan for some reason known only to Jody and Mark."

"I don't know if I'll be there or not. I feel as if I should, really, but I didn't know Darrell," Fenella said.

"Maybe I'll see you there," he said.

Fenella nodded and then she and Shelly headed for the elevators. They were silent as the car descended to the ground floor.

"Good night," they called to the bartender before they exited the building.

"That was odd," Shelly said as they turned toward home.

"Everyone wants my money," Fenella sighed.

"That must be awful for you."

"It isn't pleasant, but at least I got to ask Harry a few questions."

"And he was too worried about staying on your good side to refuse to answer them."

"Yes, there is that," Fenella smiled. They rode the elevator to the top of their apartment building and then went to their respective apartments.

"Thanks for an interesting evening," Fenella called.

"It was interesting," Shelly agreed with a laugh before she shut her door.

"What happened?" Mona demanded as Fenella slipped off her shoes.

"We had dinner and a walk and then we ran into Harry Fields at the

Tale and Tail. I suppose I need to call Daniel and tell him what Harry had to say."

"Do it quickly, so I can hear what Harry had to say," Mona replied.

"Hello?"

"Did I wake you?" Fenella asked, looking at the clock. It was just after ten. Surely Daniel hadn't already been in bed.

"I was just dozing in front of the telly. I was watching an old movie, but it clearly wasn't interesting enough to keep me awake."

"Shelly and I ran into Harry Fields at the Tale and Tail. From what he said, I think he went there looking for me," she said.

"Tell me everything."

"And then Shelly and I came home," she concluded eventually.

"You'd better ring Alfred and tell him everything you just told me," Daniel replied. "Looking at the time, maybe you'd better wait for morning, though. I'll type up everything you told me and email him a copy. That might save you some time when you speak to him."

"Thanks. I truly didn't go out looking for the man."

"I realize that. As you said, it seems as if he was looking for you, though."

"He said the memorial service is the day after tomorrow."

"It is. I was going to ring you about it tomorrow. I thought maybe we could go together."

"Sure, why not."

"Let's have dinner tomorrow, though. I don't want to wait to see you until the memorial service."

"I can do dinner tomorrow."

"You really should be less available," Mona told her.

Fenella ignored her.

"Let's just go to the Italian place near you," Daniel suggested. "I can park on the promenade and we can walk there and then to the pub."

"Perfect."

"We'll talk about the memorial service when I see you. I'll be at your flat around six, if that works for you."

"Six is good."

"Great. Good night."

"Good night."

Mona frowned as Fenella sat, still holding the phone to her ear.

"Good night," Daniel said again.

"Good night," Fenella repeated, giggling.

Mona leaned over and unplugged the phone.

"Hey, how did you do that?" Fenella demanded as she reconnected it. The line was dead and after she'd put the receiver down and picked it back up again, all she got was a dial tone.

"You aren't sixteen. Try to remember that."

"You should be happy that Daniel and I are talking more often. I thought you liked Daniel."

"I think Daniel will be good for you. He's nice, which seems to be something you find desirable. He's steady and he'll be faithful. Life with him won't be exciting, but it should be content."

"You sound as if you don't approve."

"I can't imagine settling for simply being content. Max and I were all about excitement."

"Except you weren't really a couple."

"We were a couple, just not a traditional couple. We loved one another, certainly. And we were never boring."

"Boring isn't that bad. It beats finding dead bodies, anyway."

Mona smiled at her. "I suppose I shouldn't accuse you of being boring, not when you keep stumbling over murder victims everywhere you go."

"I live with a ghost and a spoiled kitten. There's nothing boring about my life."

Mona nodded and then slowly faded away, leaving Fenella staring at the space where Mona had just been.

"How does she do that?" she asked Katie.

"Merrooww, mewwww," Katie replied.

"Why do I feel as if that was some sort of explanation? And now I'm talking to a cat. Maybe I do need more excitement in my life."

Half an hour later, she crawled into bed. She was asleep as soon as her head touched the pillow.

"I'll double your money overnight," Harry said, rubbing his hands together. "Just sign here."

"Then what happens?" Fenella asked nervously.

"We kill all the wallabies, of course. We're going to make coats out of them."

"Coats?"

"Wallaby fur coats are very popular all over the world. I'm sure Mona had a few wallaby coats in her wardrobe."

"She didn't."

"No? Never mind. We'll get you one at a discount, once you invest. Do you want a jacket or a full-length coat?"

"I don't want a coat made from wallabies."

"No? More for us to sell, then. As I said, we'll double our money in a very short space of time. Darrell didn't realize that he was providing me with a map of exactly where to find the wallabies, but thanks to all of his hard work, I know exactly where the little furry friends are hiding."

"I thought his volunteers never saw anything," Fenella protested.

"That's just it. They never saw anything. I know there aren't any wallabies living in that particular section of the Curraghs. There are several other sections that must be crawling with them, therefore. We're going to start looking near where Darrell's body was found and then move on from there. We'll go at night, since wallabies are nocturnal. I've even got William and Gail helping. They don't realize that we're actually hunting for the little beasts this time. They think we're still just trying to track them. I won't tell, if you don't."

"I'm going to tell. This is terrible. I don't want to hunt for wallabies."

"Ah, Fenella, I was afraid of that," Harry said. "Now I'm going to have to kill you. Darrell wouldn't help and I had to get rid of him, you know. I hired someone from across. He was very efficient. Too bad he had to go back home. I'm going to have to kill you myself. If you could just lie down on the ground, I'll go and get a knife."

"I'm not going to just lie down and let you stab me."

"You aren't? But you're already lying down."

Fenella stared down at her body. She was lying down. Why was she lying down? She sat up suddenly, startling Katie who shouted as Fenella opened her eyes.

"It was a dream," she told the animal.

"It was a nightmare," Mona suggested in a gentle voice.

"Yes, a nightmare. Harry wanted me to help pay for a wallaby hunt, but he wanted to really hunt wallabies. He wanted to make coats out of them."

"I don't think they make coats out of wallabies," Mona said.

"I certainly hope not. He said that Darrell had helped by finding out where the wallabies weren't, but that there were a lot of other areas where he was sure he could find them. Why did Darrell keep going back to the same section of Curraghs over and over again if no one ever saw any wallabies there?"

Mona shrugged. "That's a question for someone at the charity."

"It is. I'm going to suggest it to Daniel. Harry was right. There was a lot of area that the charity wasn't covering. Why?"

"Maybe you can ask someone at the memorial service that question."

Fenella sighed and shook her head. "I just want to sleep."

"So go back to sleep. You won't have any more nightmares tonight," Mona assured her before she faded away.

Fenella slid back under the covers. Katie crawled up and snuggled against Fenella's chest. It took her a few minutes to fall back to sleep, but once she did, she slept until Katie began to tap on her nose.

"It's eight," Fenella said happily when she looked at the clock. "Thank you."

Katie shrugged and then jumped off the bed. She was shouting loudly at her empty food bowl when Fenella joined her in the kitchen.

Once Katie had been fed, she took a shower and then made herself some breakfast. "What should I do today?" she asked the kitten.

Katie finished her meal and then jumped onto one of the couches. She curled up and went to sleep, leaving Fenella's question unanswered.

"Okay, well, that wasn't much help," Fenella laughed.

"You need to go out," Mona said.

Fenella jumped, nearly spilling her coffee. "I didn't see you come in."

"I really should find a way to announce my arrival," Mona replied thoughtfully.

"Go out where?"

Mona shrugged. "It doesn't matter. Go to the shops. Go for a walk on the promenade. Go visit a castle. Wherever you go, you're likely to trip over someone involved in the case."

"Maybe I should read another book."

"You stayed home all of yesterday and you were bored to bits. You were just too stubborn to admit it. You need to go out today."

"I went out last night."

"And immediately ran into a suspect. There are still several with whom you haven't spoken, though. You really must go out."

Fenella frowned. Mona was right. She had been a bit bored the previous day, but she'd been determined to stay home. Another day in the apartment didn't sound at all appealing, though. "I could do with a walk on the promenade," she said after a moment.

"I wonder who you'll see out there," Mona said. "Maybe Sara will feel like a stroll, too."

"Maybe I'll just have a nice walk, all by myself."

Mona laughed and then disappeared. "I'll be here when you get back," her voice floated through the apartment.

"That's creepy," Fenella called.

She heard Mona's laugh again.

It only took her a few minutes to get ready to go out. As she put on her shoes, she thought about inviting Shelly to join her. For a while, they'd walked together nearly every morning, but Shelly had gone less and less often as she'd spent more time with Tim. After a moment's hesitation, Fenella walked past Shelly's door without knocking. She set off down the promenade at a rapid pace, deliberately not looking at the other people around her. If any of the volunteers from the wallaby charity were out and about, she hoped she'd miss seeing them.

After a brisk walk to the end of the promenade, she slowed her pace for the walk back. She hadn't gone far when she heard a dog barking loudly. A moment later, she was nearly knocked over by a huge furry animal.

"Winston, how lovely to see you," she exclaimed as the dog demanded affection.

"You walked right past us," Harvey Garus, Winston's owner, told her. "Winston nearly pulled me off my feet trying to catch you."

"I'm sorry. I'm a million miles away today," Fenella replied.

"Woof," a small voice said politely.

"Hello, Fiona," Fenella greeted Winston's much smaller friend. "How are you?" she cooed as she petted the tiny animal.

"They're both fine, although I'm sure Winston would love a good run," Harvey said.

Fenella laughed. "I could do with a run, too. Let's go, big guy." She took Winston's leash from Harvey and the pair set off at a slow jog. Before long, Fenella was running hard with Winston seemingly keeping pace effortlessly. They raced back down the promenade until Fenella couldn't keep going any longer.

"Sorry, but I need a break," she told the dog, slowing her pace and struggling to catch her breath. Winston looked disappointed for a moment, but then he fell into a slow walk next to her.

"I can't believe I ever took care of the pair of them," she told Harvey when she and Winton rejoined him and Fiona. "I'm exhausted from that short run."

Fenella had looked after both dogs on a couple of occasions. She enjoyed having them to stay and she had to admit she'd never felt physically fitter than she had after a week of running with Winston every day, but the pair was hard work, too.

"And I was going to ask you to keep them again for me," Harvey told her.

"Of course I will," she said quickly.

He laughed. "I'm not actually sure that I'll need you to keep them, but I might. I should know more in another week or two. I'll let you know."

"You know I'm always happy to have them."

"I know, and I really appreciate it."

They walked back to Harvey's apartment building together. He lived in a somewhat rundown building that was right next door to Fenella's building.

"Are there any apartments for sale in your building?" she asked as she petted Winston.

"There are always flats available in my building," he replied. "Most of them need a lot of work, though. Are you looking for an investment?"

"Not at all. I have a friend who's thinking about moving down to the promenade. He has a house in Douglas now."

"If he's selling a house, he should be able to afford a flat in my building. As I said, it will need work, though."

"I'm not sure he wants to take on a project," Fenella sighed.

"Anything that's been renovated will be a lot more expensive."

She nodded. "If you hear of anything that's in decent shape and a good price, let me know."

"I will, and I'll let you know if I do have to go away, too. I know Winston and Fiona will be in good hands with you."

"Have to go away?"

He shrugged. "It will be something of a cross between a holiday and a visit with an old friend. It's a long story. I'll tell you the whole thing if I decide to go."

She gave the man a hug and then gave each animal a pat before Harvey went inside with the pair.

"How was your walk?" Mona asked as she walked back into her apartment.

"It was lovely. I saw Harvey and the dogs."

"That's always nice, but does that mean you didn't see anyone associated with the case?"

"Not a single person."

Mona frowned. "Time for the shops," she suggested.

While Fenella hated to agree with her aunt, there wasn't a great deal of food in the apartment, aside from cat food. She made a grocery list and then took herself off to the nearest store. While ShopFast was busy, Fenella managed to get through the entire shopping trip without seeing anyone connected with Darrell's death.

"I'm disappointed," Mona said when Fenella got back.

"I'm sorry, but I'm going out. I don't know what else I can do."

"At least you're going to the memorial service tomorrow. You'll see everyone there."

"Yes, I suppose I will."

"You must ask Kristen why the society focused on that section of the Curraghs."

"I must call Alfred," Fenella gasped. "I never told him about my conversation with Harry last night."

The police inspector just laughed when she apologized. "Daniel emailed me a copy of his report on the conversation. Unless you've anything to add to what you told him last night, we don't need to talk."

"I don't, at least not really. I was wondering, though, why the society always stayed in the same section of the Curraghs, especially considering they never actually saw any wallabies there."

"I discussed that with Kristen and Jody. Apparently, Darrell talked to an expert and he suggested which areas the charity should cover. From what Jody told me, I suspect Darrell was going to be making a lot of changes over the next few months, though. He'd already started redrawing the sections, after all."

Fenella nodded and then realized that Alfred couldn't see her. "Right, okay, well, that was just something I was wondering."

"I understand you're going to be accompanying Daniel to the memorial service tomorrow."

"I am, yes."

"Please do your best not to question the witnesses after the service," Alfred said.

"I have no intention..." she began.

Alfred laughed. "I'm sure you don't, but from what Daniel told me, your conversation with Harry last night was something of an interrogation."

"I didn't mean for it to be."

"I'm sure you didn't."

Fenella filled her afternoon with chores like vacuuming and dusting. She tried to read a book, but couldn't find anything that held her interest. After many hours of doing nothing much, it was eventually time to get ready for dinner with Daniel. She found a pretty red dress in Mona's wardrobe that fit perfectly, of course. When Daniel finally knocked, shortly before six, she was pacing around her living room.

❦ 9 ❦

"**Y**ou look fabulous," he said before he pulled her into a short and very sweet embrace.

"You look rather handsome yourself," she told him when he released her.

"Thanks," he replied.

"Merrooww," Katie greeted him.

Daniel bent down and scratched her under her chin. "How are you tonight? Your fur coat is especially lovely this evening."

"Meowwww," Katie replied.

"Your dinner is in the kitchen," Fenella told her. "I won't be out too late."

"You won't?" Daniel teased.

Fenella laughed. "You have to work tomorrow, don't you?"

"Yes, of course. We're going to the memorial service, remember? I'm not officially working the service, but I'll be working."

"You're always working," Fenella suggested.

He shrugged. "That goes with the job."

She grabbed her handbag and slid on the shoes that were a perfect match for the dress. Mona's shoes were as magical as her dresses, in that they were all incredibly comfortable, regardless of how high the heels were.

"So, what did you do today?" Daniel asked as they waited for the elevator.

"I took a nice long walk on the promenade, which included a run with Winston. Then I did some shopping, but otherwise, it was a fairly quiet day."

"Really? And you didn't see anyone associated with the case?" Daniel sounded shocked.

"Not a single person."

"That's almost disappointing," he said thoughtfully as they boarded the elevator car. "You always see people associated with our investigations. I was expecting you to have something to tell me tonight."

"Does that mean, since I didn't see anyone, you don't want to have dinner with me?"

Daniel laughed. "Not at all. I'm just surprised. But never mind. We can have a nice meal without ever once having to mention Darrell or wallabies."

They chatted about the weather as they walked the short distance to the restaurant. "Table for two," Daniel told the host.

"Right this way," he replied, leading them into the restaurant.

"And then her luck changed," Fenella muttered as the man stopped at a not-so-private table in the corner.

"Oh, my goodness," Gail Greer said from a table only a few feet away as she looked up at Fenella. "Hello, there."

"Hello," Fenella replied. She looked at Daniel, who shrugged and then sat down in the chair further from Gail. Fenella slid into the seat nearest Gail, swallowing a sigh as she did so.

"I'm meant to be meeting a friend," Gail said quickly. "But she hasn't arrived yet."

"I hope everything is okay," Fenella replied.

"Oh, Jane is nearly always late for everything," Gail laughed.

A waiter appeared with a drink for Gail and then took drink orders from Fenella and Daniel. When he was gone, Fenella turned back to Gail.

"How are you?" she asked.

"How am I? I'm fine, really. I'm still disappointed that the hunt was canceled so unexpectedly, but I suppose, considering the circumstances, it isn't surprising."

"I wonder what will happen to the charity now," Fenella said.

Gail looked surprised. "Why should anything happen to it? I mean, Darrell never did that much of the work anyway. Rodney did nearly everything, so he can simply continue to do so."

"Except Darrell was funding the operation, wasn't he? I suppose it will be up to his heir, whoever that is, to decide what to do."

"But he or she can't simply stop our funding. The work that we do is too important. Who will be an advocate for the wallabies if the Manx Wallaby Society closes down?"

Fenella shrugged. "Perhaps some of the volunteers could start a new charity."

Gail sat back in her seat and sipped her drink. "A new charity? That's an interesting idea. I suppose we could, if we truly had to, but I'd rather simply keep working with the existing one. I must ring Jody and ask her what's happening."

"Are you going to the memorial service tomorrow? Maybe you and some of the others can talk there."

"I'm not certain I'm going to attend. Darrell and I had a difficult relationship at times. I'm not certain that going to his memorial service is entirely appropriate under the circumstances."

"Really? I'd have thought that your shared love of wallabies would have made you friends."

Gail shook her head. "We didn't have much in common, aside from the wallabies, you see."

Fenella nodded. "You have to make your own decision about attending, I suppose."

"You're going?"

"Yes."

Gail frowned. "You only volunteered for one hunt. How well did you even know Darrell?"

"Not well, but I still feel as if I should pay my respects to his memory."

"I'm not sure about that, but you'll probably be more welcome at the service than his ex-wives will be. No doubt they'll all show up anyway, all trying to look younger and prettier than the others."

"Do you know some of his ex-wives?"

"I've met a few since I've been on the island. You met Jody, of course. The one before her was called Maria. She helped out with the charity for a while when Darrell first started it, even though he was already married to Jody by that time."

"Really? That's odd."

"It was uncomfortable, to say the least, but Darrell seemed to enjoy it. He kept Jody around as well after their divorce. I'm sure it upset Kristen, which was probably why Darrell did it."

"What's Maria like, then?"

"Oh, blonde and pretty, fairly stupid, but sweet. From what I could see, she was crazy about Darrell, even after the divorce and even though he'd remarried. She worked really hard, helping him set everything up and helping to organize the first few hunts. Rodney didn't have to do much of anything when Maria was there."

"Why did she quit helping?"

Gail frowned. "I can't remember. She may have moved across, actually. Something happened, but I'm not sure what. All I know for sure is that she was at one hunt, arranging everything from the office, and by the next hunt, she was gone."

"Was she his first wife?"

"Oh, I don't think so. I think he was married at least once or twice before. I'm sure that's what someone told me, anyway."

Fenella nodded. "It's all terribly sad."

"It will be sad if they don't keep the charity running. You don't really think they'll close it down, do you?"

"I truly have no idea."

"Are you ready to order?" the waiter asked Gail.

"Oh, but my friend isn't here yet," she replied. "I need to give Jan a few more minutes."

The waiter nodded. "Are you ready to order?" he asked Fenella and Daniel.

Fenella always ordered the same thing because she knew it would be delicious. As the waiter walked away with their orders, Gail sighed.

"Maybe she forgot about dinner tonight," she said.

"You should call her."

"I hate to bother her."

"But you had plans to do something together."

"Yes, but, well, I don't know."

"You're welcome to join us," Daniel offered. "Your friend can join us as well, when she arrives."

"Oh, no, I couldn't possibly do that," Gail said. She looked at her watch and then finished her drink. "I think I may just go home. All this talk about the charity possibly closing has upset me. And I need to decide about tomorrow. I really need to think about what I should do."

Gail put her empty glass on the table and got to her feet. "I may see you tomorrow," she said as she picked up her handbag.

"What does your friend look like? We can tell her that you've gone if she comes in later," Fenella suggested.

Gail shrugged. "I'm sure she forgot all about tonight. Thank you anyway."

Fenella watched as the woman slowly made her way out of the room.

"That was interesting," Daniel remarked as Gail disappeared.

"She called her friend Jane once and Jan once. I don't think she was meeting anyone. I think she just didn't want us to think that she was having dinner alone."

"That was just one of the odd things in the conversation, though."

The waiter came back over and picked up Gail's glass. "She decided not to stay?"

"You can put her drink on our bill," Fenella said. "She seemed to have forgotten that she had a drink."

"It was just water," he replied. "What I want to know is why she suddenly started talking about a friend. When she came in, she asked for a table for one."

Fenella grinned at him. "I don't think she wanted us to know that she was eating alone."

"She eats here by herself at least once a week," he told her. "She usually brings a book and reads. She probably had one in her handbag, actually."

"What types of books does she read?" Fenella asked.

"They're usually romance novels, you know the types with the half-naked men on the front covers. Sometimes she has books about wallabies, though. She really likes wallabies for some reason."

"And she always comes in alone?"

"She's always been alone when I've seen her, anyway. I can ask the others waiters, though. Maybe she comes with friends when I'm not here."

"I'm just being nosy," Fenella laughed. "I only just met her a few days ago and I'm not quite sure what to think of her."

He nodded. "Your food should be out in a minute."

Fenella sat back and looked at Daniel. "So she was lying about the friend."

"I can see her being self-conscious about being alone."

"And she didn't like Darrell."

"That surprised me. Not that she didn't care for him, but that she said as much to you. I'd have thought, in light of his unfortunate passing, that she'd have kept that to herself."

"She seemed surprised by the idea that the charity might close."

"And upset. I can't imagine why she didn't think of it herself, though. Darrell was the driving force behind the charity. With him gone, she must have known things were going to change."

The waiter delivered their meals, which were as wonderful as Fenella had anticipated.

"We should eat here every night," Daniel said after a few bites.

"That would be easier if you lived nearby."

"I'm meeting with an estate agent next week. I'm going to talk to him about putting my house on the market and see what's available on the promenade, as well."

"Harvey told me that there are apartments in his building, but that they all need work."

"I may not have a choice. I may not be able to afford anything new or remodeled."

"If you want the company, I'm happy to come house hunting with you. I enjoy doing it."

"Really? I didn't think anyone liked house hunting."

"I think it appeals to me because I'm nosy and I love seeing how other people live. I'm always fascinated by how people use the different spaces inside their homes and what furniture they buy, everything really."

Daniel nodded. "I can understand that, but I still don't enjoy going around a bunch of properties, most of which I can't afford, and then choosing the least awful of them."

"Maybe you'll find the perfect apartment."

"Maybe. Or maybe I'll settle for something that will do, as long as it's in a better location than my current home."

"Your current home is lovely, though. Won't you miss all the extra space?"

"I live alone and I have four bedrooms. The only time I go in most of the rooms is when I'm cleaning them, which I don't do very often. I bought the house because I thought I might meet someone and start a family, but now I'm beginning to realize that that isn't the future I really want."

"Are you quite sure?"

He shrugged. "Is it possible to be sure?"

Fenella shook her head. She still sometimes thought about adopting or fostering children, even though she'd known she'd never have children of her own for many years. Whenever she started thinking too much about wanting a child, she reminded herself that she often felt as if Katie was hard work. A child would be considerably more work. "Maybe you could find something nice near the promenade, but not right on it. I'm sure apartments just off the promenade are cheaper."

"No doubt. It will be interesting to find out what my house is worth and to see what's available in that price range. I haven't paid much attention to the property market since I bought my house in the first place."

"Pudding menu?" the waiter asked a short while later.

Fenella couldn't resist the profiteroles, which were filled with vanilla ice cream and covered in warm chocolate sauce. After dinner, they walked to the pub hand-in-hand.

Daniel got a soft drink, but Fenella decided to have a glass of wine. They found a table on the upper level.

"The only thing that would improve tonight would be if I could just walk home from here," Daniel sighed as he sipped his drink.

"Maybe you should see if you can get an earlier appointment with the estate agent."

"Unfortunately, I got the first appointment I could around my work schedule. It would be easier if I wasn't dealing with a murder investigation."

"I thought you weren't officially involved in the investigation."

"It's complicated. The chief constable wants me involved because I've had so much training recently, but I'm still a suspect, on paper, anyway."

"If you are, then I must be, as well."

"Only on paper."

Fenella sighed. "One day, many years from now, someone is going to do some historical research into crime on the island and they're going to wonder why my name keeps popping up everywhere."

Daniel chuckled. "Maybe you should write a book."

She made a face. "I tried writing a book. It isn't nearly as much fun as it seems like it should be."

"No?"

"The idea of writing was incredibly appealing, but actually sitting down and putting words on the page? That was hard work."

"I'll take your word for it."

"Shelly is trying to write a romance novel. I think she's doing better than I did with my book, anyway."

"Good for her."

They talked about everything and nothing as they sipped their drinks. Fenella did everything she could to make her glass of wine last as long as possible, but eventually she drank the last little bit.

"Did you want another?"

"Yes, but I shouldn't."

He nodded. "I'll walk you home, then."

They started out walking slowly, but they'd only gone a few steps when a heavy rain began to fall. Fenella found herself nearly running the short distance from the pub to her building with Daniel on her heels.

"The skies just opened," she gasped as they rushed into the lobby.

"I'm not sure why I bothered walking so fast. I'm soaked anyway."

Fenella looked at Daniel and began to laugh. He was right. He was completely soaked. His clothes were clinging to him and water was dripping from everywhere. She was equally wet, of course, but that just seemed to make the situation even more hilarious. They dripped their way to the elevator and rode up to the sixth floor.

"Do you want to come in and dry off?" she asked him at her door.

He hesitated and then slowly shook his head. "I'll just get wet again walking to my car. Besides, if I come in, I won't want to leave."

Fenella blushed and then turned and let herself get lost in the kiss. When Daniel lifted his head, she very nearly invited him to stay the night.

"I'll collect you at half one," he told her. "The service begins at two."

"At a church in Lonan?"

"Yes, although I'm not sure why. I believe Rodney and Mark arranged everything. I'm sure they had reasons for choosing that church."

Daniel gave her a gentle kiss and then turned and walked away. She watched him until he waved as he boarded the elevator.

"How did you get so wet?" Mona demanded when she walked into the living room. "It can't possibly be raining that heavily."

"It is, though. Daniel and I got completely drenched."

"I can see that. You sent the poor man home dripping wet?"

"I offered to let him come in and dry off."

"This will be easier once you're married."

Fenella stared at her. "No one is talking about getting married."

"No? You will be, though." Mona gave her an enigmatic smile and then faded from view, leaving Fenella frustrated and annoyed.

"That isn't any way to end a conversation," she said loudly.

"Meow?" Katie said from the kitchen doorway.

"Just yelling at Mona. Don't mind me," Fenella told her. She gave the kitten a few treats and then sat down on the couch and stared out at the sea. Katie jumped into her lap and then almost immediately jumped down again.

"I'm a bit damp from the rain," Fenella laughed as the animal gave her a puzzled look. "I probably shouldn't even be sitting on the furniture."

She got up and went into the bedroom. The rain had left her feeling slightly chilled, but the thought of taking a bath didn't appeal. Instead, she changed out of her wet clothes into her warmest pajamas before drying her hair and washing her face. After finding a book she wanted to read, she crawled into bed. Half an hour later, she found she couldn't keep her eyes open.

"And now I just have to switch off the light," she told Katie. "Much more sensible than having to get out of the bath and dry off before bed."

Katie was curled up in her spot. She opened one eye to look at Fenella for a moment and then shut it tightly again. Fenella switched off the light and snuggled down under the covers.

"How about a walk?" Shelly asked the next morning after knocking at Fenella's door.

"I was just thinking that very thing," Fenella replied. She put on shoes and followed her friend into the corridor. "How are you?"

"Tim's across and I'm feeling rather lonely, actually. The loneliness when John died was terrible, but once I'd started to feel settled in my new flat, I found that I quite enjoyed being on my own. Now I'm starting to worry that I've become too used to having Tim in my life."

"Why is that a bad thing?"

Shelly sighed. "For a whole host of reasons, really. Mostly, I'm being silly and overthinking things, though. Let's talk about you. How have you been? How's the murder investigation going? Have you seen any or all of the suspects since the murder?"

"I'm fine. I've no idea how the investigation is going. I've seen a few of the suspects since the murder, but I think I told you about everything except for seeing Gail last night."

"I was there when you saw Harry, of course," Shelly said. "Tell me about Gail, then."

"Daniel and I ran into her when we went out for dinner. She said she was meeting a friend, but then she left before her friend turned up. According to the waiter, when she'd arrived, she'd asked for a table for one. He said that she eats there often, always alone."

"But she didn't want you to know that for some reason."

"It seems so."

"Presumably, she didn't want you to think that she doesn't have any friends."

"I suppose so, although why she'd care what I think of her is beyond me."

"Did she have anything interesting to say?"

Fenella gave her friend a rundown of the conversation she'd had with Gail as they walked briskly down the promenade.

"Daniel and I are going to Darrell's memorial service today," she added as they turned around to walk back.

"You'd think he could find some place a bit more romantic to take you," Shelly said with a laugh.

"I feel a bit odd about going, especially after what Gail said last night."

"At least you'd actually met the man. Didn't you tell me that Daniel waited in the car while you spoke to Darrell? If anyone should feel awkward about being there, it's Daniel."

"He's working, though. He often goes to murder victims' funerals or memorial services, even when he has no connection to the victim at all."

"Really? I suppose I knew that, but I never really thought about it. Maybe someone will confess to the murder during the service. You don't want to miss that."

"I just hope there isn't a crowd of people there who've only turned up because Darrell was murdered."

"Oh, there'll be some for sure. Some people are fascinated by such things."

While Fenella was hoping that Shelly would be wrong, it didn't look as if she was when she and Daniel arrived at the church in Lonan shortly before two that afternoon.

"The car park is already full," Daniel sighed as he crept through the rows of parked cars. It wasn't a large area and some people had clearly decided that they could simply make their own parking spaces if none were available. Cars had been abandoned on grassy patches that were clearly not meant for parking as well as being left all along the road in front of the church. Daniel drove them a short distance away and parked.

"This will have to do," he said with a sigh. "It isn't a large church. I wonder if we'll get inside."

Feeling as if she wouldn't be terribly disappointed if they were turned away, Fenella took Daniel's arm and let him lead her to the church. There was a long line of people stretching from the church's door through the parking lot and beyond.

"Do you think we should join the queue?" Daniel asked.

Fenella looked around and then spotted Rodney at the front of the line. "Let's ask Rodney," she suggested.

"...for many years and I don't remember ever meeting you," he was telling an angry looking older lady as they approached.

"Darrin was a dear friend and I can't believe that you won't let me into the church for his memorial service," she countered, wiping her eyes with a tissue. "He meant so very much to me."

"His name was Darrell," Rodney said dryly.

"Exactly, there, you see?" the woman demanded. "We were so close that I had a special nickname for him. I always called him Darrin."

Rodney shook his head. "Once Darrell's family and friends are all seated, we'll be allowing members of the public to fill in any remaining space in the church. You're first in the queue, anyway."

The woman nodded. "You may as well just let me in now. I'm sure everyone is here already."

Fenella cleared her throat. Rodney turned around and studied her for a moment.

"Ms. Woods, how nice of you to make the effort to come," he said eventually. "You and your friend are more than welcome to find seats inside the church now."

"I know who that is," the older woman said in a loud voice as Fenella and Daniel started up the steps to the church. "That's Mona Kelly's niece. She's the one who keeps finding dead people everywhere. I wouldn't want all of Mona's money if it came with a curse like that. If

I were her, I'd go back to New York and spend Mona's money there. The curse can't follow her across the ocean."

"And that's the definite last word on curses," Daniel whispered to Fenella as he held the door for her.

Fenella swallowed a laugh as she looked around the old church. It felt even smaller than it had looked from the outside. There were folding chairs set up in rows and from where Fenella was standing, nearly all of them looked occupied.

"Two?" a man in a suit asked in a hushed voice.

"Yes."

"Friends or family?" was his next question.

"We were volunteers with Darrell's charity," Fenella replied.

He nodded. "The other volunteers are all sitting together. If you'll follow me?"

Fenella spotted William first. He was sitting on the end of the row and he stood up as soon as she and Daniel approached.

"These two next to me are empty," he told her, stepping aside to let her and Daniel move into the seats.

Once she was seated, Fenella took a good look around. Sara and Gail were in the row behind her, both staring at identical sheets of paper. Nicholas was in the row in front of them, half turned in his seat so that he could talk to William. They were talking so quietly that Fenella couldn't hear them over the low level hum of background noise.

At the front of the church, Kristen was dressed all in black, wearing a tiny hat complete with a sheer veil over her face. From where Fenella was sitting, she seemed to be wearing black lipstick and far too much eyeliner. Jody was sitting next to her in the front row, talking with the pretty blonde who was on her other side. There were two more attractive blondes in the front row.

"Do you think the front row are all Darrell's ex-wives?" she whispered to Daniel.

He studied them for a moment and then nodded. "Alfred interviewed them all. From what I can see, they're all up there, ready to pay their respects."

"The row behind them must be business associates," Fenella said, nodding toward where she could see Harry Fields talking to another man in an expensive looking suit.

"Alfred just arrived," Daniel whispered back.

She turned and watched as the police inspector chose a seat at the very back of the room. A moment later, Rodney walked into the church. He looked around and then frowned and left again.

"There aren't many empty seats. Do you think Rodney will let that woman have one?" she asked Daniel.

"I'm sure he'd rather not, but he may as well. Maybe she'll make a large donation to the wallabies in gratitude."

"Considering she couldn't get his name right, she'll probably make a donation to the capybaras by accident."

"Does the island have capybaras?"

"Not wild ones, but there are some at the wildlife park."

"Are they marsupials, too?"

"I think they're rodents, but they're pretty cute ones."

Daniel opened his mouth to reply, but he was interrupted as the service started.

"Good afternoon," the minister said into the microphone.

Conversations stopped everywhere and the building went quiet. Kristen began to sob loudly, earning herself glares from every one of the ex-wives.

"We're here today to celebrate the memory of Darrell Higgins. Mr. Higgins was a kind and generous man who was dedicated to his business and to the charity that he established, the Manx Wallaby Society. I know that a number of his former business associates are here today to honor his memory. Sadly, we were unable to include any wallabies in the service."

A few people chuckled. The minister cleared his throat and then continued.

"The family chose not to have a traditional funeral service for Mr. Higgins. They felt that it wasn't what he would have wanted. Instead, I'd like to invite his family, his friends, his business associates, and everyone else here to come forward and say a few words about Mr. Higgins."

A murmur went through the crowd. After an awkward minute,

Rodney got to his feet and joined the man at the front of the room. The pair had a short, whispered conversation before Rodney turned to face the crowd.

"Everyone who knew Darrell has to know who I am, but for those of you who only came because of morbid fascination with murder, I'm Rodney Simmons."

Fenella looked around the room. The woman who had been arguing with Rodney when she and Daniel had arrived was sitting a few seats away. She flushed and then whispered something to the woman sitting next to her.

"I was Darrell's assistant," Rodney continued. "I worked for him for more years than I want to recall. Darrell was many things. He was my employer, and a very demanding one at that. He was also my friend, who supported me through some very difficult times. I did everything that I could to support Darrell's business interests and his personal concerns. I'd done the same job for others in the past and I can honestly tell you that Darrell was far and away the best person with whom I've ever worked."

"Of course he'd say that here," Gail said in a loud whisper.

"I'm sure you all know that Darrell inherited a great deal of money. For many years, he was content to simply spend that money without putting much thought into the business of which he was nominally in charge. It was only after I began to work with him that he started to take a more active interest in the company he owned. I'd like to think that I was instrumental in helping him become more involved in his own company."

"But how involved was he, really?" Nicholas muttered.

Fenella raised an eyebrow. Why did Nicholas care?

"I would be remiss if I didn't mention the Manx Wallaby Society, of course. When I met Darrell, he was already an active supporter of a number of different charities on the island. It was only when he became interested in the island's wild wallaby population, however, that he truly felt as if he'd found something that he needed to support. He started the charity himself, and he devoted a huge number of hours to its successful running. Of course, I was still involved, but Darrell was more active with the charity than he ever had been with any other project. I'm very proud of the work that we did for the wallabies on the island." He stopped and took a step backwards, swallowing hard.

"He's upset," Gail said. "I'm sure he's said enough, anyway."

The minister said something to him and Rodney shook his head. After another moment, he stepped forward again.

"There are a number of other people who want to share their thoughts on Darrell. I believe it would be best to start with the women who shared his life."

He nodded toward the row of ex-wives. After a moment, the last woman in the row got to her feet and walked over to join him.

❧ 10 ❧

She said something to Rodney and then turned to face the room. Rodney walked back to his seat before she began to speak.

"I'm Jennifer Higgins. I was Darrell's first wife. We met at university and I had no idea that he was wealthy when we first met. We went out a few times, but it wasn't anything serious. Then I met someone else and he met someone else and we went our separate ways. We met again a few years later, when I was looking for work."

"He seems to date a lot of women he employs," Fenella whispered to Daniel.

He nodded. "I suppose a lot of people meet their significant others at work."

Fenella shrugged and then turned her attention back to Jennifer.

"I applied for a job on the Isle of Man because I wanted to get away from London. I had no idea that the company was Darrell's. They flew me over for an interview and Darrell was at the interview. After I spoke to him and to the man who was head of human resources, Darrell and I went out for drinks. He offered me the job after our third round and he asked me to marry him after our fifth. I said yes to both."

A few people laughed as Fenella and Daniel exchanged glances.

"I flew home and packed up my life. I started working for Darrell a week later and we got married a month after that. It was a whirlwind, but I'd never been happier than I was in those early days. When Darrell's focus was on you, it was wholly on you and you felt as if you were the only thing in the world that mattered to him. The problem was keeping his focus. He got bored with people, places, and things. We were married for three hundred and sixty-seven days. On day three hundred and sixty-eight, he came home from his office and told me that he wanted a divorce. I was completely blindsided. I had no idea. It was an incredibly difficult time."

She stopped and wiped her eyes with a tissue. "It was very difficult," she repeated. "He gave me a lump sum, a fairly generous one, all things considered. He let me keep my job, as well, and I was still so in love with him that I couldn't imagine leaving. I bought a little house near the office and I kept working. It wasn't that bad, actually, because Darrell wasn't really that involved with the company. I only saw him once or twice a week, really. About a month later, I found out that he was seeing someone else."

"We all knew that was coming," Gail said loudly.

"Shhhh," Sara whispered.

Jennifer nodded. "I'm sure everyone who knew Darrell expected him to replace me fairly quickly. I knew that he'd never had a relationship that lasted longer than a year when I'd married him, but the thing was, I'd married him. I was the first woman he'd actually married. I thought that meant that I was different, that I was important to him, more important than all of the other women who'd come before me. I can't believe I'm telling all of you all of this. It's ancient history anyway."

She sighed and then wiped her eyes again. "Once I learned that he had a new woman in his life, I decided that I didn't want to stay on the island any longer. I sold my little house and moved to Liverpool. This is the first time I've been back. The island is just as beautiful as I'd remembered it being. I've missed it, but I don't think I'll ever come back. There are too many bad memories for me here."

After another deep breath, she took a step backward and said something to the minister. He nodded and then she stepped forward again.

"Here's what I should have said. I fell madly in love with Darrell and we were deliriously happy for the year of our marriage. He was a good man and I don't have any regrets about marrying him and spending that year with him. I wish we could have made our relationship work for longer, but I've long ago accepted that it wasn't meant to be. I still loved Darrell and I will never stop loving him. He was a special person and I'm going to miss knowing that he's alive and well, if that makes any sense."

There were tears streaming down her face as she walked back to her seat. The next woman in the row stood up as Jennifer approached. She walked to the front as Jennifer sat back down.

"I'm not even sure what to say," she began, looking nervous. "I'm Carla Madison. I was Carla Higgins, but only for a short while. I never even got around to changing my name on my passport."

She stopped, clearly expecting a reaction from the crowd. After a moment, a few people chuckled.

"I met Darrell in London. He was visiting some friends of mine. Actually, he was involved with a friend of mine, but I didn't know that when I first met him. I thought he was charming. Jennifer was right. When Darrell was focused on you, you felt as if you were the center of the universe. We met at a party and he never left my side the entire night. He mentioned having an ex-wife, but only in passing. Mostly, we talked about me. He seemed to want to know everything about me. I told him about my childhood, about every job I'd ever held, about stupid little things that my own mother doesn't know. Darrell hung on every word. I've never experienced anything quite like it before or since."

"That's probably a good thing," Daniel whispered.

"He asked me to move to the island, to live with him, that night. I just laughed, but he wouldn't take no for an answer. At some point I told him that I wouldn't move over unless he married me. He didn't even blink, just said that that would work for him. I thought he was teasing, but when he came to collect me for dinner the next night, he brought a huge diamond engagement ring with him. I moved to the island a week later and we got married less than a month after the night we'd met. As Jennifer said, it was a whirlwind, but I was so incredibly happy that I never questioned it." She stopped to wipe her eyes.

"I'm starting to wish I'd had a chance to actually get to know Darrell. He sounds fascinating," Fenella told Daniel.

"I was just thinking the same thing," he told her.

"We went to Paris for our first wedding anniversary. We saw the sights, ate amazing food, and drank fabulous wine. On our last night, I told him that I wanted to start a family. He got really excited and agreed that we should start trying for a baby. I've never been happier than I was on our flight home. My life couldn't have been any better." Her tears were now flowing and she had to stop to wipe her eyes and take a few deep breaths.

"The poor woman," Fenella said.

"Two days later, Darrell told me he wanted a divorce. Just the same as Jennifer, I was completely blindsided. I begged him for an explanation, but he just said he didn't think it was working. I assumed he'd changed his mind about children, told him that they didn't matter, that we could work things out, but he simply kept apologizing and insisting that it wasn't me, that it was him, that he'd simply stopped loving me. And I truly believe that he was telling the truth. He'd simply stopped loving me. I didn't want to believe it, but I didn't fight the divorce. There wasn't any point. He gave me some money. I didn't ask for anything, but he insisted on giving me something. For many months, I just went through the motions, unable to think or feel anything. Then I started to hear rumors that Darrell had a new girlfriend. That was the push that I needed to leave the island. I couldn't bear the thought of seeing Darrell with another woman."

The minster handed Carla another tissue and she stopped and wiped her eyes. They had a short conversation before Carla turned back around and gave everyone a weak smile.

"I've done the same as Jennifer, said far too much. I should have simply said that my year with Darrell was the happiest year of my life. I may never recover from losing him, but it was worth it to have had him for that year. I was fortunate that he chose to make me his wife. At least I had that. I've been missing him every day since I left the island and I will miss him every day until the day I die."

She took another deep breath and then turned and walked back to her seat. The next blonde said something to her before she stood up and walked to the front.

"It's been interesting, hearing what Jennifer and Carla said," she began. "I'm Maria Higgins. I kept Darrell's name. Our story was very similar, really. I met him a few years after he and Carla had divorced. We met at a party in London. I was there with the man I thought I was going to marry, but Darrell, well, he swept me off my feet, I suppose." She stopped and shook her head. "I don't want to bore you with the whole story. I fell madly in love and we were married less than a week after we'd met. We were together for eleven months before he told me he wanted a divorce. I still loved him then, and I still love him now."

She stopped to wipe away a few tears. Fenella looked at Daniel. "I only spoke to him briefly, but he didn't seem all that amazing when I met him."

"You aren't blonde enough," Daniel replied.

Fenella swallowed a laugh as she ran a hand through her highlighted hair.

"I stayed on the island after the divorce. I suppose I didn't want to really believe that the marriage was over. I helped Darrell set up the wallaby charity and worked there for months, even after he'd met and married Jody. Eventually, I came to realize that I was wasting my time hoping he'd come back to me, so I moved back to the UK. I keep hoping, given enough time, that I'll get over him, but I'm not sure I will."

She said something to the minister and then walked back to her seat. Jody patted her arm and then stood up and walked to the front.

"I'm Jody Stevenson," she said. "I was Darrell's last wife, although we'd been divorced for several months before he died. Our story was similar to the others you've heard. We met and he proposed almost immediately. He'd only just ended things with Maria, and she was still working with him, which I found awkward, but, as everyone else has said, he had a way of making a woman feel as if she was the only woman in the world. Before we married, I did my research and I discovered that his marriages never lasted longer than a year. I suppose

I'm saying that I went into my marriage with my eyes wide open. When he asked for a divorce, three days before our wedding anniversary, I was already expecting it. Of course, I was heartbroken, but I wasn't surprised."

"She's coming across as rather cold," Fenella whispered.

"And calculating," Daniel replied.

"Darrell gave me a generous settlement when we split. I was grateful enough to him that I kept doing volunteer work with the Wallaby Society. I didn't need to find paid employment, so why not? Even though we were divorced, I still cared for Darrell and I still enjoyed his company. He was charming, when he wanted to be, and intelligent, although he hid that fact sometimes. I'm truly going to miss him and I'm angry that someone took him from all of us."

She stepped back and then returned to her seat. Now it was Kristen's turn to address the crowd.

"I'm not sure what to say," she began in a voice that quavered slightly. "Darrell and I were only just discovering one another. We were together for a few months and they were incredible months. I had hopes that we might marry one day, and that our marriage might actually last forever. Maybe I was naïve, but I truly believed that Darrell and I were meant to be together. I miss him so much now that I can't eat or sleep and I don't know that I'll ever recover."

She stopped, tears streaming down her face. The minister said something to her that made her shake her head. They had a short conversation before Kristen simply turned and walked back to her seat.

"Now what?" Fenella wondered.

"I believe some of Darrell's business associates have stories to share about Mr. Higgins," the minister said. Fenella could hear a trace of doubt in his tone.

After a moment, an older man in a dark suit in the row behind the ex-wives stood up. He looked around and then shrugged. "I can talk just as well from here," he said. "I worked with Darrell's father for many years. He was a solid businessman with good instincts and we made a fair bit of money together. When he passed away, I was happy to continue to work with Darrell. It took Darrell some time to settle into the business, but before he did that, he always hired excellent people to manage things on his behalf. In the last few years, though, Darrell began doing more and more of the work himself and I was pleased to find that he was as smart at business as his father had been. I was looking forward to working with him for a good many years to come."

"He never introduced himself," Fenella said as the man sat back down.

"I know who he is," Daniel told her.

Another man, of a similar age, wearing an almost identical suit, stood up. "I, too, worked with Darrell's father. Darrell was a good person with intense focus whenever he started on a new project. If he did, after a time, lose interest in the project, well, that was part of who Darrell was, really. I feel fortunate to have worked with him and I'll miss him."

As he sat back down Harry Fields got to his feet.

"I only met Darrell in the past year. We started talking about working together on a project and I was excited about what we were planning. I'm hopeful that I will be able to carry on with the project on my own, but I'll miss Darrell every step of the way. He was smart and funny and when he made up his mind to do something, he made sure it got done."

Another three men in suits took it in turns to say much the same thing about the dead man. Fenella was only half listening as they basically repeated what everyone else had already said. What kept nagging at her was the idea that Darrell was never interested in anything for more than a year. Was the Wallaby Society the only exception, or was he planning to shut it down soon?

"Next, I believe Mark Masterson wants to say a few words," they were told.

Mark walked up to the front of the church. Fenella thought he looked arrogant as he faced the room. "Darrell was my client, but he was also my friend. I worked hard, as his advocate, to help him in a myriad of different ways, but we used to spend time together, just as friends, too. Darrell could be very demanding, but that was because he had very high standards. I'm going to miss him, both personally and professionally." He walked back to his seat as the minister stepped forward again.

"We've heard a bit about Darrell's charity, the Manx Wallaby Society," he said. "I'm sure a representative from the society would like to share his or her thoughts with all of us."

Several people around Fenella exchanged glances. After a moment, William got to his feet. Fenella noted the scowl on Gail's face that was quickly replaced by a neutral expression.

"I'm William Faragher," he said. "I've been doing my best to keep track of the wallabies for years. I was happy when Darrell took an interest and I enjoyed working with him and the Manx Wallaby Society. I suppose I'll be looking after the wallabies on my own again now, though. I'll miss Darrell and all of his support."

Gail made a face. As William sat down, she jumped to her feet. "William isn't the only one who cares about the wallabies. There are a lot of us here who've been a part of the Manx Wallaby Society, and we all intend to continue to do our vital work to protect the wallabies, with or without Darrell's support."

It will be without, Fenella thought.

After taking a deep breath, Gail looked around the church and then blushed brightly. She dropped back into her seat and bent her head, staring at the ground.

"Excellent," the minister said brightly. "I must admit that I was unaware of the island's wild wallaby population until recently. I'm pleased to learn that there are so many people concerned with their welfare. We're put here to take care of all of God's creatures, of course. Does anyone else want to take a moment to remember Darrell?"

People looked around the room. Fenella found herself studying the ex-wives who were all sitting and staring straight ahead. It seemed odd to her that each one had only been a part of Darrell's life for almost exactly a year. Kristen must have known that her days were numbered. What did that mean for the Wallaby Society?

"Well, then, Darrell's family and friends invite everyone to join them in the church hall for tea and biscuits. I believe there may be a few announcements that will be made at that time. Thank you all for coming today. I'll just conclude with a prayer."

"Ready for some tea and biscuits?" Daniel whispered to Fenella as the minister concluded his prayer.

She nodded. It wasn't that she was hungry. She was simply curious about the announcements that were going to be made.

It was a short walk across the parking lot to the church hall. It seemed as if everyone headed there as they left the church.

"I wonder if Rodney will be trying to keep people out of the hall, too," Fenella whispered as she and Daniel joined a long line of people waiting for the doors to open.

She got her answer a moment later as Rodney, the minister, and Mark appeared in the doorway.

"We appreciate that some of you came to pay your respects to Darrell without actually knowing him personally," Mark said. "While we appreciate the gesture, we respectfully ask that you not attend this reception, which is intended for Darrell's family and friends. We all need the time and the space to mourn and I think we'd all prefer to do that away from strangers."

The woman standing next to Fenella made a noise. "Come on, Ethel," she said loudly. "Clearly, we aren't welcome here because we aren't wealthy enough to have been Darrell Higgins's friends when he was alive."

She turned and walked away, her friend on her heels. Daniel raised an eyebrow. "I'm surprised more people aren't leaving," he whispered to Fenella.

"I feel as if we should leave," she whispered back.

He shook his head. "I'm working, remember? I really want to hear whatever announcements are going to be made."

"I hope they aren't closing down the charity."

"That's certainly one possibility."

The line began to inch forward. Fenella could hear more than one person arguing with the men at the door about his or her relationship with Darrell. After a moment, Alfred walked over and said something to Mark. He nodded and then turned and walked into the church hall. Alfred took his place next to Rodney, which seemed to intimidate the woman who was talking to Darrell's former assistant.

"I'm sorry, but I don't remember ever meeting you," Rodney said.

"Yes, well, maybe I'll just go," the woman said, blinking nervously at the inspector next to Rodney. "I mean, it isn't as if Darrell and I were close friends or anything. I simply wanted to pay my respects." She clutched her handbag tightly and walked quickly away. As she went, several other men and women fell into step behind her, shortening the line noticeably.

Only a few minutes later, Fenella and Daniel reached the doors.

"Ah, yes, welcome," Rodney said, nodding at Fenella. "You two can go right in."

"Need a hand out here?" Daniel asked Alfred.

"I think most of the morbidly nosy have left," he replied. "I certainly hope so, anyway."

Daniel nodded and then he and Fenella walked into the hall. It was basically one large room. A table had been set up along the wall at the back with hot drinks and plates of biscuits. As she and Daniel slowly crossed the room, Fenella looked around.

There were folding chairs set up in several small clusters. Near the back of the room, sitting together, were the ex-wives. They didn't seem to be speaking to one another, and several of them had teacups in their hands. On the other side of the room, a small cluster of Darrell's former business associates were standing together. It seemed to Fenella that they were all only just managing to resist the urge to check their watches every two seconds. The men and women from the Wallaby Society appeared to be gathering in another group of chairs.

Fenella and Daniel each got a cup of tea. "Want to share a plate?" he asked her as she reached for one for her biscuits.

"Sure," she replied.

They each added a few biscuits to the plate and then strolled slowly around the room.

Kristen was sitting near the ex-wives, but didn't seem to be actually with them. Fenella gave her a sympathetic smile as they walked past her.

"Fenella, thank you for coming," she said, getting to her feet. "You were incredibly kind to me the other day and I don't believe I ever thanked you."

"You've been through a lot lately. No thanks were needed," Fenella assured her.

"But I truly did appreciate you rescuing me from my disastrous dinner and also for meeting me for tea the next day. I feel as if I'm rushing around, trying to keep myself busy, so that I don't have time to think."

"I'm sure today was difficult."

Kristen glanced over at the ex-wives and then sighed. "I feel as if none of them truly appreciate how much Darrell cared for me. They all think that he would have grown tired of me soon, simply because he grew tired of each of them after a year. Darrell had changed, though, and we were going to be together forever."

"I'm sure you'd have had a very long and happy life together," Fenella lied politely.

Kristen nodded. "I know you're right. Darrell loved me. I'm certain of that."

"Of course he did," Jody said as she joined them. "This week, anyway."

Kristen flushed. "He told me that I was the first woman who truly mattered to him."

"He told me the same thing," Jody replied. "I can even remember his exact words. 'Jody, you're the first woman I've ever actually cared about. I feel as if all of the women who came before you were simply there to help me recognize the real thing when I found it.' Those were his exact words."

"Sounds familiar," Maria said from her chair. "I'll bet he said it while staring into your eyes with such intensity that you almost had to blink."

"He did that with me," Carla said, getting to her feet and joining them. "If I'm honest, it was almost creepy how he'd stare and stare and never blink. At the time, though, it felt intense and wonderful."

"Are you talking about that staring thing he did?" Jennifer asked. "He did it for the first time with me on our wedding night. It was almost weird, but he sounded so sincere as he told me how much I meant to him and how he knew he'd never find another woman he could ever love as much."

"He said that to me, too," Maria exclaimed. "In almost those exact words."

"I suppose it was easier to keep using the same lines over and over again," Carla sighed. "Maybe that was why none of us lasted longer than a year. Maybe he could only come up with a year's worth of sweet nothings."

A few of the women chuckled. "When this is over, let's go and get a drink somewhere," Jody said. "There's a nice pub in Douglas called the Tale and Tail. I assume you're all staying in Douglas?"

The other three women all nodded. Carla named a hotel that Fenella knew was near her apartment building. Jennifer mentioned one that was a bit further away and that was the same one where Maria was staying.

"You're all within walking distance of the pub, then," Jody said. "I am, too. Let's go and get drunk and compare notes on the, um, lovely man to whom we were all married."

"Does that mean that I'm not invited?" Kristen asked.

Jody glanced at her and then looked at the other women.

"You're more than welcome," Carla told Kristen. "Just don't be surprised if you hear things that upset you. I suspect we were all told the same sweet lies that Darrell told you."

Kristen shook her head. "He meant everything he said to me."

"Of course he did," Jennifer replied, patting her arm. "I truly believe that he meant everything he said to all of us, at the time he said it, anyway. The problem was, when he started to get bored, he stopped caring and he had a very short attention span."

"You should bring your friend," Jody suggested, nodding toward Fenella. "If things get too difficult for you, she can cover your ears and sing 'la la la' until you feel better."

Kristen flushed. "You've never liked me," she said angrily. "It wasn't my fault that Darrell stopped loving you."

"I never said it was, although I do think you could have waited to start seeing him until after we were divorced," Jody replied.

"How many times do I have to tell you that I didn't start seeing Darrell until after your divorce?" Kristen demanded.

"During the last months of our marriage, Darrell started staying out late. He also suddenly started 'working' every weekend," Jody said, putting air quotes around the word working. "If he wasn't seeing you, then he was seeing someone else."

Kristen shrugged. "He wasn't seeing me," she said firmly.

"It wasn't like Darrell to cheat," Maria said. "I mean, he moved from woman to woman at an astonishing pace, but as far as I knew, he never moved on to a new woman until he'd ended things with his previous one. I'm surprised to hear you say that he cheated on you."

"So maybe he didn't," Jody said. "Maybe he truly was working every weekend and two or three nights a week."

"That doesn't sound like the Darrell I knew and loved," Jennifer laughed. "When I knew Darrell, he never wanted to work, ever. He was all about living a life of leisure and spending all of his inheritance."

"He worked very hard," Kristen protested. "When we were together, he often worked weekends or had late meetings in the evenings."

Maria opened her mouth to say something, but Mark, who'd moved into the middle of the room and loudly cleared his throat, interrupted her.

"Ah, right, I've just a few things to say to everyone," he said when the room went quiet. "First of all, thank you all for coming. I'm sure Darrell would have been deeply touched to see all of you here, paying your respects to his memory. There's been a great deal of speculation in the press about Darrell's estate. I'd like to set some of the rumors to rest, if I may."

"Did he leave a will?" someone asked.

Mark flushed. "I took my job as Darrell's advocate seriously. One of the first things I did when I began working with Darrell was insist that he create a will. Once he understood the importance of having such a document, he made certain that he updated his will on a regular basis. His most recent update took place only a month ago and I'm happy that it reflects his wishes at the time of his death."

"That's good news," Kristen murmured.

"Are you sure about that?" Jody asked.

Kristen flushed.

"I need to arrange meetings with all of the various beneficiaries. It might be easiest to hold them in small groups, actually. I hope that all of Darrell's former wives are planning to remain on the island for a few days?"

"He named all of us in his will?" Jennifer asked.

"He did. We can meet tomorrow to discuss things if that works for all of you," Mark replied.

The women all looked at one another.

"It works for me," Jennifer replied. "I'm staying at least a few more days."

"Tomorrow is fine," Maria told him.

"I can do tomorrow, too," Carla said.

"And I live here, so tomorrow is as good a day as any," Jody added.

"Kristen, I'd like to include you with the ex-wives, if you don't mind," Mark said.

Kristen took a deep breath and then blew it out. "I don't believe that I belong with them, but if that's more convenient for you, I suppose I shouldn't object."

"It is more convenient for me, thank you," Mark replied. "Rodney and I will be arranging individual meetings with each of Darrell's business associates. I'll probably start arranging those for early next week. If any of you would prefer to do something sooner, please ring my office and I'll do what I can to accommodate you. Harry, we'll meet right after this, if that works for you."

Harry nodded. "That's fine."

Mark looked down at the sheet of paper in his hand. "That just leaves the Manx Wallaby Society. Rodney and I are arranging a small gathering for all of the members of the society. It will be held tomorrow evening at the office in Ballaugh. Everyone who has ever volunteered in any capacity, even if it was for a single hour during just one hunt, should attend. There are specific provisions in Darrell's will for dealing with the charity in the event of his untimely death. I believe you all should hear them."

❧ 11 ❧

A buzz went around the room and Fenella had to force herself not to rush over to where the charity volunteers were sitting to hear what they were saying.

"Interesting," Daniel whispered in her ear.

"Again, thank you all for coming," Mark said. He looked around the room and then walked away, heading straight for Harry.

"I better have been left more than the damned wallabies," Kristen muttered.

"I thought you loved the furry little darlings," Jody said mockingly.

"I do, of course, but they don't need the money as badly as I do," Kristen told her.

Jody laughed. "Tomorrow should be interesting. I wonder what dearest Darrell left me. Probably his wedding ring from our marriage. I'm sure he'd have found that amusing."

"I'm surprised he left any of us anything, really," Maria said. "We all got decent settlements when we divorced, after all."

"What else was he going to do with the money, though?" Carla asked. "He didn't have any children to inherit his fortune. I can't see him leaving large lump sums to his business colleagues, can you? He probably left quite a lot to the Wallaby Society, as that was his favorite project when he died, wasn't it?"

"He'd been running it for a year," Jody said. "What does that tell you?"

"That he was about to jettison it for something new," Jennifer said with a chuckle. "Unless he truly had changed from when I knew him."

"Let's have this conversation over something stronger," Jody suggested. "Does anyone need direction to the pub?"

The women all shook their heads.

"You are coming, aren't you?" Kristen asked Fenella.

She was shocked. "I suppose I can," she said hesitantly. "But not right away."

"It's four o'clock. Let's meet at the pub at eight," Jody suggested. "That way everyone can have some dinner and change into more comfortable clothes."

"Perfect," Jennifer said. "I can't wait to get out of these shoes."

Maria nodded. "I only wore heels because I knew Darrell would have expected as much."

As the women began to leave, Daniel touched Fenella's arm. "Let's go talk to our fellow volunteers," he suggested.

They crossed the room and slid into chairs around the vaguely circle-shaped cluster. William was talking.

"...what is said and then go from there," he said. He looked over at Fenella and Daniel and smiled. "We were all just taking wild guesses at what the provisions for the charity in Darrell's will might be," he told them. "Want to throw in a guess?"

"What does everyone else think?" Fenella asked.

"I don't know what to think," Sara said. "I hope that he provided funding for us for another ten or twenty years, but that might be a bit optimistic."

"I think it's very optimistic," William told her. "I think we'll be lucky to have been left enough to keep the charity running through the end of the calendar year."

"There's little point in speculating," Gail said. "We'll find out tomorrow night."

"And then we'll have to make some decisions," Nicholas said. "I donate my time to the charity because I can't afford to donate any money. I suspect many of us are in the same boat. If Darrell didn't provide any funds, what do we do next?"

"Some of us could afford to fund the charity going forward," Sara said, looking pointedly at Fenella.

She flushed. "I don't think I'm in a position to fund an entire charity," she said quickly.

"You could afford to rehome all of the wallabies in a luxury mansion with their own maids and butlers," Sara countered.

"Wallabies don't want to live in a mansion," Gail snapped.

"What makes you so sure about that?" William asked. "I mean, given the opportunity, that might be exactly what they want."

"They're wild creatures. They need to live in the wild," Gail replied.

"Fenella could afford to buy up a huge section of the Curraghs to designate as a sanctuary for wallabies," Sara suggested.

"I don't believe the Curraghs are for sale," Fenella protested.

"Some parts are protected, but not all of it. Anyway, if you offered the government enough money, they'd probably take it, as long as you weren't planning to develop the site," Sara replied.

Fenella shook her head. "Let's see what happens tomorrow," she suggested, looking at Daniel a bit desperately.

"I hope you all can attend tomorrow night," Mark said as he joined them. "Let's say seven o'clock, if that works for everyone?"

"I dare say we can all manage that," William replied.

"Half seven would be better," Gail said.

Mark looked around the circle. "Would half seven be better for anyone else? I'd much prefer seven."

"Seven is better for me," William said cheerfully.

"I'd prefer seven, actually," Sara said, sounding apologetic. "I'd rather not be out too late."

"We'll make it seven, then," Mark said. "Gail, if you're late, I'm sure someone will fill you in on whatever you miss."

Gail frowned, but nodded.

"And with that, I'm going to have to go," Mark announced. "I have a great many things to do before tomorrow."

"Can't you give us a hint as to what's going to happen with the charity?" Gail asked as Mark stood up. "We're all ever so worried about everything."

"I'm sorry, but I believe it will be best to wait until tomorrow to say anything. I know there are a few other volunteers. I do hope someone will try to invite them to attend tomorrow's meeting."

"Betty is still away," Sara told him. "I'm not sure when they're meant to be coming back, actually. Jake is still in Birmingham. Apparently, there were some complications with the baby. Everything is fine now, but he's not returned, yet. I'm pretty certain that Dave is still in hospital, although I haven't spoken to his daughter in a few days. There are a few former volunteers who've moved away over the past year. What about them?"

"We have all of Rodney's records from the past year. We'll be contacting anyone who isn't still on the island after tomorrow," Mark told her.

"Does that mean that Darrell left each of the volunteers something in his will?" Sara demanded.

Mark smiled at her. "I truly can't say anything until tomorrow. You'll just have to wait and see." He walked away before anyone could reply.

"I'm going to have to ring Doug in Liverpool and tell him that he could be about to inherit a fortune," Sara said.

"Don't get his hopes up," William suggested. "Wait until after tomorrow. Knowing Darrell, if he did leave anything to the volunteers, it will be pictures of wallabies or some such thing."

"I'd love that," Gail said loudly.

"You'd love a few thousand pounds even more," William said. "You could buy your own picture and then have a holiday."

"Would that be enough to get me to Australia?" Gail asked. "Could Darrell have really left us each thousands of pounds?"

"If he did, I shall donate my share back to the charity," Sara said firmly. "Unless he also left enough money to fund that, too."

Gail's smile faded. "Yes, of course, that's the right thing to do, if he didn't fund the charity."

"Let's just wait and see what happens tomorrow," Daniel said firmly. "We'll see you all at the office tomorrow evening."

"It's getting late," William said as he looked at the clock on the wall. "I'll see you all tomorrow."

Fenella and Daniel sat and watched as the charity volunteers slowly made their way out of the room. The rest of the room had emptied, as well. Only a few people were left, all standing in front of the table in the back, eating biscuits, and talking quietly amongst themselves.

"That was all very interesting," Alfred said as he sat down next to Fenella. "Tell me about the conversations you had with everyone."

Sighing, Fenella glanced at Daniel, but he simply nodded and then sat back in his seat. "We didn't really talk to anyone in the church," Fenella began. It felt as if it took her a long time to get through the church service and all of the conversations that she'd had in the church hall. Daniel interrupted a few times when she forgot things, but mostly she simply talked for what felt like hours.

When she was done, Alfred smiled at her. "Thank you. They're a fascinating bunch and one of them is a killer. I wish I knew which one."

"You don't suspect any of the ex-wives, do you?" Fenella asked.

"Jennifer, Carla, and Maria were all across when Darrell died. None of them are on the list of suspects," Alfred told her.

"Which leaves Jody and Kristen on the list," Fenella replied thoughtfully.

"And you're going out for drinks with them tonight," Daniel interjected. "Be very careful."

Fenella nodded. While she didn't feel as if she was in any danger from any of the women, especially in the pub, she'd still be extra cautious in their company.

"I'd like to come along, but I don't think I'd be welcome," Daniel added.

"Probably not. I'm not sure why I've been invited along," Fenella replied.

"Kristen seems to regard you as a friend, even though you've only just met," he told her.

"I suppose she doesn't know many people on the island," Fenella said thoughtfully.

"Did Mark give you any hints as to what's in the will?" Daniel asked Alfred.

The other man shook his head. "I'm planning to attend his meeting with the ex-wives tomorrow. You'll be at the Wallaby Society one. I'm going to guess that we're going to hear things at both meetings that will suggest motives for Darrell's murder."

Daniel nodded. "Which will help, as we've nothing concrete at the moment."

"It will all come down to money," Alfred sighed. "We just have to see how much has been left to each of the interested parties."

"From what Mark said, no one besides him knew the content of Darrell's will," Fenella said.

"Which is why Mark is on the list," Alfred told her.

Fenella gasped. She hadn't really thought about the advocate when she'd been considering suspects.

Alfred laughed. "And on that note, I'd better get to the office and start working on my reports. Ring Daniel when you get home from the pub," he told Fenella.

"Of course," she replied.

Fenella and Daniel talked about everything that had happened at the service and the reception after it on the drive back to Douglas.

"I just keep thinking about how everyone kept talking about Darrell's short attention span," Fenella said eventually. "I keep wondering what that would have meant for the charity in the future."

"So you think that one of the charity volunteers killed him because he was going to stop supporting the charity?" Daniel asked.

"It sounds insane, but it's possible, isn't it?"

"Anything is possible. Some of the volunteers are passionate about wallabies."

"Gail is, anyway."

"If she killed Darrell, she must have done it right before she came to take our place," Daniel pointed out.

"And she didn't act like someone who'd just murdered someone."

"Which proves nothing, of course."

Fenella sighed. "The killer almost has to have been someone from the charity. Who else would have known where to find Darrell?"

"Anyone who rang him and asked him where he was?"

Fenella laughed. "Okay, I suppose that's true. But I still think the charity volunteers seem the most likely suspects."

"Including Jody and Kristen and Harry?"

"Definitely, although Jody and Kristen might be able to alibi one another. I'm not sure when Harry arrived at the office, though."

"Let's just say, for sake of argument, that no one has an unbreakable alibi."

Fenella gave his words some thought. "It could have been any one of them, couldn't it? Nicholas or William or Gail or Sara or Harry or Rodney. Have I forgotten anyone?"

"There are a lot of others on the list," Daniel told her. "You saw how many of Darrell's former business associates were at the memorial service. They're all being discreetly investigated."

"Maybe one of them had a better motive than protecting a few random marsupials, too."

"Maybe. We should know a lot more about motive once the contents of the will are made known."

Daniel found a parking space on the promenade. "Dinner?" he asked.

"I'm starving," Fenella told him. "Lunch seems to have been a long time ago and the biscuits at the memorial service weren't very good."

"Where do you want to go?"

"What if we just got something and took it back to my apartment," Fenella suggested. "I'm going to the pub later and I spent the last few hours in a crowd. I think I'd like some time to unwind away from people."

"Does that include me?"

"No, never you," she said, blushing as she realized what she'd said.

Daniel smiled at her. "That's good to hear," he said softly.

They walked to a nearby pizza place and got pizza and garlic bread to take back to Fenella's apartment.

"Merrow," Katie said as a greeting.

"Want to find plates and things while I feed the monster?" Fenella asked Daniel as he followed her into the kitchen.

A few minutes later, they were sitting at the counter with plates full of pizza while Katie delicately nibbled her way through a bowl of cat food.

"What shall we talk about?" Daniel asked after a few bites.

"Anything other than murder," Fenella replied.

"How disappointing," Mona said as she slid onto the stool next to Fenella. "I wanted to hear all about the memorial service. I assume it's too much to hope that someone confessed."

Fenella swallowed the reply that sprang to her lips. Daniel couldn't see Mona. If she didn't want him to think she was crazy, she needed to remember not to reply to the woman when he was in the apartment.

"How's Jack doing?" Daniel asked.

"Good. He's interviewing for a job in Pittsburgh soon, or maybe he's already done it. He actually went out to Las Vegas for an interview recently, too."

"I didn't realize he was looking for another job."

"I don't think he knows what he wants. Coming to the island was an eye-opening experience for him. I think he's realized that he's missed out on a lot of opportunities over the years. It's made him question everything, really."

"I hope he finds something that makes him happy."

"Me, too. I'll always have a soft spot in my heart for him."

Daniel nodded. "I feel that way about my ex-wife," he admitted. "And about Nancy."

"Tell me more about Nancy."

He shrugged. "She's a few years older than I am. In some ways, she's similar to Jack, really. She's lived on her island in Scotland for her entire life aside from when she went to university. Policing was all that she ever wanted to do and she was fortunate to get the part-time constable's job within days after she got home from university. A few years later, after holding down two other part-time jobs to make ends meet, the island's inspector retired and she was offered the position."

"And it's a very small island?"

"Pretty small, anyway. They definitely don't need more than one inspector," Daniel replied.

Which was why, in spite of being attracted to Nancy, Daniel hadn't pursued her. Fenella was slightly uncomfortable talking about her, but she was also oddly curious about the woman who'd attracted Daniel's attention during the classes he'd taken in Milton Keynes.

"Did she enjoy her time in Milton Keynes?" she asked.

He chuckled. "It was quite overwhelming for her, really. She flew in and hired a car, but she hated trying to drive around the city. The traffic scared her."

"I can sympathize," Fenella said. She'd had to work hard to earn her Manx driver's license and the thought of driving on the UK mainland terrified her.

"I thought you might. You have other things in common with her, too. She has two older brothers."

"Really? Only two?" Fenella laughed. There were days when she missed her four older brothers terribly and other times when she barely thought about them. If pressed, she would admit that she missed some of them more than she missed others. The one that she missed the least was also the only one who'd visited her on the island since she'd moved.

"Only two, but they both live on the island with her."

"Really? Does anyone leave?"

Daniel shrugged. "It's a small town, really, the island. People who move there tend to fall in love with the place and stay forever or leave within a month or two of arrival. A huge percentage of the children who grow up there end up moving back at some point, often when they're ready to have children of their own. The island has excellent schools, even if the kids do have to leave for university."

"What do her brothers do?"

"Her oldest brother runs the family farm. They have cattle and sheep. Her younger brother is a nurse."

"Has Nancy ever been married?"

"No, although she nearly married the man who owns the farm next to her family's farm when she was in her early twenties. That was back when she was working three jobs to make ends meet and living in a tiny flat on her own. She didn't love him, but she loved the idea of not being alone and of having a house to call her own."

"But she didn't marry him?"

"She found out he was seeing someone else behind her back. When she tells the story, she insists that they ended things as friends, but, well, I don't know." He sighed. "I don't know why we're even talking about her."

"I was just curious. Do you talk to her often?"

"I haven't spoken to her in several weeks. We were texting one another once in a while, but we haven't even done that lately. We both know we can't make a relationship work and I, well, I have another relationship that I'm focused on." He patted her hand.

She smiled. When she opened her mouth, Mona held up a hand.

"Don't say another word about Nancy," she said firmly. "The last thing you want to do is to keep reminding him about her. She's part of his past. Don't talk about her or about his ex-wife."

But I have more questions, Fenella thought. "Is your sister planning to visit again anytime soon?" she asked instead.

"She might try to bring the kids over in the summer. Her husband may not be able to get time off work, but she thinks the kids would enjoy another visit to the island. What about your brothers? Any of them planning a visit?"

Fenella shrugged. "They all keep talking about coming, but they're all busy with their own lives. I think I'm going to have to go back to the US in order to see them all again."

"Are you planning a trip to the US, then?"

"Not planning, exactly, more like bouncing the idea around at the back of my mind."

He nodded. "Of course, you can go any time. You don't need to worry about taking time off work."

"Which is probably why I can't seem to make any decisions," Fenella said. "If I had to actually plan something, I might actually do it. As it is, I simply keep putting everything off."

Daniel helped Fenella tidy away the empty pizza boxes and load the dirty dishes into the dishwasher. Then they sat on a couch and watched the sea together.

"You should probably get ready to go," he said after a while.

"I should," she agreed. She stood up and stretched. "I'm ready for bed," she sighed.

Daniel stood up and pulled her into a kiss. "Me, too," he said huskily when he lifted his head.

She felt herself blushing. "I have to go and meet the ex-wives," she reminded him.

He nodded. "Let's go away for a weekend," he suggested. "After the case is solved, of course. We could go to London, maybe or Edinburgh."

"I've never been to Edinburgh. I've heard it's wonderful."

"It's a beautiful city, full of history."

"That sounds perfect."

"Let's plan something for the end of the month," he suggested.

"What exactly are you proposing?" she asked.

He chuckled. "I want our first nights together to be special. I feel as if this could be the start of something wonderful. This is your space and my house is my space. I think it would be good if we were on neutral ground as we see where our relationship is going."

Fenella nodded. She'd been thinking along the same lines, although her reasoning was more to do with getting away from Mona if she was actually going to sleep with Daniel than anything else. "Let's get through this murder investigation first," she said.

"I may put in for a few days off, now, otherwise I might not be able to get them."

"Okay," Fenella said, trying to ignore the sick feeling in her stomach that accompanied the simple word.

He kissed her again, which changed the sick feeling to something else altogether. "You need to go," he reminded her a while later.

She glanced at the clock and sighed. "I'm going to be late. I hope I don't miss anything important. Shall I call you when I get home?"

"Or I could simply wait here for you to get back," he suggested. "I could watch the waves and keep Katie company."

"If you want to," Fenella said, not entirely sure how she felt about the idea. In her bedroom, she flipped through Mona's wardrobe, wondering what to wear to the pub.

"It's sweet that he wants to stay," Mona said. "And he wants to take you away for a romantic weekend. You should go."

"I'm considering it."

"He's just about perfect for you."

"And that scares the heck out of me."

Mona laughed. "You're falling in love with him. I'm really happy for you."

"Thanks. I think."

"Wear the blue jumper with the dark grey trousers," Mona told her.

Fenella found both items right in front of the wardrobe. "I've never seen these before," she said as she changed into the sweater.

"They've always been there, they simply aren't all that interesting so you've never noticed them before. That's what makes them perfect for tonight."

"I can't believe you owned anything that wasn't interesting."

Mona laughed. "On me, that jumper was interesting," she told Fenella.

Fenella frowned at herself in the mirror. There was nothing wrong with the outfit, but Mona was right, she looked boring. The clothes were remarkably similar to Fenella's own things.

"But much better quality," Mona told her.

"Stop reading my mind," Fenella complained. Daniel was right. They needed to go away if they were going to spend a night or two together.

"If you want to have Daniel here overnight, you simply have to let me know. I can go away for a few days. I've been thinking about going to a spa, anyway."

"There are spas for ghosts?"

"We have everything we could possibly want, well, mostly. It's complicated."

"I'm sure." Mona often told her things about the ghost world, knowing that Fenella had no way of knowing if she was lying or telling the truth. For the most part, Fenella didn't really want to know.

"I don't want to get in the way of your relationship with Daniel. If I was sure that you two were going to get married and live happily ever after, I'd move on to the next part of my afterlife."

"It's too soon to be thinking about happily ever after."

"Exactly, which means I need to stay here for a while longer. Max will be happy anyway."

"Because he's still here due to the fact that he doesn't realize he's dead."

"Exactly."

"Will you tell him, when you move on?"

"I can't imagine moving on without him. Of course, once we both move on, I'll have to share him with Bryan again. I know it's selfish of me, but I'm enjoying having him all to myself."

Fenella stared at her aunt. She'd learned a lot about Mona and her relationship with Max in the past year. While Mona had been madly in love with Max, apparently, Max had been devoted to his partner Bryan. "Doesn't he miss Bryan?" she asked after a moment.

"He thinks Bryan is on holiday, which he is, in a way." Mona sighed. "Once you're settled properly, I'll move on and I'll take Max with me. I'm sure he and Bryan will be delighted to see one another again."

Mona looked sad for a moment and then she tossed her head and smiled brightly at Fenella. "But you're going to be late for your evening with the ex-wives. Maybe one of them will confess to murder or at the very least say something interesting. Off you go."

"What are you going to do tonight?" Fenella asked as she touched up her makeup.

"I'm just going to stay here and keep Daniel company."

"Don't start changing him the way you changed Jack."

"Jack needed changing. Daniel is fine."

"He is, isn't he?" Fenella asked softly.

Mona smiled. "You'd enjoy Edinburgh, but Paris is more romantic."

Fenella sighed. "First Daniel and Alfred have to solve a murder."

She checked her appearance in the mirror and then walked back out to the living room. Daniel had switched on the television and was flipping through the channels.

"I hope you don't mind," he said, nodding toward the big screen.

"Not at all. Make yourself at home. There are snacks in the kitchen. Help yourself."

"Meoowwww," Katie said.

Fenella laughed. "I'll leave Katie's treats on the counter. If you get yourself something, she can have a handful of her treats."

He nodded. "We'll be fine. Have fun. I'm hoping someone will say something interesting tonight."

"Do you have anything you want me to ask them about?"

"If Darrell was planning to shut down the charity, I have to believe that either Jody or Kristen knew about it. They both may have known, actually. I'd be curious what the other wives thought of the charity. Maria helped to set it up, of course, but I wonder what Jennifer and Carla thought about it."

"I'll see what I can find out," Fenella promised.

"There will be a female constable at one of the other tables at the pub," he told her. "You may recognize whoever they send, but she'll be in plainclothes and she won't acknowledge you."

Fenella nodded. She'd been expecting as much, really.

Daniel walked her to the door and then pulled her into a kiss. "Or you could stay here with me," he whispered in her ear.

"I could, but then we'd never know what we missed. What if I miss the one thing that solves the case?"

"If we weren't planning to go away when the case was solved, I might try to change your mind. As it is, I have even more incentive for wanting the case solved."

Fenella gave him a quick kiss and then opened the door. She could feel Daniel's eyes on her as she walked down the corridor. When she'd boarded the elevator car, she turned around and waved to him. He waved back as the doors slid shut.

It didn't take her long to walk to the pub. Her mind was racing as she thought about Daniel. The possibility of going away with him was exciting but terrifying. Walking into the Tale and Tail helped calm her. She looked around the room and sighed. While she had a good deal more money than she'd ever imagined having, she didn't have enough to buy the pub, which was probably for the best. If she owned it, she'd probably want to try to read every single book on the shelves and there was no way she'd manage that in her lifetime.

"The usual?" the bartender asked as she approached the bar.

"Yes, please. I'm meeting some friends, a group of thirty-something blonde women," she told him.

He raised an eyebrow. "The Darrell Higgins' ex-wives club?" he asked. "They arrived a few minutes ago. They're upstairs."

Fenella took her glass of wine and headed for the stairs. As she began to climb, she could hear raised voices.

"I'm not going to stay if you're going to be horrible to me."

It was Kristen's voice and Fenella felt torn between hurrying up the stairs and turning around and going back home.

❧ 12 ❧

"You could have waited to start arguing until I got here," Fenella said loudly as she crossed the room to where the women were sitting together on several couches.

"It's just Jody and Kristen snapping at one another," Jennifer told her. "I have some sympathy for both of them, really."

"I've been there," Maria sighed. "I still can't believe that I stayed and helped set up the charity after Darrell divorced me."

"Because he still needed you," Jody said.

"Exactly that," Maria agreed. "He had me convinced that the charity needed me, which meant that he still needed me, even if we weren't together any longer. I needed him to need me, which is truly pathetic."

"That was Darrell, though," Carla said. "He made you desperate to be a part of his life so that once he'd cast you aside, you'd do anything to cling to the fringes of his existence for as long as possible. It was horrible."

"I wasn't clinging to anything," Jody said coolly.

"You *were* clinging," Kristen almost shouted. "You hated that Darrell had moved on and fallen in love with me. You did everything you could to get between us."

Jody shrugged. "I didn't have to do much to get between you and Darrell. He was simply amusing himself with you until he found his next wife."

"I was going to be his next wife," Kristen insisted.

"If he didn't propose in the first few days after you'd met, he wasn't going to propose," Jody told her. "He went out with dozens of women in between wives, but when he met someone he wanted to marry, he proposed almost immediately."

"He'd changed," Kristen said firmly.

"You can believe whatever you want," Jody told her. "We all know the truth."

"He was going to propose soon," Kristen said with tears in her eyes. "You believe me, don't you?" she asked the other women.

"I think you'll be a good deal better off without him," Jennifer replied. "He was never going to be the man you wanted him to be."

"Why doesn't anyone believe that he'd changed?" Kristen asked.

"I don't think we would have believed it until you'd been together for over a year," Maria said.

Kristen took a deep breath and then sighed. "He was going to end things with me, wasn't he?" She sat back in her seat as tears began to stream down her cheeks.

Fenella sat down next to her and handed her a tissue.

"Oh, darling, don't cry," Jennifer said. "Darrell was simply Darrell. I'm sure he loved you dearly and would have continued to do so for months yet. He simply couldn't manage to stay in love, that's all."

"Why not?" Kristen wailed.

Jennifer looked at the others. "I think it had to do with his childhood," she said. "He was essentially raised by a succession of nannies. His parents had little time for him, and they apparently had trouble keeping nannies, as well. He told me once that he never had the same nanny for more than a year."

"That explains everything," Carla sighed.

"It does, rather," Maria agreed. "He never told me anything about his childhood. I asked questions, but he always changed the subject. I didn't think about it at the time, but now it seems significant."

"He told me that he went to boarding school when he was ten," Kristen sniffed.

"He told me that, too. They had housemothers to look after them, but they changed houses every six months for some reason or another," Maria said. "He did tell me that one of the housemothers was especially sweet, but when he got moved to a new house, he never saw her again."

"The poor child," Fenella said.

"It all sounded rather awful, but Darrell always insisted that he'd been given the best possible education," Carla said.

"It's hardly surprising he had difficulty with long-term relationships," Jennifer said thoughtfully. "I should have tried harder, really."

"I think we all feel that way," Maria said with a rueful smile. "Unfortunately, I don't think we were really given a chance."

"You're right, of course. I thought things were wonderful between us right up until they weren't," Jennifer sighed. "If I'd had any idea that Darrell was getting bored, I might have tried to do something, but I'm not really sure what I could have done."

"I could see the end coming, but I still couldn't do anything to stop it," Jody told her. "Whenever I tried to talk to Darrell, he swore up and down that things were perfect between us, that he was finally in a relationship that was going to last forever. He said all of the right things, and I actually thought he meant them, right up until he asked for a divorce."

"He did mean them," Carla said. "That was the thing with Darrell. He meant everything he was saying, when he said it, but once he'd changed his mind, he wouldn't change it back."

"I tried so hard to get him to change his mind," Jennifer sighed.

"We all did," Maria told her.

"Some of his business associates that spoke at the memorial service today said something similar about his approach to his business," Fenella said.

Jennifer shrugged. "When we were married, he didn't really have anything to do with running his company. He wasn't all that interested in it, as long as it was paying for his lifestyle. I believe he did change in that respect, anyway."

"He did," Maria agreed. "He hadn't become a serious businessman or anything, but he'd started getting more involved in managing some of the things his company did. Before that, he was mostly interested in helping out various charities. His father always insisted that he give generously, and Darrell had taken that lesson to heart."

"He was very generous," Jody agreed.

"But his short attention span was still a factor," Jennifer added. "At least when we were together."

"What do you mean?" Fenella asked.

"I said we met at a party. It was a charity event. My parents were donors on a very small scale, but they'd managed to get an invitation. Darrell had just handed the charity a huge check. At the time, I thought that meant he was passionate about the charity in the same way that my parents and I were. They'd been supporting it since before I was born and I'd been raised with the idea of giving to them whenever possible," Jennifer explained.

"What charity?" Maria asked.

Jennifer named one of the largest cancer charities in the UK. "My mother lost her mother to cancer. She wanted to do everything she could to help with the fight against it. The night we met, Darrell and I talked for hours about the charity and all of the good that it does. He knew even more about the charity than I did and he seemed very proud to be supporting them."

"And then what happened?" Jody demanded.

"About three months after we were married, he came home one day talking about guide dogs. He'd met a man who used one and the whole thing fascinated him. By the end of the week, he'd learned more about guide dogs and the charities that provide them than I'd imagined possible. A few weeks after that, he wrote a huge check to one of the charities. When I asked him about the cancer charity, he told me that he'd done enough for them and was moving on."

"Let me guess, he'd been giving to the cancer charity for about a year," Maria said with a small laugh.

Jennifer nodded. "Of course, I didn't know anything about his short attention span in those days. He'd told me that he'd never had a relationship last longer than a year, but that didn't seem all that unusual. My longest relationship, before I met Darrell, had only lasted sixteen months." She made a face. "I suppose that's still my longest relationship, isn't it?"

"And for how long did he support the guide dogs charity?" Carla asked.

"He was still giving to them when we divorced, but I know he started helping a children's charity not long after we split," Jennifer said.

"Do any of you know of any charity he supported for longer than a year?" Fenella asked.

The women all exchanged glances.

"He usually wrote a big check at the beginning and end of the year," Maria told her. "I'm sure the charities were all grateful for whatever he gave them."

"No doubt," Fenella agreed. "Surely he couldn't behave the same way with his business interests?"

"When we were together, he didn't really have business interests," Jennifer laughed.

"He used to go into the office once or twice a week when we were married," Carla said. "Sometimes he'd come home talking about a project, but I don't remember hearing about the same one more than once or twice. If anything, he was worse with his business things. He had a board of directors to deal with everything, of course."

"And then he found Rodney," Maria added. "Rodney made everything so much easier for him. When we were together, he got involved in some retail project that was being constructed in Manchester. He flew back and forth probably half a dozen times and he spent hours at night studying architectural drawings. Then, one day, he simply stopped talking about it. When I asked him about the project, he just told me that Rodney was handling it."

"He did that a lot," Jody said. "He'd get really involved in something and then, something else would grab his attention and he'd leave the first thing to Rodney while he went after whatever was shiny and new. As Carla said, he was probably worse about his business deals than he ever was with the charities."

"Or his wives," Jody laughed.

"At least we all got a whole year out of him," Maria said.

"His girlfriends didn't usually last that long, though," Carla told her. "I know several women who only went out with him for a month or so before he lost interest."

"I wonder how he decided which women he wanted to marry," Jody said thoughtfully.

"I don't think anyone will ever understand how Darrell's mind worked," Maria said.

"Did the man ever do anything for more than a year?" Fenella asked.

The women all laughed. "I doubt it," Jennifer told her.

"Darrell and I talked about it once," Jody said. "I pointed out that he never committed to anything for more than twelve months. He took that as a challenge, really. Oh, he still dumped me after a year, but he kept the Wallaby Society going, even after its first anniversary."

"How long has it been going, then?" Jennifer asked.

"Thirteen months, more or less," Jody replied.

"It's almost exactly thirteen months since Darrell first mentioned it to me," Maria interjected. "He rang me and told me that he was starting his own charity, one that would support a cause that was really close to his heart."

"And did you immediately guess that he was talking about wallabies?" Fenella had to ask.

Maria laughed. "Not at all. I'm not sure what I would have guessed, if anyone would have asked, but up until that day, I had no idea that he was interested in wallabies."

"I was as shocked as Maria when he started talking about wallabies," Jody said. "When we first met, he was supporting a charity for the homeless, but that didn't last long."

"He only supported them for a few weeks," Maria said. "He lost interest in that one really quickly."

"Or maybe he simply discovered that he loved wallabies more than homeless people," Kristen suggested.

"Oh, he definitely loved wallabies more than homeless people," Maria told her. "But he usually did his best to avoid actually coming into contact with anyone who might actually need the services that whatever charity he was supporting offered. He liked to go to big charity parties, but he never actually volunteered to help with the day-to-day running of them or with their mission."

"We visited a guide dog training center," Jennifer said. "It was a beautiful facility full of puppies and trainers. Darrell loved it. At the end, though, when we met a few of the people who needed the dogs, Darrell was clearly uncomfortable. I don't think he'd ever had much experience with people outside of his social circle."

"Which made the homeless a real challenge," Jody laughed.

"If he could have simply written large checks, he might have stuck with the homeless charity for longer, but the director was very keen on having Darrell meet the people he was helping. Darrell was excited about the idea, right up until he actually had to go and talk to men and women who'd been living on the street," Maria said. "They were all lovely people, by the way, but Darrell found it very difficult."

"We volunteered together in a soup kitchen once, just after we were married," Carla said. "I should say that I volunteered us, really. A very persuasive young man from the charity rang our house. He'd heard that Darrell and I were newly married and he invited us to share our good fortune with others. It was something along those lines, anyway. I fell for it and signed Darrell and myself up for three days of volunteering."

"I'm going to guess it didn't go well," Jody said.

"Darrell went the first day and he did his best, but you could tell that he was uncomfortable. He struggled to make conversation with the people running the soup kitchen, let alone the men and women who were using it."

"And you'd signed up for three days?" Kristen asked.

Carla nodded. "At the end of our first day, Darrell asked the man running the place if he'd rather have us back for two more days or a check for fifty thousand pounds. Obviously, he took the money, and I learned to never volunteer Darrell for anything."

"So was he still as devoted as ever to the wallabies?" Fenella asked.

"Why? What have you heard?" Jody demanded.

"I haven't heard anything. I was just wondering, since it's been over a year since he started the charity," Fenella replied.

Jody and Kristen exchanged glances.

"I'd be lying if I said I hadn't given that question a lot of thought lately," Jody told her. "One of the reasons I volunteered with the charity was so I could keep an eye on what Darrell was doing with it. As I said earlier, I'd teased him about his inability to commit to anything for more than a year. He was determined to prove me wrong. I was certain that he'd turn the whole thing over to Rodney soon, even if he didn't close it down."

"But he'd already made it past a year," Fenella said.

"Yes, but he knew I wasn't going to be impressed if he'd only managed thirteen months. I believe I'd said something to him about him having to go for at least two years before I'd be impressed," Jody said.

"And why he still cared about impressing you is another question," Kristen said under her breath.

"He was all ego," Jody replied, waving a hand. "He always wanted to impress everyone. I'm pretty certain that I struck a nerve when I mentioned his inability to commit to things long-term. He'd still ended things with me, but that didn't mean he was going to admit that I was right about anything."

"So you think he was going to turn it all over to Rodney?" Fenella asked.

Jody shrugged. "That was one option, anyway."

Fenella frowned. "I thought Rodney had been running it for the most part, anyway."

"He did nearly all of the work, but Darrell was very proud of the fact that he took part in every hunt himself. He used to go out in the field for at least a few hours, and when he wasn't out in the field, he used to sit in the office for the entire day, monitoring everything," Kristen told her.

"But this time he'd taken on even more responsibility," Fenella remarked.

"Yeah, I wish I knew why," Kristen said.

"He told me that he was concerned because no one ever saw anything," Jody said. "He wanted to change the boundaries of the sections to see if that might help."

"I understand that, but I don't know why he didn't just tell Rodney to redraw the boundaries," Kristen replied.

"Do either of you know why the charity always stayed in the same place?" Fenella asked. "The Curraghs are huge, and yet you only covered a small section of them. Why didn't you try moving around, especially since no one ever saw anything?"

"When Darrell first started, he looked at where other people had seen wallabies in the past before he chose the area we would cover," Maria told her. "He told me he wanted to keep revisiting the same areas every month for a full year before making any changes. We were certain, back then, that we'd see lots of wallabies, of course, or at least, evidence of their presence."

"Is that why he was finally making changes, then?" Fenella asked.

Maria shrugged. "I'm not sure."

"He wasn't changing the area we were covering, though," Jody told her. "He was just changing how it was divided up between the volunteers."

Fenella nodded. "Even though no one ever saw anything."

"We might have seen more if we'd had full cover for every hunt," Kristen said. "As it was, we always had gaps in the schedule. Darrell didn't like to talk about that, though."

"Surely, he should have told people in an effort to get more volunteers on board," Fenella suggested.

Kristen shrugged. "He said he didn't want to do anything that might make people question our results," she explained. "He wanted our study to be scientific."

"But it isn't scientific if some areas weren't actually being covered," Fenella said.

"Yes, well, Darrell didn't see it that way," Kristen told her.

Fenella swallowed a sigh. "Where did he find his volunteers?"

"You can answer that better than I can," Kristen replied. "You simply turned up at the last hunt. Where did Darrell find you?"

"He sent me a letter," Fenella explained. "I get a lot of mail from charities around the island, but Darrell's was different. He didn't ask me for any money, for a start."

"He would have," Jody laughed. "He was probably hoping you'd feel the same way he does about charitable giving. Writing a check is preferable to actually doing anything useful."

"He did seem surprised when I called and offered to help with the hunt," Fenella told her.

"I'm sure he was. We rarely got new volunteers. I believe everyone else has been with us since the first few hunts," Jody said.

"Except for Harry," Kristen reminded her. "He only started helping last month."

"So where did all of the others come from when Darrell first started the charity?" Fenella asked.

"I believe William knew most of them. William contacted Darrell when Darrell first started working on the charity. I'm not sure how he'd heard about Darrell's plans, but he rang up and made an appointment to talk to Darrell. He was a huge help, actually, even if he and Darrell had issues, especially in the beginning," Maria said.

"What sort of issues?" was Fenella's next question.

Maria shrugged. "William had been tracking the wallabies for years. He had his own ideas about the best ways to do the job. He also thought that one day a month wasn't enough to get an accurate look at the wild population. I'm pretty sure that William goes out to look for wallabies every single day. He has a little cottage in the Curraghs, you know."

"I didn't know that. So he's seen them in the wild, anyway," Fenella said.

"He has, many times, usually at dusk or after dark. That was another area where he and Darrell disagreed. Darrell was just too lazy to organize hunts after dark," Maria told her.

"And William knew the other volunteers?"

"He knew many of them, anyway," Maria said. "He and Darrell discussed lots of things, from building wallaby shelters around the Curraghs to trying to tag the wild population to Darrell's monthly hunts. When Darrell decided that he wanted to establish the hunts, he rang William and asked him if he'd be interested in volunteering. William agreed and offered to bring a few friends to the first hunt."

"That was nice of him," Carla said.

"He's really devoted to the wallabies," Maria told her. "While he didn't think the hunts were going to do much good, I think he was simply happy to see the wallabies getting some attention."

"So which of the volunteers did he recruit?" Fenella asked.

"You're asking me to remember a bunch of people I haven't seen in almost a year," Maria protested. "Jody, who was still volunteering? Maybe, if I hear the names, I'll remember if they came with William or not."

"I was in charge of the volunteers," Kristen said tightly.

Maria nodded at her. "Sorry, I wasn't aware of that. Can you tell me who the current volunteers were, then?"

Kristen sighed and then finished her drink with a long swallow. "After I get another," she said, getting to her feet.

"She could have offered to get a round," Jennifer said as Kristen walked away.

"She probably can't afford it," Carla said. "At least not until tomorrow, when the will is read."

"Do you really think Darrell left her anything?" Jody asked. "He wasn't serious about her."

"But he was generous with his money. I suspect he'll have left her something," Jennifer said. "A better question is whether he left any of us anything."

"It sounded as if he might have left the charity volunteers something," Maria said. "Mark said that anyone who'd ever volunteered, even just for an hour, with the charity should attend the session tomorrow."

"So you'll be there?" Jody asked.

"I wouldn't miss it for the world," Maria replied.

"Sadly, I never helped with the Wallaby Society," Jennifer said. "You'll have to ring me when the meeting is over and tell me what happened."

"If she doesn't, I will," Jody offered.

"I think we do need another round," Jennifer said after she'd finished her drink.

"And you got the first round, so it's my turn," Carla said with a laugh. "I was the second wife, after all."

Everyone laughed as Carla got to her feet. "I know what the others are drinking, but what do you want?" she asked Fenella.

"Just tell the bartender that it's for me," Fenella replied. "He knows what I drink."

"You're a regular here, then?" Jennifer asked as Carla walked away.

"I am. My apartment is just a short distance away," Fenella replied.

"Of course, because you inherited Mona's flat on the promenade, didn't you? Mona was amazing," Jennifer told her. "Darrell found her fascinating, but then, I think all men found her fascinating. There was something almost magical about her."

"Everyone tells me that. I only met her a few times, when I was a child," Fenella said. "I wish I'd had a chance to get to know her."

"And Max," Jennifer added. "He was utterly gorgeous, even though he was far too old for me. He only had eyes for Mona, though. She'd go around a room, flirting with everyone, while he sat at the table watching her. I used to hear all sorts of stories about them having screaming rows when they were younger, but those days were over by the time I moved to the island. They were so devoted to one another, I always wondered why they never married."

"I suppose they had their reasons," Fenella replied.

"Maybe one of them was already secretly married to someone else," Maria suggested.

"Or maybe a dozen other things," Jennifer laughed. "Ah, here's Kristen and Carla back."

Kristen sat back down as Carla passed around the drinks she'd carried up on a large tray. When she was done, she put the tray on an empty table and then took her seat.

"What did I miss?" she demanded before she took a sip of her fresh drink.

"We were talking about Max and Mona," Jennifer told her. "But now we can talk about the volunteers."

"Sara Hampton," Kristen said.

"She was one of William's recruits," Maria replied. "She's a lovely woman. I saw her at the memorial service today, but I didn't get a chance to speak to her."

"Maybe you'll be able to talk to her tomorrow night," Jennifer said.

"I hope so."

"Tomorrow night?" Kristen repeated. "Are you planning to come to the office for the charity meeting, then?"

"Mark said that anyone who'd ever volunteered should be there. I'm sure I qualify," Maria replied.

Kristen scowled and then took a big drink from her glass. "Nicholas Fitzgerald," she said after a moment.

"Also one of William's friends," Maria said.

"Jake Christian," was Kristen's next name.

"Again, one of William's recruits," Maria said. "I never gave it much thought, but William seems to have found just about everyone for Darrell."

"Dave Johnson used to be a volunteer, but he's been poorly for a while now," Kristen said.

"He was another one who came with William to the first meeting," Maria said.

"Doug Hempstead moved away, but he volunteered in the early days," was Kristen's next name.

"William, again," Maria laughed.

"Betty Argon, although she's married now. I don't know if she'll change her name," Kristen said.

"Betty is married now?" Maria echoed. "I find that difficult to believe."

"Apparently, she met someone in ShopFast and they got married a few weeks later," Kristen told her. "They're on their honeymoon right now."

Maria shook her head. "That's almost the most surprising news I've had in a long time. Darrell's death was a bigger surprise, but not by much, really. I thought I knew Betty reasonably well."

"But is she one of William's friends?" Fenella asked.

Maria nodded. "She is."

"There's Gail, too," Kristen added. "Gail Greer."

"Who was not one of William's friends," Maria said. "I'm not sure how she found out about the Wallaby Society, actually. When Darrell had the first meeting for volunteers, she simply turned up. Now that I think about it, everyone else knew

William. They all sat together, chatting, while Gail sat by herself in the corner."

"How would she have known about the meeting, then?" Fenella asked.

Maria shrugged. "It's a small island that thrives on gossip. I'm sure a great many people knew about the meeting. I know Darrell was hoping that more would turn up than actually did."

"It sounds as if you never had enough people to cover the entire section you wanted to cover," Fenella said, trying to count the number of people that Kristen had named.

"We never did while I was working there," Maria confirmed. "Darrell always insisted that we'd get more volunteers as time went on and they got more publicity."

"Were there other volunteers over the last year that we haven't discussed?" Fenella asked.

Kristen shrugged. "Those are all of the ones that I can remember."

"There was a woman called Annie something who helped with one or two about six months or so ago. I believe she was another of William's friends, actually."

"She only helped a few times?" Fenella asked.

"Yes, and then she died," Jody replied.

Kristen gasped. "How awful. What happened to her?"

"I believe it was cancer," Jody said. "She'd been poorly for a long time, which was why she didn't help with the earlier hunts. Then she was in remission for a short while, so she came to a few before she had relapse."

"I don't remember her," Kristen said.

Jody shrugged. "She's the only person I can remember other than the ones we've already mentioned."

"It doesn't sound as if Darrell did very much to recruit more volunteers, then," Fenella remarked.

"Rodney used to offer to try to find more volunteers, but Darrell never agreed. He kept saying that he wanted to keep things small and manageable," Jody told her.

"Even if that meant not having adequate numbers to monitor the Curraghs successfully," Fenella said.

"Because he didn't really care," Maria said softly. "He knew his interest in the wallaby population was going to be fleeting, no matter what he said otherwise. He'd set up the charity and he used it to keep himself busy sometimes, but he wasn't truly interested in wallabies any more than he'd been interested in fighting cancer or training guide dogs. At the end of the day, he was too shallow to care about anything."

After a moment of stunned silence, Jody raised her glass. "I'll drink to that," she said before she downed its contents.

The other women all followed suit, aside from Fenella, who only took a sip of her drink. She was afraid she might miss something important if she drank too much.

"And on that note, I'm going back to my hotel to cry into my pillow," Carla said, standing up. "It's been, well, interesting talking with all of you. I don't know if I feel better or worse for it."

"See you tomorrow," Jennifer said.

"Oh, yes, at the reading of the will," Carla replied. "I do hope, since I'm feeling as if I'm being forced to be there, that darling Darrell left me a little something."

"I'm hoping for a good deal more than that," Jody said.

"Yes, but you would be, wouldn't you?" Carla replied with an enigmatic smile.

She turned and walked away before Jody could reply. That seemed to be everyone else's cue to leave. Fenella sipped her drink as the other women all stood up and began gathering up their belongings.

"Thank you for coming," Kristen said to Fenella. "I wish you could be there tomorrow when Mark reads the will."

"I'm pretty sure he wouldn't allow that."

Kristen shrugged. "I'll see you in the evening at the office, then."

"I'm looking forward to it."

Fenella waited until the others had all left before she finished her drink. Then she collected all of the glasses on the table, putting them on the tray that Carla had left behind. When she carried the tray back down to the lower level, the bartender laughed.

"You didn't have to do that," he said.

"I know, but I didn't want to leave a mess."

"That's why you're one of my favorite customers," he replied.

❧ 13 ❧

It only took Fenella a few minutes to walk back to her apartment building. When she walked into her living room, Daniel was fast asleep in front of the television, with Katie on his lap. Mona was sitting on a chair nearby, an amused expression on her face. Fenella looked at her and raised an eyebrow.

"He fell asleep at least an hour ago," Mona said. "Katie curled up in his lap and went to sleep while he was watching the television. Eventually, he simply dropped off as well."

Should I wake him, she thought.

Mona didn't reply.

I thought you could read my mind, she said in her head. After a moment, she sighed deeply and then walked back over to the door. She opened it and then shut it considerably more loudly than she had when she'd come in a minute earlier.

"Oh, hello," Daniel said sleepily as she crossed the room.

"Hello," she replied.

"How was the pub?"

"It was interesting. The women told me a lot more about Darrell, but I'm not sure any of it is relevant to his murder."

He nodded and then looked down at Katie. "I need to get out a notebook and take notes," he said apologetically.

"I'll take her," Fenella said. She picked up the still sleeping kitten and cuddled her. "Hello, my darling. I'm home now. Why don't you go and curl up on the bed? I'll be in soon."

Katie opened one eye and then squeezed it shut again, snuggling into Fenella's arms. She laughed and then sat down next to Daniel, settling the animal on her lap as she did so.

"Right, tell me everything," Daniel said.

Mona sat forward in her chair as Fenella began to speak. "I should have grabbed a glass of water before I started," she said when she was finally finished.

"I'll get you one," Daniel offered. As he disappeared into the kitchen, Mona cleared her throat.

"Tomorrow should be interesting. If any of the ex-wives have been left anything in Darrell's will, we'll have a motive for his murder."

Fenella didn't reply. She'd been thinking something similar, though. "Do you think Darrell did leave his ex-wives anything in his will?" she asked Daniel after she'd drunk half of the water in the glass he'd brought her.

"I've no idea what Darrell might have done. My ex-wife is the last person I'd leave anything to in my will, but Darrell may have had other ideas."

"Will you be there when they read the will to the women?"

"Alfred will be there. I'll be at the evening event with you, obviously."

"Someone suggested that Darrell might have left something to the charity's volunteers. That seems very unlikely to me."

Daniel shrugged. "We'll find out tomorrow." He yawned. "I should have dozens of questions for you about the session at the pub, but I'm too tired to think straight. Do you think you learned anything interesting?"

"What they told me simply reinforced the notion that Darrell had a short attention span. I have to believe that he was getting ready to shut down the charity, but I don't know if that matters."

"The charity volunteers had the best opportunity to find Darrell in the Curraghs, but his mobile phone records show that he'd spoken to dozens of different people that morning and even more the night before. He could have arranged to meet anyone out there."

"By anyone, I assume you mean his business associates?"

"Business associates and other acquaintances. I haven't actually found anyone who has described himself or herself as Darrell's friend, aside from his advocate, whom Darrell also spoke to the morning that he died."

"Why did he call his advocate that morning? Surely he was too busy with the hunt to be worried about legal matters."

"From what I could see from the mobile records, he rang Mark Masterson at least once a day, every day. According to Mark, they talked about a few business matters, but nothing important."

"Does Mark have an alibi?"

Daniel shook his head and then frowned. "I'm so tired that I'm telling you things I shouldn't be telling you," he said, getting to his feet. "I need to go home before I start telling you the really important things."

"What really important things?" Mona demanded.

Fenella bit her tongue and then followed Daniel to the door, still carrying her sleeping cat. He leaned over and gave her a gentle kiss.

"I wish I had the energy to do more, but I'm out on my feet," he said.

"Do you want to stay in the spare bedroom?" she asked.

He started to shake his head and then stopped. "Actually, maybe I should. I know my house isn't far away, but I'm not sure I should be driving. I'm a good deal more tired than I ought to be, really."

"I hope you haven't caught anything," Fenella said worriedly.

"Me, too. I don't have time to be poorly."

"The bed is made," she told him as she led him to the spare bedroom. "There are pairs of pajamas in the bottom drawer of the wardrobe. They came with the apartment. I'm not sure I want to know why Mona had them."

Daniel grinned. "I really wish I'd had a chance to meet her. She must have been amazing."

"That's what I've been told."

"Thank you for this. I'll see you in the morning."

"Do you need me to wake you at a certain time?"

"I'll set the alarm on my phone. I'll have to go home to shower and change before work, but I can go in a bit late tomorrow since I'll be working in the evening."

Fenella nodded and then headed to her own bedroom, stopping to set Katie down as she passed through the living room. Katie blinked a few times and then ran into the spare bedroom.

"Hello," Daniel said. "Are you sleeping with me tonight, then?"

Frowning, Fenella went into her own room and shut the door. If Katie wanted to stay with Daniel, that was fine, she told herself. Normally, she slept with the door open, but that felt weird with Daniel there. She got ready for bed and then crawled under the covers. The bed felt huge and empty as she tried to get comfortable. She was thinking about going over and demanding her cat back as she fell asleep.

It was nearly eight o'clock when she opened her eyes the next morning. Fenella gasped and then jumped out of bed. Katie always woke her at seven, but of course, Katie was with Daniel. She took a quick shower and threw on the first clothes she came to in her wardrobe. Just before she opened her door, she took several deep breaths.

"Ah, good morning," Daniel said. He was standing near the windows in his crumpled clothes from the previous day.

"Maybe you should leave some clothes here," she blurted out without thinking.

He looked surprised and then shrugged. "I need to go home and check on a few things before work anyway. I can shower there and change into clean clothes."

Blushing and feeling like an idiot, Fenella nodded. "Katie must be starving," she said, looking at the kitten who was sleeping on one of the chairs.

"I gave her some breakfast," Daniel said. "I left the packets on the counter so you could see what I gave her. I hope I did okay."

"As Katie clearly isn't objecting, I'm sure you did fine."

He nodded. "Thank you for letting me stay, but I really need to go."

She walked with him to the door.

"I may well be brewing something, so I won't kiss you," he said.

"Brewing something?"

"A cold or the flu."

"Oh, dear. I hope not."

"I'll collect you around six tonight for the charity meeting."

"Great. I'll see you then."

She opened the door and then watched him walk down the corridor. He waved as he boarded the elevator. As Fenella moved to close her door, Shelly's door swung open.

"Was that Daniel leaving?" she asked. She looked at Fenella and blushed. "It isn't really any of my business, is it?"

Fenella grinned at her. "Sure it is, and yes, it was, but it wasn't what you're thinking. I went to the pub last night with all of Darrell's ex-wives. Daniel stayed here to hear what they had to say, and by the time I was finished telling him, he was too tired to drive home. He slept in my spare room."

Shelly frowned. "Is that what you wanted?"

"Yes, maybe, probably. I don't know."

"Do you want to talk about it?"

"Not really."

"Do you want to talk about the murder, instead? I'd love to hear what the ex-wives had to say."

Fenella swallowed a sigh. "Come on in. I'll make coffee and we can talk."

Shelly smiled brightly. "I know I'm just being nosy, but I was reading all about the case and all of the ex-wives in the local paper yesterday, and I'd love to get the inside story."

"I don't have the inside story, but I can tell you about the wives, if you want."

Fenella made coffee and then poured herself a bowl of cereal. "Do you want anything?" she asked Shelly.

"I had breakfast, thanks."

While she ate, she told Shelly all about her evening with the ex-wives.

"So who had a motive for murdering Darrell?" Shelly asked at the end.

"We'll know more once the will has been read, but if Darrell left his ex-wives anything, that might have given one of them a motive."

"Or all of them," Mona suggested.

"Or all of them," Fenella agreed, frowning when she remembered that Shelly couldn't see or hear Mona.

"But the first three were all across when he died, right?" Shelly asked.

"I think so. That still leaves Jody and Kristen, though, and they were both in Ballaugh that morning. Either one of them could have slipped away, killed Darrell, and then gone back to the office."

"Was Jody still in love with him?" Shelly asked.

"I don't know that she was ever in love with him," Fenella replied thoughtfully. "I can't help but feel that she only married him for his money. The other three women seem genuinely upset about his death, but Jody doesn't. Maybe that's just her, though. In answer to your question, no, I don't think she was."

"So why was she working for the charity?"

"Because she loves wallabies?"

Mona laughed. "Not a chance."

"Maybe," Shelly said. "Or maybe there was something else going on between her and Darrell."

"You think they were still involved, even though they were divorced?"

"Probably not romantically, but maybe Jody was involved in his business deals or something," Shelly suggested.

"Maybe."

"If she didn't kill Darrell, who did?" Shelly asked.

Fenella shook her head. "I've no idea. I don't think Jody did it, actually, but that doesn't mean I have suspicions about anyone else. Kristen is a possibility, I suppose, but I really think she loved Darrell. She seems quite upset about his death."

"She could just be a very good actress," Shelly said. "If it wasn't one of them, who could it have been? What about the charity volunteers?"

"I've been wondering about them. After everything I've heard about Darrell, I have to think that he was getting ready to close the charity down. I can see the volunteers being upset, but I can't see any of them killing him over it. Someone suggested, when we were all invited to the office tonight, that Darrell might have left something to the volunteers in his will. If that's the case, then the volunteers have another motive."

"If they knew about the will," Shelly said.

"Yes, and I'm not sure how they would have, actually," Fenella admitted.

"Maybe Darrell said something to one of them. He or she would never admit to the conversation now."

"Very true. Aside from the ex-wives and the charity volunteers, Darrell had a lot of business associates. I can't imagine why any of them would have killed him, though. I don't think many people get murdered over business deals."

"Maybe one of them got tired of him moving from thing to thing all the time," Shelly suggested. "Maybe they were working on a deal and then Darrell lost interest and the killer lost a lot of money. Or maybe he was going to lose a lot of money because Darrell had lost interest, but by killing him, he'll be able to take the deal forward, working with Darrell's estate."

"I don't know enough about Darrell's business interests to know if that's possible or not. Rodney would know."

"We didn't talk about Rodney. The paper yesterday said that he was devoted to Darrell. Why?"

"I'm not sure. Darrell probably paid him very well, but beyond that I don't know."

"I met Rodney once. He was the type of person who loves to be needed. No doubt he felt needed by Darrell, who was incapable of running his own company," Mona said. "I'm sure Rodney loved making himself indispensable to Darrell."

Fenella nodded and then tried to think of a way to suggest as much to Shelly.

"I don't want to consider Mark Masterson as a suspect, not when I knew him as a child," Shelly said.

"We don't have to talk about him."

Shelly sighed. "I don't think we've solved the case," she said.

"I'm sure we haven't," Fenella laughed. "Maybe we'll all know more once the will is read."

"I wish I could be there for the readings."

"I'd love to be there with the ex-wives," Fenella admitted. "I'm really curious what Darrell had to say about them in his will, if he even mentioned them at all."

"He must have mentioned them, otherwise Mark wouldn't be having them meet for a reading."

"I suppose so. I'll see Jody and Kristen later. I'm sure one of them will tell me what happened."

"And then you'll tell me, right?"

Fenella laughed. "Of course I will. We can walk tomorrow morning, if you want."

"I do want. I was coming to see if you wanted to walk this morning, actually, before you tempted me to stay inside with your promise of coffee."

"We could walk now," Fenella offered.

Shelly glanced at her watch. "I'm afraid I don't have time now. I promised myself that I'd finish the chapter I'm in the middle of before lunch. Tomorrow at eight?"

"Perfect. I'll see you then."

Fenella walked her friend to the door and then shut it behind her.

"You need to find out more about Darrell's business," Mona told her as she walked back into the kitchen. "What was he currently working on?"

"I'm not getting involved in the investigation any more than I already am," she countered. "I'm going shopping."

She didn't actually need anything. She simply wanted to get away from Mona. Darrell's murder had been horrible and it didn't seem as if the investigation was going anywhere. Mona would happily sit and talk about suspects and alibis and motives all day, but Fenella wanted to put the whole thing out of her head.

It only took her a few minutes to walk into the town center. She strolled along the streets, looking into shop windows as she went. After buying herself a selection of chocolates from the chocolate shop, she kept walking. None of the other shops held any appeal, but she was feeling too restless to simply go back to her apartment. After another look into every window, she headed for the Manx Museum.

A slow walk through the exhibits took up the rest of the morning. She treated herself to lunch in the small café and then walked back down into town feeling a bit better. Mona was nowhere to be seen when she got back to her apartment. She curled up with a book until it was time for dinner.

"Hello," Daniel said when she opened the door to his knock just before six.

"Hello," she replied.

"Never mind that," Mona snapped. "Ask him about the will. Did the ex-wives get anything?"

"How was your day?" Fenella asked.

"It was interesting," he replied. "I can't tell you about it, though. I'm not even meant to know anything. Alfred told me a few things he shouldn't have."

"You need to marry the man so that he'll tell you things," Mona said.

Fenella only just managed not to reply. "Are the ex-wives likely to be keeping things quiet, too?" she asked Daniel.

He shrugged. "I believe Mark asked them not to repeat anything from today's meeting, but legally he can't stop them from talking about what happened. I think he's just hoping to keep everything out of the newspapers for the time being, anyway."

"Should we go, then?" Fenella asked.

He nodded. "I'm sure you're eager to talk to Jody and Kristen."

"If they want to talk to me."

They were in Daniel's car, heading for Ballaugh when she spoke again. "But how are you feeling? You were very tired last night."

"I'm doing okay. I haven't been sleeping well lately, and I think it all just caught up with me. I slept like a log in your spare room, though, so I'm feeling better today."

"That's good to hear. I was worried that you were getting sick."

"I may still be, but I hope not."

They chatted about the weather as a steady rain fell during the drive. The parking lot in front of the office was about half full when Daniel found a parking space.

"Ready?" he asked her.

"I suppose so. You don't really think that Darrell left anything to the volunteers, do you?"

He shrugged. "Let's just say that his will has been surprising thus far, shall we?"

Fenella got out of the car feeling eager to speak to either Jody or Kristen. Surely, one of them would tell her about the will.

Daniel held the door open for her and then followed her into the office. Jody was sitting on one side of the room, staring at her phone. Kristen was behind the desk in the corner, glaring at the computer's screen. Mark and Rodney were sitting together on one of the couches, talking.

"Ah, our first volunteers," Mark said as he stood up. "Obviously, we need to wait until everyone arrives before we begin. I'll just take your names and some other information, please."

Daniel told him their names, which Mark carefully wrote on a sheet of paper.

"And how many hunts did you help with?" he asked next.

"This one was our first," Fenella replied. "We only signed up for an hour, because we weren't sure what to expect."

Mark nodded. "That's fine. I'm sure Darrell was grateful that you were willing to give up any time at all. Did you fill out your sightings report after you finished your hour?"

"Yes," Fenella said.

"So Kristen will have it?"

"I assume so."

"Excellent. One report between the two of you?"

"Yes, because we were together for the entire time."

"Good, good," he said, making a note. "That's all I need for now. Just make yourselves comfortable while we wait for the others."

Fenella nodded and then she and Daniel settled on a couch in the corner.

"That was odd," he said in a low voice.

"It was," she agreed. She sat back and looked over at Jody.

"Go ahead," Daniel told her. "I know you're dying to talk to her."

Fenella gave him an apologetic smile as she got to her feet. "Hello," she said as she approached Jody. "How are you today?"

Jody looked up at her shrugged. "Shell shocked, really."

"Oh?"

"You haven't heard? I'd have thought you'd have spoken to someone by now."

"I haven't, though."

"We aren't meant to talk about it, but I feel as if I need to tell someone what happened." She slid closer to Fenella and then looked over at Mark. He was frowning at them. Jody laughed. "Let's go outside," she suggested.

"It's raining," Fenella told her as they both stood up.

"We can sit in my car. I need to talk to someone before I explode. We'll be able to see the others as they arrive, so we can make sure we come back once everyone is here."

Fenella followed the woman out to the parking lot and then slid into the passenger seat of the luxury car that Jody unlocked.

Jody sat behind the steering wheel and rested her head against the headrest, shutting her eyes.

"Are you okay?" Fenella asked as a single tear slid down Jody's face.

"Not really. I've always prided myself on being tough enough to take whatever life throws at me, but today was hard. I truly did love Darrell, you know. I knew I'd be lucky to get more than a year out of the marriage, but I decided it was worth the risk. Financially, I did really well out of the deal, too. Emotionally, it was harder than I'd been expecting, but the day we got married I started a countdown to our first anniversary, knowing that he was going to end things by the time I got to zero."

"You were trying to protect your heart."

"I was, and for the most part, I succeeded. I did love him, but I was able to keep some distance between us, if that makes sense. I didn't let myself fall in love with him. I knew I couldn't do that."

Fenella nodded. "I'm not sure how you managed it, but, of course, you were right about the countdown."

"I was, and I told myself at the time that it didn't matter, that I'd been expecting it anyway, that I was sad, but not devastated. I almost believed that, too, even though I couldn't quite bring myself to stop seeing Darrell. I kept working with the charity so I'd have an excuse to see him. I stayed involved in a few of his business deals, too. But I kept telling myself that I didn't really care and I truly believed myself, too."

"And now you don't?"

Jody sighed. "Darrell's will was not at all what I'd been expecting."

"No?"

"I was hoping he might have left each of his ex-wives a little something. He didn't have any children, after all. Who else was he going to leave his money to? Rodney? I thought I might get enough for a holiday or something. He'd already given me a very generous settlement when we divorced, so I wasn't expecting much."

"And what did you get?" Fenella had to ask.

Jody gave her a tight smile. "A million pounds. He left all four of his ex-wives a million pounds each. That was the good news."

"Was there bad news?"

"I don't know what to call it," Jody sighed. "Along with the money, he left us each a letter. We had to read it immediately, in front of Mark. It was pretty awful."

A million questions sprang into Fenella's head, but she wasn't sure how to ask anything that wouldn't sound rude. "A letter?" she repeated after a moment.

"Yeah, a letter all about how much he'd loved me," Jody said bitterly. "He talked about some of the fun we had when we were married and then mentioned a few of the less than fun times, too, saying how much he'd loved sharing the good and the bad with me. It was every good thing that the man ever said to me, all written down and it broke me."

Jody burst into tears, leaving Fenella digging around in her handbag for a tissue. When she finally found one and handed it to Jody, the other woman laughed.

"I need more than just a few tissues," she said, wiping her eyes and then holding up the now sodden mass. Fenella handed her the packet and Jody took a moment to dry her eyes and blow her nose.

"Mark told us that Darrell wrote the letters within days after each of his divorces. He wanted to capture his feelings while they were still fresh in his mind. The problem is, the letter read more as if it had been written while we were still happy, not after he'd ended things. He listed a dozen things he loved about me and talked about how happy being with me made him. We were divorced before he'd written it, but it really didn't read that way."

"How odd."

"It was odd," Jody agreed. "We compared notes afterwards and the other ex-wives all said the same thing. We all felt confused and hurt and lost. Jennifer couldn't stop crying and Maria got really angry. She couldn't understand how he could have written about how much he loved her after he'd divorced her. None of us could understand, really."

"What did Mark say?"

"That Darrell never stopped loving any of us, but that he felt the need to move on to new things all the time. I suppose that makes some sense, but it doesn't make me feel any better. I'm not even sure that I want the money, which is crazy, but I'm just a complete emotional wreck right now. I swore, when I married Darrell, that I wasn't going to let him destroy me the way he'd destroyed his first three wives. Up until today, I thought I was doing okay."

She wiped away another tear and then took a deep breath. "There's Maria. I'm going to go back inside and redo my makeup. I don't want her to see me this way."

Jody climbed out of the car and rushed back into the building as Fenella watched Maria park her rental car and slowly get out.

"Hello," she said as she climbed out of Jody's car. "How are you?"

Maria stared at her for a moment and then shook her head. "I need a drink," she said softly. "Or maybe a dozen drinks. Maybe I should just drink until I can't feel anything anymore."

"I'm sorry."

"He left me a million pounds and then broke my heart all over again," she replied. "I knew I'd never get over him, but I thought I was ready to move on. I'd even been out with a very nice man a few times. I was sure I was finally getting over Darrell, at least as much as I ever would."

"And now you don't feel that way?"

"He wrote all about every good thing that had ever happened between us, reminding me of silly little things we'd shared, things I'd forgotten about, even. And he kept saying, over and over again, how much he loved me. I was sure he'd written it when we were still married, back when we were crazy in love, but Mark assured me that the letters were all written after each divorce. How could you write about how much you love someone after you'd left them?"

"I've no idea."

"I've been in my room all afternoon, sobbing into my pillow. I don't know if I'm angry or heartbroken or something else I haven't thought of yet. If Darrell were here right now, I might just kill him myself, given the chance."

"We should get out of the rain," Fenella suggested.

Maria looked up at the sky. "Is it raining? I hadn't noticed."

It was raining heavily and both she and Maria were getting soaked, but Fenella simply took the woman's arm and led her into the office. Daniel was still sitting where she'd left him, his phone in his hand.

"Ah, Maria, there you are," Mark said. "I have a few questions for you about your volunteer work with the charity."

Maria shrugged. "I don't really want to talk about anything right now."

"It won't take long," Mark promised as he took Maria's arm and led her to a couch.

Fenella glanced around the room. Most of the volunteers had arrived. They were all sitting together in the corner. Harry was standing near them, staring at his phone. When she looked over at Kristen, she got an angry glare in return.

Unable to resist, she walked over to the desk. "Are you okay?"

Kristen shrugged. "No doubt they've been telling you about their love letters and their million pound payday," she said angrily, nodding toward Maria and Jody.

"They have. Should I assume you didn't get either?"

Kristen's laugh was brittle and angry. "I got a hundred thousand pounds, which is more a slap in the face than anything else."

"It sounds quite generous to me," Fenella told her.

"He was worth millions. The ex-wives got a million each. I should have been given at least that much. He hadn't fallen out of love with me yet."

Fenella nodded slowly. The woman's words made some sense. "I'm sorry," she said after a moment.

"I didn't get a letter, either. I've nothing to read and reread and cling to when I'm feeling all alone. He just said something in the will about leaving the money to 'Kristen, the woman who has been most recently sharing my life.' He didn't even bother to say that he'd loved me."

Fenella thought about reaching for the tissues, but she didn't need them. Kristen was too angry to cry, at least for the moment. "I truly am sorry. Maybe he was going to write you a letter, but never found the time. As I understand it, though, he only wrote the letters after he'd ended things. You were lucky you didn't get one, surely."

Kristen shrugged. "I don't want to talk about it."

The door behind Fenella swung open and Gail walked in. "Am I late?" she asked.

"Yes," Kristen snapped.

Fenella glanced at the wall clock. It was two minutes past seven.

"I have a few questions for you," Mark told Gail. "Once that's out of the way, I think we can begin."

❧ 14 ❧

Fenella sat down next to Daniel as Gail spoke to Mark. "Who's the man next to Sara?" she whispered.

"That's Jake, the one whose daughter just had a baby. Don't make eye contact with him unless you want to see pictures of the baby, lots of pictures of the baby," Daniel replied.

Fenella laughed. "I won't look directly at him until after the meeting, then."

"Did Jody have anything interesting to say?"

"You know what she told me. She got a million pounds and a letter that broke her heart."

"That isn't exactly how Alfred described it, but it's close."

"Where is Alfred? I thought he'd be here tonight."

"I think he's still recovering from this afternoon. Apparently, there were many tears, lots of shouting, and then more tears."

"I can believe it. Jody is still upset and Maria seems angry and sad at the same time. Kristen is just mad, but then she didn't get a million pounds or a letter."

He nodded. "Alfred said she was furious this afternoon. I gather she got very upset with the other women, even though they didn't do anything."

"She should be angry at Darrell, but that won't do her any good."

"Exactly, although I do believe she's pretty mad at him, anyway."

The door opened again and Alfred walked into the room. Mark frowned at him. "Inspector Patrick, I wasn't expecting you here tonight."

"I thought, after the tensions this afternoon, that it made sense for me to be here," he replied. He nodded at Daniel and then dropped into the chair nearest to the door.

Mark made another note and then got to his feet. "I believe I've spoken to all of you. We are missing a few volunteers, but I'll be tracking them down over the next few days to ask them the same questions I've just asked all of you."

"What questions?" Alfred asked.

"I asked each volunteer how many hours they'd volunteered with the charity's hunts and whether or not they'd filled out the reports that Darrell used to track the wallabies," Mark explained. "You'll understand why in a moment."

Alfred nodded. "Sorry I interrupted."

"Right, so now that I have that information, we can get started," Mark said. "Darrell's will was complicated and it involved several different groups of people. I've already spoken to his former wives and to his most recent girlfriend. They've been informed as to what they've inherited. Some of them are here tonight, of course, because they were also a part of the Manx Wallaby Society. As such, they'll be entitled to some additional inheritance, under the terms of the will."

"Additional inheritance?" Maria repeated.

Mark nodded. "We'll get there," he promised. "I want to start by reading you what Darrell wrote about the Manx Wallaby Society in his will." He opened his briefcase and pulled out a stack of papers.

As he shuffled through them, Fenella looked at Daniel. "This could be emotional for some of the volunteers," she whispered.

"Here we are," Mark said. "'I founded the Manx Wallaby Society in order to track and protect the wild wallaby population on the Isle of Man. These small marsupials found a very special place in my heart and I was happy to dedicate many hours of my time and a great deal of money to their cause. The Curraghs are a wonderful wetland area and it was always a joy to spend time there, watching for wallabies and enjoying being out in nature.'" Mark stopped and took a sip of coffee.

"He didn't spend much time in the field," Gail complained loudly.

Mark smiled at her. "He did what he could. Let me continue, though. 'The Society was blessed with a number of very dedicated volunteers. I can't express my thanks and admiration for these people enough. They put in many long hours, month after month, trying to track our elusive marsupial friends. William Faragher was a pioneer in studying the wallabies and I'm grateful to him for not only assisting me in my efforts, but also for bringing so many of his friends to our hunts each month. I'm not exaggerating when I say that the wallaby hunts would never have happened if it weren't for William.'"

"That's very kind of him," William said gruffly.

"We all worked hard," Gail interjected.

Mark nodded. "Of course you did. I'm afraid I urged Darrell not to write too much. He wanted to mention every single person by name and talk about his or her individual contribution to the charity, but I insisted that he keep things brief. I believe he was planning to write individual letters to each of you, in the same way he'd written to each of his former wives, but I'm sure he assumed he had many years in which to write those letters."

Gail shrugged. "What did he say to his ex-wives?" she asked, looking at Jody.

"I don't want to talk about it," Jody said flatly.

"Did he leave you any money?" Gail asked.

Jody flushed. "That isn't any of your business."

Gail frowned.

"She got a million quid," Kristen said bitterly.

"A million pounds?" Gail gasped. "Really?"

Jody shot an angry look at Kristen before she turned back to Gail. "Yes, a million pounds. It doesn't seem much after having lived with the man for a year."

"Did all of the wives get that sort of money?" Gail asked Kristen.

Kristen nodded. "A million pounds each." She muttered something under her breath that Fenella decided she was glad she hadn't heard.

"What did you get?" Gail demanded.

"Barely anything," Kristen said.

"A hundred thousand pounds isn't barely anything," Jody protested.

Kristen shrugged as Gail gasped again.

"A hundred thousand pounds? And you weren't even married to the man," Gail said.

"I'm sorry to interrupt, but I think we should get back to the business at hand," Mark said with a small chuckle.

Gail sat back in her seat, muttering something to herself.

"The next section of the will details how Darrell wanted to thank the hard working volunteers who helped him with the charity," Mark said. "I can read the entire section if you want, but it's probably easier if I simply summarize things."

"We can get copies of the relevant section, can't we?" Sara asked.

"The entire document will be public record eventually," Mark replied. "Before that happens, if anyone has any questions or concerns about its contents, you're more than welcome to come to my office and read through a copy yourself."

"Thank you," Sara said.

"To summarize then, every volunteer who dedicated an hour or more to any hunt over the past year will be getting ten thousand pounds. That includes every person here, aside from Kristen, who never took part in the hunts," Mark said.

"That isn't fair," Kristen wailed.

Mark held up a hand. "There's more," he said. "You, Jody, and Maria will each receive twenty thousand pounds for your hard work in the office here. Jody and Maria will get both amounts because they each spent at least one hour in the field."

"Not fair," Kristen said again. "Darrell didn't want me in the field. He wanted me here, coordinating everything."

"Yes, well, I'm only following his instructions," Mark said, sounding slightly smug.

Kristen blinked hard and then sighed. "It isn't fair," she said again in a low voice.

"What about Rodney?" Jody asked. "He didn't usually go out in the field, of course."

"Darrell made separate provisions for Rodney," Mark replied.

"I can't complain," Rodney said.

"Don't tell me you got a million pounds, too?" Kristen shouted. "I don't believe it."

Rodney flushed. "As you'll find out eventually anyway, I may as well tell you that I've been left two million pounds for my years of dedicated service."

Kristen threw her coffee cup across the room. It hit the wall and shattered.

Alfred got to his feet. "I appreciate that this is difficult for you, but someone could have been injured," he said as Maria began to clear up the mess.

Kristen only stared at him for a minute and then slowly shook her head.

"Maybe I should have simply spoken to each of you individually," Mark said, sounding as if he was enjoying himself immensely.

"Is that all?" Alfred asked.

Mark shook his head. "I asked you all about the forms that Darrell asked you to complete. There's a thousand pound bonus for each form that you completed over the past year. I'm going to have Kristen or Jody go through the files to count the forms and tally each person's individual total."

"William, you'll be rich," Sara said.

William laughed. "It's a good deal more than I was expecting, but then I wasn't expecting anything at all. It was kind, but totally unnecessary of Darrell to thank all of us in this way."

Mark nodded. "We talked frequently about his estate. As he didn't have children, he wanted his money to go to the people with whom he'd shared his life. That was why his former wives were all given gifts and why each of you will receive something. Does anyone have any questions about that section of the will?"

"What do I have to do to contest it?" Kristen asked flatly.

Mark chuckled. "You'd have to talk to your own advocate about that. I can almost guarantee that fighting it would cost you a good deal more than what you've inherited, though. What would you be hoping to accomplish?"

"She wants her own million pounds," Jody said.

"I earned at least that," Kristen snapped. "You all got paid to go away when Darrell got tired of you and now you're getting even more money. It isn't fair."

"Life isn't fair," William suggested. "Darrell didn't have to leave you anything."

Kristen opened her mouth to reply, but Mark held up a hand. "Let's move on, shall we?"

"There's more?" Sara asked.

"The next section of the will deals with what happens to the charity now," Mark explained.

"Ah, so now we'll find out that every penny we've just been given is going to be needed in order to keep the charity running," William suggested.

"The money is yours and you may do anything you'd like with it. Darrell suggested in his will that you might want to use some of it to start a new charity for the wallabies. The Manx Wallaby Society will cease to exist on the first of next month."

There were gasps of surprise from around the room. The noises were quickly replaced by angry voices.

"He can't do that," Gail shouted.

"Surely we can simply take over the operation," William argued.

"I can't believe Darrell would simply shut the charity down," Sara said. "He loved the wallabies."

Mark held up a hand. "I understand that you're shocked and upset, but there's nothing I can do. The charity was entirely Darrell's concern and as such, he had every right to deal with it in his will. He chose to end it after his death, rather than leave it to others to continue running it. You can, of course, start your own charity that does the same things. I'd be more than happy to advise you on the best way to set things up."

"For a fee," Jody suggested.

Mark flushed. "I'd be prepared to donate some hours to help get things started. I appreciate that you're all upset and that the work that Darrell was doing was important to you."

"It was important to the wallabies," Gail said.

"Yes, of course," Mark agreed.

"Could we start a new charity doing the same thing?" William asked.

"Of course you could," Mark replied. "You'd need to find an office to run it out of and you'd probably need at least one paid member of staff."

"An office? What's going to happen to this building?" Sara demanded.

"It's going to be sold or developed," Mark replied.

"Sold or developed?" William repeated. "What does that mean?"

"It means that it will no longer be available to the charity," Mark replied. "All of the furniture belongs to Darrell's estate, but if someone here wants the paperwork associated with the charity, I'm sure we can arrange something. It would be a shame to lose all of the records of your hard work over the past year."

Harry stood up and walked over to Mark. He said something in a low voice that made Mark nod.

"Right, so does anyone have any questions about the disposition of the charity?" Mark asked as Harry sat back down.

"If we want to keep things running, we need to find an office and hire staff, that's what you're saying, isn't it?" William asked.

"If you want to continue doing the same things that you were doing with Darrell, yes."

"Jody, you were a volunteer. Would you be willing to volunteer to help us with the new charity?" Sara asked.

Jody frowned and then slowly shook her head. "I helped with the charity because I felt a sense of obligation to Darrell after his generosity when we divorced. While I think wallabies are sweet, I think I'm going to do some traveling and then I may move somewhere far away where I don't have to think about Darrell ever again."

"Kristen, what about you?" Sara asked.

Kristen stared at her for a moment and then laughed. "You weren't listening, were you? I didn't get anything, or not much, anyway. I'm going to have to find myself a paying job and soon. I'll be going back across, of course. This island holds nothing but bad memories for me now."

"Maybe we can take turns doing the paperwork and things," Sara said. "I have a spare bedroom in my house. We can use that as a temporary office."

"I don't know if it's going to be worth the effort," William sighed.

Gail had tears running down her cheeks. "We have to make it work. The wallabies need us."

"They seem to be doing fine on their own, actually," William said. "We never did see a single one during any of Darrell's hunts, after all."

"But if we're running things, we can plan hunts for evenings or even overnight. I'm sure we'll see something if we're there overnight," Gail said.

"Are you quite certain that Darrell didn't leave any money just for the charity?" Sara asked. "I can't believe he didn't leave us enough to start a new charity."

"He left a few charitable bequests, but nothing for the wallabies," Mark told her.

"But that doesn't even make sense," Sara told him. "He loved the wallabies. Why would he leave money to other charities and not to the wallabies?"

Mark shrugged. "He didn't really discuss his bequests with me. He simply told me what he wanted and I wrote his will accordingly."

"I'm sure he had bequests for the wallabies six months ago, didn't he?" Jody asked.

Mark looked at her and then nodded slowly. "He changed his will just about every month. Until recently, his will included a provision for keeping the charity running."

"And then he got bored with it," Jody sighed.

"We can still make it work, in spite of him," Gail said passionately. "We don't need Darrell."

"But we sure could use his money," Jake suggested.

"I'll donate everything I'm getting from Darrell's estate," Gail said. "That should pay for something."

"We need to have a meeting of all interested parties," William suggested. "Maybe we can find another benefactor to help us get started." He glanced at Fenella, who sighed deeply.

"Oh, dear," Daniel whispered.

"I've been expecting that all night," she told him.

"Maybe, if we had enough funding, we could buy this cottage and all of the furnishings," Sara suggested.

Mark shook his head. "As I said, this cottage will be sold or redeveloped."

"If it's for sale, we can make an offer," Sara said.

"It isn't going to be sold individually," Mark said. "It's part of a business deal that Darrell was involved in before his death. That deal will still be moving forward, assuming that planning permissions can be obtained."

"Planning permissions for what?" William asked.

"This isn't the time or the place to discuss that," Mark replied.

"You said redevelopment," Sara said. "Darrell wasn't considering building something on this land, was he? It's part of the Curraghs. It borders the areas we've been monitoring for the past year."

"As I said, this isn't the time for that discussion," Mark said firmly.

"Let's set up a time and a place for another meeting," William said. "We've a great deal to discuss. I'm available tomorrow night."

"That won't work for me," Gail said.

"I can do tomorrow," Sara told William.

"So can I," Nicholas said.

Gail shook her head. "You can't have the meeting without me," she insisted.

"It's just a preliminary meeting," William said. "We need to discuss our options, that's all. I'm sure you'll be able to come to the next one."

"Or you could hold the meeting another day," Gail said. "That would be for the best."

"For whom?" Sara asked. "If the rest of us can do tomorrow, then I can't see the harm in having the first, preliminary meeting tomorrow."

Gail blinked back tears. "But I want to be there," she cried.

"If I were to meet with you privately, would you be prepared to tell me more about what might be happening to this cottage?" William asked Mark.

Mark shook his head. "I'm afraid I'm not at liberty to discuss that at the moment."

"But you won't allow us to make an offer to purchase it?" was William's next question.

"I'm sorry, but that's not an option, not unless something changes," Mark said.

"What aren't you telling us?" Sara demanded. "There's something odd going on here."

"I think that's everything for tonight," Mark said. "Did anyone have any questions about the will?"

"Many, but I think I'll wait and read the whole thing in your office before I ask them," William said.

"I want to know what's going to happen to this cottage. Why is it such a big secret?" Sara asked.

Mark opened his mouth to reply, but Gail interrupted by laughing loudly. "I know why he won't tell you," she said. "But as you aren't interested in having me be a part of the new charity, I don't know that I want to tell you anything."

"What do you know?" William asked.

Gail shook her head. "I'd tell you at the first meeting of the new charity, if I were going to be there," she said, folding her arms across her chest.

"Let's consider this the first meeting of the new charity," Jake suggested. "What do you know about Darrell's plans for this building?"

"It isn't just this building," Gail said, looking excited at being at the center of attention. "Darrell was planning to start developing the entire area."

"Developing it?" William echoed. "But it's protected land."

"Is it, though?" Gail asked. "He didn't seem to think so. He seemed to think that he'd done enough to prove that the wallabies weren't using it, anyway. As long as he kept certain sections of the area as wetlands, he was sure he'd be able to develop most of the area that we've been monitoring."

There was a moment of stunned silence and then everyone began to speak at once. Daniel got up and walked to the table. He took a bottle of water and then went and stood behind Gail as people began to shout over one another.

"That's enough," Mark said loudly. "I'm not certain what Gail thinks she heard, but there's no need for a discussion of that right now."

"He was using us," Jody said in a dazed voice. "He was using us to track the wallabies so that he could obtain proof that they weren't using this section of the wetlands as their home."

Harry laughed. "It was really too easy," he said. "Oh, when he first started out, Darrell had the best of intentions. He was really excited about his new charity and he couldn't wait to see a wallaby in the wild. It was only after the first six months or so, when no one saw a bloody thing that he started to wonder if he was wasting his time. That was when we first met and began to talk about the land that Darrell owned out here. He'd bought it all when he'd started the charity, from a farmer who'd given up on farming out here."

"He bought it so that he could build houses on it," Sara said.

"Oh, no, he bought it because he was sure he'd have wild wallabies living on it. The idea excited him. It was the farmer who'd sold him the land who'd told him all about the wallabies, you see. As I said, for the first six months or so, he was all about the stupid wallabies. After he discovered that he didn't actually have any living on his land, that's when he started wondering what else he could do with the property," Harry explained.

"And while he was talking with you about building a huge housing estate in the area, we were still going out every month and watching for wallabies," Sara said bitterly.

"He was starting to worry that one of you might actually see something," Harry laughed. "Rodney saw him working on the plans for the various housing estates one day so he told Rodney that he was redrawing the sections for the hunt instead. Obviously, the new sections didn't make any sense, but they weren't meant for watching for wallabies."

"We would have seen wallabies one day," Gail shouted. "They're out there and they need us."

Harry nodded. "Yes, well, since you didn't have any luck finding any, I don't believe we're going to have any trouble getting planning permission for the first of our planned housing estates. Darrell signed all of the agreements before he died, so now I can carry on, working with his estate."

"Is that true?" Gail demanded.

Mark nodded. "Darrell's will contains several provisions for the continued operation of his company following his death. He set up a complicated trust that will run until it's no longer needed."

"I estimate we'll be done with our planned trio of housing estates in the area in about ten years," Harry said.

"Three housing estates?" Sara repeated. "You can't be serious."

Harry shrugged. "They were Darrell's plans, not mine."

"It was all for nothing," Gail said softly, tears streaming down her cheeks. "I never should have done it. I didn't know what else to do. The wallabies needed me. I had to do what I did for them."

"What did you do?" Sara asked.

Gail looked at her for a minute and then slowly shook her head. "Nothing," she said. "I didn't do anything."

"How did you know about Darrell's plans?" Harry asked. "I can't imagine that he discussed them with you."

Gail blinked at him. "I overheard him on his mobile. He was discussing his plans with someone," she said after a moment.

"When was that?" Harry asked.

"A while ago," she mumbled.

"It can't have been too long ago," Harry said. "In fact, I only remember discussing it with him by telephone once. That was the day he died."

"You killed Darrell," Kristen shouted at Gail.

"Don't be ridiculous," Gail snapped. "I was walking to my section that morning and I came up behind Darrell. He was talking to someone about his horrible plans. I listened for a moment and then I ran away."

"And then a wallaby came out of the trees and killed him?" Jody asked.

"I've no idea what happened. I was upset, but I wasn't really clear on what I'd heard. It wasn't until Harry started telling us about Darrell's plans that it made sense."

"I think we should go back to my office and have a chat," Alfred said, moving to stand next to Gail. "You neglected to mention seeing Darrell that morning in your original statement."

Gail flushed. "It didn't seem important. Anyway, I don't have time to talk to you right now. I need to leave." She got to her feet and headed for the door.

Alfred took her arm before she'd gone more than a few steps. "I'm sorry, but I'm going to insist that you come with me to the station."

"Are you arresting me?" Gail demanded.

"Not if you cooperate, not at this point. If you don't want to cooperate, I will arrest you, however," Alfred replied.

"I have nothing to say to you," Gail said. She sat back down in her seat and folded her arms.

"What do you have to say to me?" Kristen shouted. "You killed the man I loved. You may as well admit to it. We all know you did it."

Gail pressed her lips together and shook her head.

"I can recommend a few advocates," Mark said. "I think you're going to need one."

Color flooded into Gail's cheeks, but she still didn't speak.

"And now you're going to go to prison for a very long time," Jody said. "I wonder if the wallabies ever go as far north as Jurby."

"They've been spotted that far north," William said.

"So at least, when you're sitting around in your prison cell, you'll have something to do," Jody told Gail. "You can watch for wallabies all day long."

"I'm not going to prison. I didn't do anything," Gail said shakily.

"Let's go and talk about that in my office," Alfred said.

She looked up at him and then began to cry. "I was so angry. I thought Darrell was so wonderful, but there he was, talking about how many houses he thought could be squeezed into the various sections he'd mapped out. I stood behind him and listened as he talked about putting a road right where we were standing. He'd be putting so many wallabies in danger."

"Let's go," Alfred said softly.

Gail got to her feet. "I was certain that I'd misunderstood what he was saying," she said. "When he put his phone back in his pocket, I asked him what he'd been talking about. He stared at me for a minute and then started to laugh. 'That's the cat out of the bag, then,' he said and then he laughed again and said 'or should I say, the wallaby out of the bag?' I was so angry. How dare he laugh at the wallabies?"

"So you killed him," Jody said flatly.

"I had a knife in my hand. I was cutting up an apple while I walked. It was just a little paring knife. I didn't think it would kill him. I just wanted to hurt him, make him stop laughing, make him change his mind about building on the site. I never meant to kill him," Gail said through her tears.

"Time to go," Alfred said firmly. "We'll get you an advocate before I take your formal statement."

Gail looked as if she wanted to say something, but after a moment, she simply nodded and let Alfred lead her out of the room.

"Gail? Gail killed him?" Maria said as the door shut behind them. "I don't believe it."

"I'm afraid it's all too believable," William replied. "If I'd have known what Darrell was planning, I might have been tempted to kill him myself."

"It's just a stupid housing estate," Kristen exploded. "I know it might have displaced a few wild wallabies, but it isn't something to kill a man over."

Glances were exchanged and then Daniel cleared his throat.

"I'm sure everyone is upset about everything that's happened here tonight. Perhaps it would be best if we simply ended things here for now," he said.

"Yes, I believe that would be for the best," Mark said quickly.

A few people muttered under their breaths, but eventually everyone began to get up and collect their belongings. Fenella stayed where she was, watching the others.

"I can't believe she killed him over a few houses," Kristen said as she picked up her handbag.

"She killed him over a few wallabies," Maria countered. "Let's go and get drunk somewhere," she added.

Kristen nodded. "I definitely need a drink. Jody, are you coming?"

Jody looked surprised by the invitation. "You know, a bottle or two of wine is exactly what I need right now," she said. "I shouldn't drink alone, should I?"

The trio walked out together as William stood up.

"I'll ring everyone in a day or two," he announced. "I'm not certain now whether it would be better to try to continue what we were doing or whether we should be getting ready to appear before the planning board to fight Harry's plans. I'm going to have to give the matter some thought."

"There aren't any wallabies in any of the sections that you people monitored," Harry said, sounding frustrated.

"Of course there are," William countered. "We may have to organize a round the clock watch for a few days in order to prove it, but we will prove it, mark my words."

Harry sighed and then reached for his coat. "Darrell was right. The only way we were ever going to succeed is if we kept the whole thing quiet until it was a done deal."

"We would have noticed when Darrell applied for planning permission," Sara said.

Harry shrugged. "Whatever." He picked up his briefcase and stomped out of the room.

"We would have noticed," Sara said again. "And we would have stopped them."

"And we will stop them," William said confidently. "We'll meet early next week and start making our plans."

"Ring me first," Mark suggested. "Harry may have given up on the idea by then. This was really Darrell's project, not his."

The volunteers slowly made their way out of the building, leaving Fenella and Daniel with Rodney.

"I can't believe he was working on something like that and didn't tell me," Rodney said as Fenella and Daniel headed for the door. "I thought he told me everything."

"Perhaps he didn't think you would have approved," Fenella said.

"I wouldn't have approved," Rodney replied. "I've become quite fond of wallabies over the past year. I never would have agreed to building on their land."

❧ 15 ❧

The car was silent as Daniel drove Fenella home. "I won't
even come up," he said. "I'm going to go and see if Alfred
needs any help. He'll want statements from everyone who
was there tonight, but they can wait until tomorrow."

"It was a horrible evening," Fenella said.

"It was pretty awful," he agreed, pulling her into a hug. For several
minutes, she rested in his arms.

"I really do have to go," he whispered.

"I know," she sighed.

"I'll probably come over tomorrow to get your statement," he
added. "Sleep well."

"You, too."

"I just hope I can get some sleep at some point," Daniel sighed.

"What happened?" Mona demanded as Fenella let herself into her
apartment. "You look upset."

"Gail confessed to killing Darrell."

"Gail? The wallaby lover from across?"

Fenella sighed. She was tired and upset and she really didn't want to
talk about everything that had happened that evening, but she knew

Mona wouldn't stop asking questions until Fenella had told her everything.

"I need a drink," she said, heading for the kitchen.

"Drinking alone isn't wise," Mona said.

"I'm not alone. You're here and so is Katie."

Fenella gave Katie a few treats and then poured herself a glass of wine. She took a healthy swallow before she turned to her aunt. "Okay, sit down and I'll tell you everything."

An hour later, Fenella was yawning over her second glass of wine.

"You need to get some sleep," Mona said. "I still can't quite believe that Gail killed him."

"Me either, and I was there when she confessed."

"Would she have confessed to protect someone else?"

Fenella shrugged. "I doubt it. Unless a wallaby did it."

Daniel visited the next afternoon. "I just need a short statement from you about last night," he said after he'd greeted her with a quick kiss. "Gail has given Alfred a full confession, so it's just paperwork at this point."

"She actually killed Darrell?"

"She did. She had the knife hidden in her house, but she told Alfred where to find it. I was amazed that she'd managed to kill someone with it. It was just a small paring knife and it wasn't even very sharp. The coroner said that she'd hit just the right spot to kill Darrell instantly."

"Was she smart or lucky?"

"That's a good question. She's insisting that she hadn't meant to kill him, that she just wanted to hurt him, but Alfred suspects that she may have had some medical training at some point. He's looking into it, anyway."

They sat together on a couch while Fenella gave her formal statement.

"I was thinking about something," Daniel said when she was finished.

"What?"

"According to what Mark said last night, I'm going to inherit ten thousand pounds from Darrell's estate."

"Yes, I suppose you are."

Daniel grinned at her. "Even if I'm quite sensible and put half of it in the bank, that still leaves a nice amount for a short holiday somewhere, doesn't it? We could go to Paris, maybe?"

Fenella blushed. "I can put my inheritance from Darrell toward the trip, too. I don't need it otherwise. We could take more than just a short holiday."

"I'm not sure how much time I can get off work, but let's start planning something soon," he said as he walked to the door. "I probably have to work tonight, but maybe we could have dinner together tomorrow night."

"I'd like that," she said in the doorway.

He pulled her into an extended embrace that left her head spinning.

"I'll ring you," he said huskily as he raised his head.

"Good," she replied.

He turned and pulled the door open and then looked back over his shoulder. "Oh, by the way," he said casually, "Nancy rang me last night. She's coming over for a fortnight's holiday soon."

Fenella felt her jaw drop as she watched Daniel walk down the corridor toward the elevators.

ACKNOWLEDGMENTS

Linda at Tell-Tale Book Covers continues to do a wonderful job with my covers. Thank you!

Thank you to my new editor, Dan Hilton, who did a great job on this title (and several others).

And thank you to my readers who follow Fenella and Mona.

NEIGHBORS AND NIGHTMARES

Release date: May 15, 2020

Fenella Woods has been having nightmares for the past two weeks. She and Daniel Robinson, her police inspector boyfriend, have been getting along really well, even starting to plan a vacation together. That was before he announced that the woman he'd met while taking classes in Milton Keynes was coming to visit the Isle of Man.

Daniel and Nancy Weston had become friends while they were in Milton Keynes, but according to Daniel, they'd agreed not to pursue a relationship, as neither was prepared to move in order for them to be together. That's not the way Nancy tells the story, though. When she and her friends arrive on the island, she announces that she's given up her job and is ready to make big changes in her life, changes that seem to include Daniel.

When Nancy turns up dead on the beach where she and her friends are staying, Daniel and Fenella are both suspects. Inspector Mark Hammersmith is in charge and Daniel finds himself suspended from his duties while the case is under investigation.

Can Fenella and Daniel work out what happened to Nancy? Her

friends seem to be the most likely suspects, but they're a tight-knit group who don't want to confide in anyone. It becomes increasingly clear that the group has a number of secrets, but surely they wouldn't work together to cover a murder, would they?

ALSO BY DIANA XARISSA

The Isle of Man Ghostly Cozy Mysteries

The Isle of Man Cozy Mysteries

The Markham Sisters Cozy Mystery Novellas

ABOUT THE AUTHOR

Diana grew up in Northwestern Pennsylvania and moved to Washington, DC, after college. There she met a wonderful Englishman who was visiting the city. After a whirlwind romance, they got married and Diana moved to the Chesterfield area of Derbyshire to begin a new life with her husband. A short time later, they relocated to the Isle of Man.

After over ten years on the island, it was time for a change. With their two children in tow, Diana and her husband moved to suburbs of Buffalo, New York. Diana now spends her days writing about the island she loves.

She also writes mystery/thrillers set in the not-too-distant future as Diana X. Dunn and middle grade and Young Adult books as D.X. Dunn.

Diana is always happy to hear from readers. You can write to her at:

Diana Xarissa Dunn
PO Box 72
Clarence, NY 14031.
Find Diana at: DianaXarissa.com
E-mail: Diana@dianaxarissa.com

214

Made in United States
Troutdale, OR
06/18/2025

32238595R00130